SAVAGE SAINT

STEEL ROSES MOTORCYCLE CLUB
BOOK 2

JENA DOYLE

DIRTY WORDS PUBLISHING

Line Editor: Misha Robinson, Verity Ink Editorial

Proofreader: Kimberly Hunt, Revision Division

❁ Formatted with Vellum

For anyone who's ever wanted to fuck someone inappropriate...

STEEL ROSES FAMILY TREE

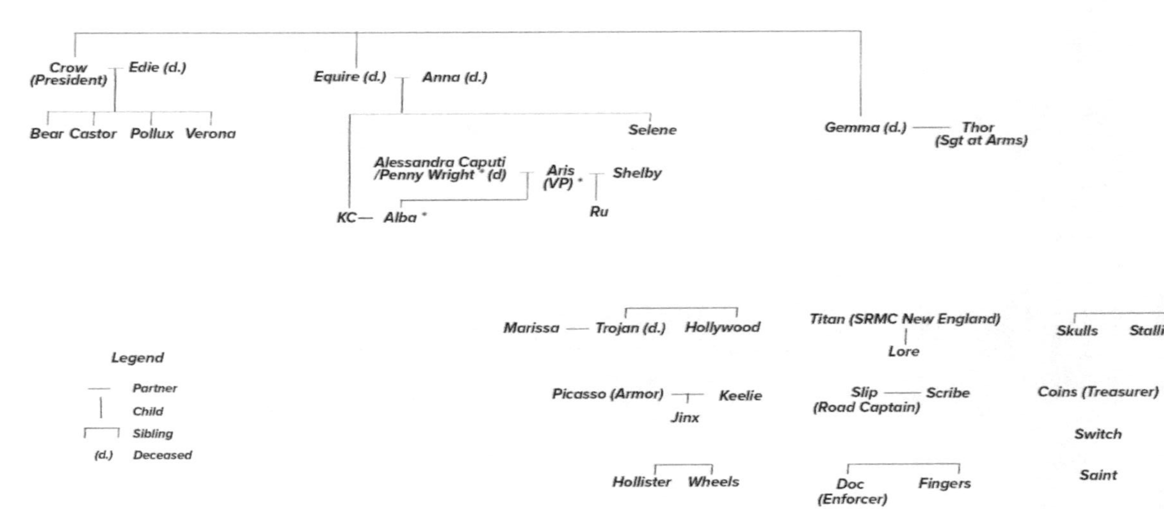

CAPUTI FAMILY TREE

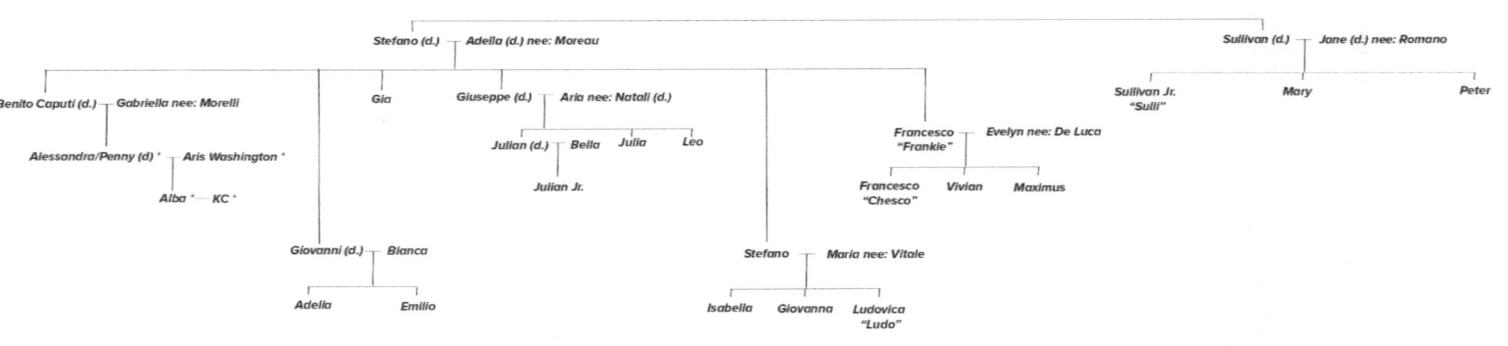

Legend

—	Partner
|	Child
⌐	Sibling
(d.)	Deceased
nee.	Maiden Name

* Member of Steel Roses Family Tree

1

RU

"What the hell?" I ran my hands through my hair and narrowed my eyes at the profit and loss statement from the last six months. Holy crap, there was a lot of red. Even though I was supposed to be bartending, the strip club owned by Steel Roses Motorcycle Club didn't have many customers tonight, so I'd spent the majority of my shift digging through reports.

Sales were dismal. The dancers had reduced their hours or quit altogether. My dad's best friend, Saint, had stepped up as general manager, but between the crumbling building and the lack of staff, he was overwhelmed. He worked here at the Beacon in addition to his MC responsibilities. Pretty soon, there wouldn't be a Beacon. No one knew how to run it like my dad, Aris—no one except me.

"This can't be right." I grimaced and went to the next page. The building had become costly to maintain, and Dad hadn't done anything to modernize it in years. No wonder Saint was having such a hard time.

"Hey, can I get a drink?" one of the regulars said.

"Last call was ten minutes ago, Rodney."

"C'mon, Ru!" He wagged his eyebrows. "Your old man never gave a shit."

"My old man's not here," I said. "And if you don't stop talking to me in that tone, I'm gonna bend you over my sink and scrub your mouth out like your momma shoulda done." He was an old-timer and had been coming here since I was in pigtails. I wasn't scared of his drunk ass.

Rodney slammed his hand on the bar and gave a loud guffaw before turning and walking toward the door, grabbing his belly as he stumbled away and hooted.

My dad and I didn't have a typical father-daughter relationship. My mom had split soon after I was born, and last I heard, she was doing fifteen to twenty for manslaughter. Because of this, I'd done a lot of my own raising. My dad called me an old soul, but I called it having to grow up before I was supposed to. Dad and I were more like a team. I cooked and cleaned before I was ten, and sometimes, I was pretty sure he forgot which one of us was the parent.

Last year, I learned he had a secret life I hadn't known about—a lover named Penny, a child named Alba, a whole other personality. There was so much to unpack that I could fund a therapist's salary for years. My dad had never dated anyone else after my mom, and once I'd met Penny, I understood. Dad had loved her since he met her. This past July, she died of cancer and his grief forced him to take a step back from running things at the Beacon. Hence the reason I'd started working here again as soon as I graduated from college and moved home permanently.

Aside from the decrepit building and failing finances, the enormous alpha asshole of a problem with this place was my new boss, Saint—the same sexy biker that called himself my dad's brother by oath, the one that had been at every Thanksgiving and Christmas since I was a teenager. Eighteen months ago, we'd secretly started an affair that lasted for a while after that. I had irrevocably fallen in love with him, and he had crushed my silly heart under his steel-toed boot.

"Hey you," came the familiar voice from my right.

"Hey." I locked eyes with Lore, the newest member of the Roses, and leaned over the bar to kiss him on the cheek. Originally a part of the New England chapter, he had transferred to Madison County two years ago when his security job brought him to the area. He was tall with dark hair and a matching beard, completely covered in tats... yeah, I had a type, even if it wasn't like that between Lore and me.

"You ready?" Lore nodded toward the door and grinned, winking as he tapped his tattooed knuckles on the bar.

"Almost," I said. Rodney was the last customer, and he'd taken my threat serious enough to waddle his way to the door a while ago. "Let me count down my till and take it upstairs." Saint had disappeared up there earlier, but at this time of night he'd probably hit the road. That was good, because if he saw the affection between Lore and me, he'd get pissed. I didn't have the energy to deal with him.

Lore smiled and nodded, shoving his hands in his pockets as he sat on a stool. I put the excess cash into a plastic bag and taped it closed before grabbing the till out of the register and walking to the front door so I could lock it on my way toward the stairs.

Last year had brought me more than heartache. I'd gotten abducted by the MC's enemy, Benito Caputi, and the rest of the Caputi crime family. I spent sixteen hours in a cold, dank basement, huddled against my sister, believing we were both going to die. Luckily, we survived (mostly) unscathed.

When I wanted to go back to Mount Vernon for my senior year at Thomas Washington University, it had taken nearly the entire club to convince my father to let me go. Dad eventually relented when I agreed to take a brother with me. Lore had patched in right around the same time, so being a brat, I'd chosen the brother who looked the most like Saint and knew the least about me.

I thought it would piss him off, that maybe he'd see a younger version of himself in Lore and come running back out of jealousy. Like a lot of things related to Saint, he'd disappointed me, and all these months later, I was still the stupid woman addicted to a man who'd never feel the same way.

Unrequited love was such bullshit.

Perhaps, in another life, it could have been more between Lore and me, but the precise reason I'd picked him turned into why we couldn't be more than friends. He reminded me *too* much of Saint, and if I ever thought about taking things further, that fact threw cold water on the whole thing. It was like being addicted to name-brand soda and only having the dollar store version as an option. It *sort of* tasted right, but something always smelled off.

When I got to the office on the second floor, I froze just inside the door. Saint leaned back against the desk, his long legs stretched out in front of him, his big arms crossed over his chest. He raised an eyebrow at my entrance and tilted his head to the side, running his heated dark eyes down the length of me, burning me where I stood.

I tried not to let my tremble show, tensing my muscles to keep from shaking.

"What's he doing here?" he growled.

"He's my friend." I swallowed, my throat dry and scratchy, and forced my legs to move toward the safe behind the desk.

Saint tracked me as I walked. "Hmm."

I'd known him long enough to understand the noises he made. This one said he didn't like that I was friends with Lore, and he had more questions.

"Hmm," I mocked, mine saying I didn't give a rat's ass what he liked. I punched in the combination on the safe and twisted open the door. My heart pounded so hard I heard it in my head, but I forced myself to focus on putting the money away.

"You two together?"

I debated how to react. The fire that surged in my chest wanted me to turn around and kick him in the shin. For the eight months we were hooking up, he'd had every opportunity to openly claim me. When I told him I wouldn't be his secret anymore, he broke it off like it meant nothing and sent me packing to college. *Go have fun,* he'd told me with that annoying apathetic look in his eyes. *Go be twenty-two.* That was what made it hurt so much—as if the eight months I'd spent on my knees for him weren't enjoyable, like the time we'd had together was an insignificant blip on his radar. He didn't even fight to keep me. He'd had his chance, and he blew it.

I turned so I could look at him.

The glint in Saint's expression said he expected an answer. Once upon a time, we'd promised each other the truth, only ever the truth between us. Now, we'd smushed that all to hell. Perhaps he didn't deserve my wrath, but he certainly didn't deserve to know my secrets anymore.

"That's none of your business." I put the till next to the others and placed the deposit on top of the stacks of cash on the upper shelf. Then I closed the door and twisted the handle shut.

"Hmm." Another noncommittal sound. This one meant he'd picked up on the animosity in my voice and was now considering how he wanted to respond. When we were together, he would have wrapped his hand around my throat and pushed me to the ground, reminding me exactly what I could do with my attitude. Now, he only took a deep breath and let it out on a disappointed sigh. "Next time, tell him to leave the cut at home. It distracts the clientele."

I made a sad laughing noise and raised an eyebrow, taking a step toward the lockers. "There's no clientele. We haven't made money in six months."

He shot his hand out, wrapping his fingers around my wrist as I passed. The touch startled me, and I gasped before I could stop it.

"Careful," he murmured. "I'm patient, but I have my limits."

"Limits?" The brat inside me blinked awake at the threat. I had once lived to test his boundaries, breaking his rules and reveling in the punishment. Saint and I had a kink dynamic few others would understand, especially given the age difference between us. He gave me rules, I broke them, and both of us loved the punishment that came after that.

Even now that we were broken up, I couldn't help myself. I struggled in his hold, trying to yank away from him. "What are you gonna do, huh? Bend me over my daddy's desk and hold me down while you spank me?" I took a step closer, pleased when his jaw tightened and his lips turned into a thin line. I stuck my lower lip out, half taunting him, half pretending to pout. "Please, sir. I've been so bad."

That tipped the scales. He launched off the desk, snarling as he got in my face and seared me with his gaze, the pain and hunger of the months apart behind it. He didn't say anything, but he didn't have to. I understood what his growl meant. *Don't throw that in my face.*

A jolt of lust hit me between the legs, my cunt clenching. I stared right back, squeezing my thighs together in a pathetic attempt to soothe the pain, but even my lady parts admitted he had a point. I bared my teeth, jerking against his hold again. This time, he let me go with a tiny shove, and I stumbled back, taking a deep breath as I righted myself and brushed my hands over my corset top.

"Tell your boyfriend the next time he wears his cut in here, I'll rip it off and shove it up his ass." Saint straightened and circled around behind the desk, focusing his attention on some papers. I didn't say anything, just grabbed my purse from my locker and slammed it shut, stalking to the door and giving Saint my best "eat shit" look as I did.

How dare he?

Lore was more than just my friend and former bodyguard. He was technically Saint's brother by oath. Saint couldn't threaten whomever he wanted. I didn't give a shit who my dad had left in charge. I was so pissed and turned on and frustrated that if he *did* throw me over the desk and fuck me on it, I wouldn't have stopped him.

Fuck Saint. Fuck his gorgeous mouth and that incinerating stare. Fuck everything about him.

When I'd asked him to go public and tell my dad about us, he said it was too fucked-up, too depraved, Aris would never forgive him, blah, blah, blah. Those were his hang-ups, not mine, but it told me something about him. I didn't like what I'd learned. In the battle between my father and me, Saint would always choose him. I wouldn't be with someone who didn't put me first.

I saw the love my dad had for Penny, what Alba had with her fiancé, KC. I wanted that with a desperation that chafed. If Saint wouldn't give it to me, I'd find someone who would. Being abducted by Benito Caputi had put a lot of things into perspective and made me question my choices. I wouldn't be anyone's dirty little secret, not anymore. Life was too damn short.

"You ready?" I asked Lore when he stood.

"Yeah. Let's roll." He wrapped an arm over my shoulders, and I grabbed his fingers, a blatant display of familiarity between us.

Feast your eyes on that, you fucker.

"Oh, and Ru?" Saint's voice came from the doorway to the stairs, and I stopped, shooting a death glare in his direction. His predatory stare hit me in the gut, like he meant to circle me until I got weak enough for him to make an easy strike. "Clean the floors when you open tomorrow."

Fury surged in my veins, and I clamped my teeth together so hard that I thought I might break a molar. He'd given me a direct order in front of someone he believed I was fucking. As my sort-of boss, he had that right, but that wasn't the tone he'd used. No, that meant, *Get on your fucking knees.*

2
____

RU

"All right, spill." Lore shoved a fry into his mouth and sat back on the barstool. "What's up with you and old man Scrooge?"

I laughed and flicked a fry at him. "He's not old."

"What is he? Forty?"

"Thirty-seven."

"He's old as fuck." Lore studied me, amusement flickering over his lips. "You in love with him?"

I sighed and shook my head. "I used to be."

"Used to be?"

I took a big bite of my burger, apathetic about the sauce dripping down my chin or the unladylike way I was eating it. Lore had held my hair back on many a drunken night. The boundaries between us were long since gone, but in a fraternal sort of way.

"Not anymore?"

I shrugged. "It's complicated."

Lore crossed his arms over his chest, an incredulous look making my cheeks burn with shame. "Go on."

I sighed and told him the whole thing. I'd met Saint at fourteen. He'd been twenty-nine at the time, so much older than me in my young eyes. It was a crush at first. He was *that* guy, the one every girl had, the one that set the bar for all the guys that came after. He gave me attention like no one ever had before. He *saw* me, truly saw me, and affection like that at such a pivotal point in my life had left a lasting impact.

"Then, a year and a half ago"—I chomped on another fry—"we were driving around in his truck during a blizzard and got stuck in the snow. We started drinking whiskey to keep warm."

"As one does."

I nodded, taking another big bite of burger. "I threw myself at him."

"Poor guy." Lore laughed and shook his head. "Never stood a chance."

"We fucked, and when we got home, we fucked some more." I told him that from December through to the following August, we were together, and Jesus Christ, I'd thought there was no feeling greater than having his hands on my body. "Until he broke my heart. That fucking sucked."

Lore blew out a breath and ran a hand over his hair. "No kidding."

"I went back to college for senior year like nothing ever happened, and now I can't even have a civil conversation with him, let alone forgive him." I swallowed down the rising bile and pain with a gulp of beer. "My dad doesn't know. I wanted to tell him, but Saint thought I should find someone my age." I avoided Lore's gaze for fear of the judgment I might see there. "When we're around everyone else we act normal, but it's pretend. That hurts the worst. I'll never get back what we had."

Before we were together, Saint and I were friends—almost as close as he was with my dad. Deep down, I wasted away without him, and even though it had been ten months, our breakup could have happened yesterday for how badly it had ripped my soul to shreds. I did my best not to be alone with him, not anymore.

"That's what that was all about." He nodded, finally understanding. When we'd met, I'd been obviously heartbroken over someone back home. I never talked about it because I *couldn't*. Lore had been kind enough not to push. "I get it. I, uh...I've been there." When I finally lifted my eyes, there was only understanding and maybe a bit of amusement.

Relief settled in my chest. "Really?"

He nodded. "My sister's best friend back home. It's a nightmare."

I laughed because it felt good to talk to someone who had an objective viewpoint. Only a handful of people knew the truth, like KC and my good friend, Hollywood. As fellow MC members and Saint's sworn brothers, they wouldn't be caught dead discussing it. My best friend, Selene, had wanted to surgically remove Saint's cock after we broke up. Alba knew, too, but she'd always been Team Saint, so she gave advice to nudge us back together. That was a pipe dream at this point.

Lore took a deep breath and let it out on a sigh. "Well, that's a shame. Here I was hoping you'd fall for my devilish charms."

"Yeah fucking right," I said through a deep belly laugh. "Believe me, if it were that easy, we'd already be married. I am sorry, though."

"You're the veep's daughter. It was never gonna work anyway." He softened his expression and winked, tapping his beer against mine before taking a drink. "Only a brother like Saint could get away with that."

I smiled at the memory that bubbled up from the night Saint and I had first gotten together. *"No one casually fucks the veep's daughter and gets away with it,"* he'd told me at the time. Turned out, not even he had the balls to face my father.

"I saw the way you looked at him when he called out for you." Lore wagged a finger at me. "You still care what he thinks, which means you're not over him."

I cleared my throat, my skin burning hotter because I might never be over him.

"I bet I only have to come around a few more times before he starts pissing on his territory." He paused, narrowing his eyes before adding, "Respectfully."

I imagined the look on Saint's face if I brought him around again, a small jolt of excitement settling in my gut. I tempered that down because I liked Lore, and I didn't want anything bad to happen to him. "Thanks, I appreciate it, but you don't have to do that."

"I only do the things I want, Ru." He winked again, and I wished I didn't have this hang-up with Saint. In another world, Lore and I would have hit it out of the park. Giggling, I flicked another fry at him, and he caught it with his mouth, giving me a smile as he chomped it down.

After dinner, he drove me home on his bike. Dad and I lived on the other side of the mountain, about ten miles from Alba's old place. It used to be a three-bedroom rancher, but Dad had turned his grief into productivity, channeling his rage into renovations. Now, we had a second floor and a huge two-story deck out back, overlooking the woods and the valley below.

I spotted Saint's bike when we pulled up, the distinctive indigo and silver flames going down the tank visible in the faint moonlight. My heart sank into my gut, and I trembled, knowing we'd have a confrontation when I went inside. I almost asked Lore to take me to his place instead, but this was going to happen sooner or later. I might as well get it over with.

"You all right?" Lore turned off the bike, and I climbed to the side, unhooking the helmet to hand to him.

"Yeah." I shook out my hair. "He'd never hurt me."

"Hmm, okay." He grabbed me by the back of the neck. "One more thing." I tumbled forward as he brought my lips to his, devouring them, biting and licking and marking. If I hadn't just bared my aching, bleeding heart to him, I might have been turned on by it.

When he let me go, I took a deep breath and steadied myself before muttering, "What was that for?"

"I hope he saw it." Lore gave me a quick peck. "I hope he rocks your world." Then he kicked his bike to life and took off, leaving me standing there, anxious to greet the monster lurking in the shadows.

I didn't have to look very far. I made it two feet toward the porch before he emerged from the corner, a cigarette between his fingers, his boots echoing off the hardwood. My heart banged against my ribs, and I froze at the sight of him—six feet two, dark and menacing, inked from neck to waist, including a giant cross on his chest I'd once loved to lick.

"What are you doing here?" I took another step, putting my hand on the railing to hold myself upright. My knees shook, and any second, I'd crumble to the ground in front of him like I used to do.

No. Stay strong.

"Aris invited me over." The hiss of the cigarette drew my attention as he inhaled, his chiseled features and obsidian beard illuminated in the faint glow. God, he was pissed. He only smoked when he was furious or worried, and tonight, I might have been cause for both.

"Right." I looked at the front door, forcing my legs to stay in place. If I stepped back, he'd chase. If I gave an inch, he'd take a mile. I knew better than to tempt the dominant in him, especially given what he'd just seen. "Where's my dad?"

"Asleep. Passed out about an hour ago." That sounded about right. When he wasn't working on the house, he was drunk. Sometimes, both.

"And you're still here."

He took another long draw on the cigarette. "I'm still here."

"Why?"

Saint didn't answer, but I knew him so well, he didn't need to. He'd stayed because he wanted to make sure I got home okay, that Lore kept his hands to himself. A shiver skated down my back despite the sticky June heat.

He took another step closer and stabbed the cigarette out in the ashtray, the heavy sounds of his heel-toe pounding in time with my pulse. When he stood in front of me, staring down from under hooded lids, the rush of all I'd ever felt for him surged back to life despite our fight in the office two hours ago.

I wanted him to take me on the porch, to hold his hand over my mouth and rail me from behind, hissing words about not waking my dad. I wanted what we used to have with such a perverse desperation that I was afraid I'd do anything to get it back again.

"We broke up, Saint." I admired my strength.

"We did."

"I won't be anyone's secret."

"I know." He ran his knuckles down the side of my face, brushing my curly brown hair behind my ear. "Doesn't mean I like the sight of you on another man's bike."

"Hmm." I nodded, and this time, my sound meant, *If only there was something you could do about that.*

My attitude used to be one of his favorite things about me, and when he dropped his gaze to my lips, I recognized the look that flickered behind it. He picked up the message loud and clear and clenched his hands into fists at his sides. I bet they itched to spear through my hair and force me to my knees. I bet it hurt to deny himself.

Good.

He stepped back and gave me one solemn nod before turning to walk down the porch stairs. "Have a nice night, Ru."

I didn't speak because if I did, I would have told him to take me inside and make it all up to me. I would have forgiven him for everything, and he hadn't earned that.

"Hello!" I called when I got to Crimson's studio early the next morning. Maybe owning a cam business with my sister should have sounded fucked-up, but I'd joined her before I knew she was my sister, so I figured I couldn't be held accountable. I stopped caring a long time ago.

I walked through the foyer area, smiling at the fuzzy pink wall Alba had insisted on installing in the waiting area. Every time I saw it, I giggled at the argument she had with KC when they bought it. He obviously wanted something more neutral but wilted for his "sunshine" all the same.

When no one called back, I looked into the break room and found it empty. Coffee steamed in the pot, set to auto brew, but this early, it wasn't a surprise that no one was here yet. We were a bunch of night owls, we wild things.

Alba had begun the site a few years ago as a way to make money when her mother was dying of cancer. She needed a partner and went to a party to find one, only to meet KC. They hit it off, and he signed on to help her by being her sexy cam guy. I came into the business a few months after that with lofty ideas about a toy line and a homestyle setup with multiple live feeds going at all hours. We wanted to give the power back to the performers, and now they were pulling high five figures each, myself included. In the next eighteen months, I hoped to triple or quadruple what we were doing.

I didn't care that people wanted to jerk off to me rubbing one out. If anything, it sated the exhibitionist side of me. I only needed to do a few scenes a week to save enough money for my move-out plans, knowing I could do a live stream if I needed the extra cash for something. It wasn't like I was making much money at the Beacon these days, and I really needed to get out of my dad's place.

I walked down the hallway to my favorite room, the one painted in grays and whites with the big fluffy comforter on the bed, and stepped inside, locking the door behind me. Then, I came face first with Crimson's slogan.

Real people. Real orgasms.

My cheeks burned because I knew the truth. I'd done nearly a hundred and fifty videos in the months I'd been camming, and not a single performance had been real. Luckily, none of my fans could tell the difference, and if they did, they didn't seem to mind.

After I recorded three scenes, I cleaned the space and showered, preparing to head to the Beacon to open. I had so much to do on top of dreading the fact I would run into Saint at some point. Tonight, I didn't have backup behind the bar, which meant he'd have to help if we got busy enough, and that would make it more difficult to ignore him from afar. When Lore showed up again, like he'd said he would, Saint would get grumpy and...

And what?

Sulk and pine for me on my porch? Make demands and snarl in my face?

Bring it on.

By noon, I had performed most of my normal activities, wiping down the bottles before cleaning the surfaces under the bar and filling up the sinks. Then I went to the closet to get the mop and water bin, remembering Saint's order to clean the floors.

God, that tone sent chills down my spine, like some kind of Pavlovian response etched into my neural pathways. I'd heard it and wanted to mouth off, to break every boundary he had just to get him to react. Those days were gone.

I cranked the music overhead, some old-fashioned rock and roll to get my day going, and dipped the mop in the bucket. I'd always been the type of person to use my chores as an impromptu solo concert featuring yours truly. I belted my way through the greatest hits from my childhood while I shook my ass and bobbed my head to my very own air guitar. It took over my soul, compelling the movement from me without my consciously knowing it. I sang at the top of my lungs and danced like an idiot until I turned around and saw Saint leaning up against the doorjamb to the back.

"Ah!" I jumped and grabbed my chest, a sharp slice of fear piercing through me. "What are you doing here?"

He snorted out a laugh. "I work here."

I rolled my eyes. "I wasn't expecting you until two."

He shrugged as he straightened and walked closer, my gaze catching on the tattoos snaking down his arms and the way they complemented the black T-shirt he had on. "I couldn't miss the show."

"Har har." I sneered and went back to cleaning, drenching the mop in the bucket before sloshing it on the floor again, dragging it back and forth. I ignored the burn in my cheeks and the roll in my stomach that preened for his attention. "You always loved my singing."

I grimaced as soon as the words left my mouth. He didn't love *me*, not anymore, and the mention of our shared history picked at the gaping hole in my heart.

"I love everything your mouth can do," came his reply.

I stopped, tightening my fingers around the wooden handle and straightening my spine.

"Sorry." He sighed and walked behind the bar, grabbing a glass and putting it under the faucet for some water. "That was...inappropriate."

Clearing my throat, I forced myself to keep mopping while the silence dragged on between us, growing more suffocating by the second. In all the years I'd known him, we'd never *not* talked. I used to text him twenty to thirty times a day, and I'd always get a response within fifteen minutes. Now, it had been a week since we'd had a conversation over dinner at the clubhouse, where we pretended to be the former versions of ourselves in front of our family.

I didn't know what to say. I loved him, I wanted him, and it skewered me to know he didn't feel the same, or if he did, he wasn't brave enough to tell everyone about it.

I deserved better, Goddamn it.

"It's okay." I shook my head and sighed. "It's weird between us now."

"It is." He spread his hands over the bar and leaned forward. "Isn't it?"

I pursed my lips and dipped the mop in the bucket again.

"Why are sales so dismal, Saint?" I shifted my gaze to his, unsurprised to find that same stoic calmness in his eyes. Nothing rattled him, nothing except me.

He sighed and stood up, running a hand over the back of his head. "Look around. The place is a fucking dive. I don't have the time or the money to do this by myself."

"Why isn't Dad helping?"

Saint shook his head. "It was hard right after you left. He isn't always..." He cleared his throat and added a quiet, "Sober."

I swallowed, considering this. Dad had never been an alcoholic, but I could also see him drowning in his grief. He was the type of person to keep it from those closest to him, so they didn't worry.

"Being here stressed him out and made it worse." Saint took a deep breath and let it out. "He's doing better now."

That eased the tension in my gut, but not enough to make me forget about it. I'd have to talk to him the next time I could. Looking back at Saint, I debated whether it was the right time to bring this up. I had the plan, the math, and the strategy. "I can help you."

He raised an eyebrow and took a drink. I watched the muscles in his neck work while he swallowed, remembering how rough his beard felt against my lips. "I'm listening."

I leaned the mop against the counter and put my hands in the back pockets of my cutoffs, taking a few steps closer and looking around at the old memorabilia from ages gone by. "This place hasn't changed in twenty years."

His eyes narrowed. "And?"

"That's a problem." I put my elbows on the bar and leaned toward him, keeping his gaze as I continued. "The old-timers are retired. No one wants to come to the strip club where their grandpa got his jollies off."

That made Saint chuckle low in his chest. "What do you suggest?"

I pursed my lips. "Ask the MC for a loan to renovate the place. Make it more modern. Tear out the wood paneling, add a new spot system, the whole thing."

"Hmm." He narrowed his eyes again while he considered, but that noise meant I hadn't driven it all the way home yet.

"You need to do something new with it."

"Like what?" He took another sip of water.

"I don't know. Turn it into a sex club or something."

He coughed, spitting water back into the glass, his face turning red as he struggled for air. "Fuck."

"Yeah." I grinned and shrugged playfully. "You could call it Saints and Sinners."

"What do you know about sex clubs?" he growled, his eyes turning angry for half a heartbeat before he locked it down. In the months we'd been together, Saint had exposed me to the kink life-style, but we'd never taken it public. After it ended, the idiot glutton in me thought I could fill the hole he left in my heart with another dominant. I thought someone else could replace him. I was wrong.

I ignored his question and kept talking.

"I'd turn that storage space into a specialty room and add an addition in the back for *VIP activities.*" Winking, I turned toward the front. "I'd wall this part off and make it members only. Maybe we could advertise it on Crimson, and once word got out, everyone would want in." I kept going, the ideas pouring out of me quicker than I could think them. "We could have male and female enter-tainers and create a healthy place for people to explore their sexuali-ties. It needs to be upscale and classy, but still have a grunge that makes it the Roses'."

Saint eyed me up and down, his expression turning more serious. "You've thought a lot about this."

I shrugged. "I grew up in this place. I don't want to see it closed."

He nodded, but before he could say anything else, the front door opened again and my father strolled through, tugging off his aviators.

"Hey, Ruthie." He smiled and walked to my side to give me a hug and a kiss on the head. "How's it going?"

"Fine, Dad. How are you?" I forced a smile and stepped back from the bar, pretending Saint and I had never had anything but friend-ship between us. Tall and bulky, Dad had gone gray early in his life. He'd once had curly chestnut locks like me, but that wasn't the only evidence that I belonged to him. We both had the same ivory skin tone, and our icy-blue stares had been known to freeze assholes where they stood.

"Busy as fuck." Dad shifted his gaze to Saint and held out his hand. "What's up, brother?"

"How are you?" Saint took it with a shake.

"Oh, you know. Just getting ready." Dad looked between us and leaned against a stool. "You tell her yet?"

That piqued my interest. "Tell me what?"

"I have to make a run down south," he said.

"Okay." I gave him a warm smile. "Safe travels. See you when you get back."

"Hah! Nice try."

I swallowed, still not understanding why he was telling me this.

"I'm gonna need you to move your boxes from the guest room into the garage for the time being."

My stomach dropped, and my mouth hung open as I clenched my fingers around the arms on the seat. He couldn't be saying what I thought he was saying...could he?

"What do you mean?" I looked at Saint for help, but he crossed his arms over his chest and stared, holding that practiced poker face.

"Saint's gonna stay in the guest room while I'm gone."

"No, he's not." It came out panicked before I could stop it. Saint cut his gaze to me, and Dad's features twisted in confusion as he raised an eyebrow.

"Of course he is." He chuckled like I was joking. "What's gotten into you?"

I shook my head. "Nothing. It's just... Doesn't Saint have other stuff to do? I can have Lore—"

"Lore is doing enough for the club these days." Dad glanced at my former lover, who rubbed at the back of his head and straightened. "Am I missing something here? I thought you two were like peas and carrots or some shit."

"We are." I took a deep breath, praying it would steady the building anxiety in my chest. "It's just..."

"We got into a fight," Saint cut in.

"A fight?" My dad barked out a laugh. "About what?"

"She can't bring her fuck buddy around here, wearing his cut. It scares the customers."

Dad gave me a side-eye like I should have known better, and I leveled Saint with my best "fuck you" glare.

"No colors in the Beacon, got it?" Dad pointed a mock chastising finger at me before returning his attention to his friend. "Make up with my daughter. She can fuck who she wants."

Ohh, I could have kissed my dad for saying that. I squared my jaw in Saint's direction, a look he quickly answered with a silent, *It's one thing to fuck a twenty-four-year-old prick. It's another to fuck your dad's best friend.*

Dad turned to head across the floor, yelling, "Get your shit out of the guest room by tomorrow, okay? I have to leave in the morning," before he pushed open the door leading upstairs and disappeared behind it, abandoning me there with Saint.

Quiet stretched on forever as he stared at me and thinned his lips. My blood thundered through my veins while I considered what to do next.

"Snitch." I was only half teasing.

He didn't react to my name-calling, just took a deep breath and let it out slowly through his nose. If there was one thing I hated about him, truly despised, it was his ability to keep silent. The man had infinite patience. On the other hand, I couldn't control my mouth half the time. Words flew out like there wasn't a filter between them and my brain.

"You can't live at my house."

"You don't have a choice." Saint crossed his arms over his chest, and I focused on the words on his fingers—HOPE and VICE. *"The two worst things in life,"* he'd once told me. I couldn't argue.

"Why are you doing this?" I sighed, letting the weight of these last few months settle between us. "If you want me, say you want me, Saint. Tell the whole world I'm yours." I didn't know how much clearer I could be. "If you don't, then let me go."

I went back to the mop and picked it up so I could finish cleaning the floors, blinking back the tears welling in the corners of my eyes. Saint didn't answer, just followed my father up the stairs, closing the door quietly behind him.

3

SAINT

I was a bad man.

Two days ago, Aris had asked me to watch the house while he went on his run, and I turned him down. Ru wouldn't have liked it. She'd have seen it as an invasion of her privacy, some real obsessive stalker shit. She'd have been right.

When I saw her with one of my brothers, I rethought that decision real quick. I certainly didn't feel threatened by Lore. He ranked lower in the club than me. I could tell him to fuck off to another chapter, and he'd have to listen. But demanding that would raise a lot of questions, and I didn't have any good answers.

That didn't mean I wanted him touching someone that didn't belong to him, and last night, I coulda slit his throat for kissing her in front of me. I had to hand it to him, he had some fucking balls, and I woulda been impressed if it wasn't Ru he was touching. Lord help me, it took all my willpower to go home instead of tracking his ass down. Ru wouldn't like that, either. Even then, I maintained that Aris needed to find someone else to stay with Ru while he was out of town.

It was when she looked at me like she did last night on her porch that changed my mind—her mouth hanging open, her cheeks flushed, her skin so fucking warm. I wanted to take her right then and there. She had that haze in her eyes that reminded me of the days when they'd shimmered every time they settled on me. Now, they shot daggers if we were in the same space. Not that I blamed her for that, either. I was tired of my shit, too.

This morning, I'd told Aris my plans had changed. I needed to see it in her eyes again to know it was still there, that I hadn't irreversibly fucked things up.

"Leo Caputi's on a yacht in Miami with Nikki and her baby," I said, turning the picture around so my brothers could see the grainy telephoto shot of Benito's nephew with a bottle of champagne in his hand. The backstabbing bitch, Nikki, sat next to Leo with her infant on her lap.

"Who brings a baby on a party yacht?" Bear shook his head and sighed. As the president's eldest son, he wore the crown of heir apparent. When the patriarch, Crow, stepped down, Bear would take his place. Everyone knew that, and we accepted it. Even though he was big and broad, Bear had a calm demeanor and a good head on his shoulders. I'd follow him into hell and back. "What's the plan?"

"We lie low." The sergeant at arms, Thor, sipped his beer, his long dark blond hair pulled back at the base of his neck. He'd been given the nickname because he was a tall Viking motherfucker that had spent the early part of his life in the military special ops. He never talked about his time overseas, and we never asked.

Bear seemed nonplussed at the anticlimactic answer, and KC balked, but I got distracted by Ru behind the bar. She smiled at a customer and refilled his beer while he flirted with her. I watched her use her precious finger to tuck a chestnut curl behind her ear, and I pretended not to care she'd be here so much. It didn't bother me one bit.

Nope.

I didn't ache for the days we were together like my skin was on fire. I didn't immediately get hard at the sight of her parted lips. I didn't care that she'd come home and requested the new guy stay on as her bodyguard, the one who'd been assigned to protect her while she was at college.

Even on its best day, the Beacon didn't make much money, but that wasn't the point. We needed the place to launder cash, and if we didn't do an obvious amount of business, that would draw the Feds. We didn't want any more pig shit around here. If I was being honest, it had been sinking long before Aris stepped back, and once he did, that was the final nail in the coffin.

I had tried to turn things around, but my heart wasn't in it, either. Ru existed everywhere inside these walls for me. I had once held my hand over her mouth and fucked her in that dark corner across the room. I couldn't count the times I'd gripped her by the throat and eaten her pussy in one of the VIP areas. After she left, it physically hurt to be here, but I'd promised Aris to look after the place, so I kept trying my best.

"What do you mean there's no plan?" Bear shook his head. "There's gotta be a plan."

KC nodded. "I don't like doing nothing, sarge."

"We're hanging tight until they make a move." Thor looked from me to the younger brothers and back again.

"They're backing off," I explained. Since I'd been an investigator in a former life, I knew how to find the worst parts of anyone and dig deep without getting caught. Because of this background, the MC had put me to work researching Benito's widow, Gabriella Caputi, and her new gang of thugs. I hadn't learned much in the ten months since we'd killed her husband. They were good at hiding their tracks, and even my most loyal informants reported little activity.

"What about Gabriella's threat?" Bear looked between KC, Thor, and me, expecting an explanation.

The Caputis and the Roses had a blood feud going back some forty years. It had started over a love triangle in the seventies but escalated in the early nineties after Aris fell in love with Benito's daughter. Knowing they could never be together, she faked her death, moved to Rose territory under the name Penny, and raised Alba as a single mother. She tragically died of cancer last year, and once Benito learned of Alba's existence, he'd come after both of Aris's children as payback. The Roses went after them, killing Benito in the process and leaving only his nephew, Leo, to take up the mantle as kingpin.

Benito had two backstabbing pieces of shit on the inside of the SRMC, a brother named Pie and his wife, Nikki. She'd been a hangaround as long as anyone could remember. After we found out about their betrayal, Nikki knew what would happen to her. She ran to the fuckers that had put him up to it, and they'd taken her in. Those Caputi fucks would only keep Nikki around as long as they could use her. Blood meant something different to them, and if someone wasn't genuine Caputi, they weren't family and they never would be.

Shortly after that, Gabriella had tracked us down. Grief-stricken by both the loss of her husband and a daughter she thought had died decades ago, she'd shown up at Alba's house and told us to watch our backs. *It is not the men that hold the true power,* she said, tears in her eyes. *And soon, you will know what a mother's grief can do.*

Perhaps Benito Caputi had never been in charge. Perhaps it had been Gabriella all along. If that were true, she'd kept it a secret. The rumor in the dark fucked-up underworld said Leo had taken over, and he didn't have the same stomach for bloodshed as his uncle. He wanted to party. He wanted to snort away his inheritance, and judging by the photos I'd discovered, Gabriella hadn't done much to stop him.

"We haven't seen her." KC took another drink. "She's staying outta sight."

"I don't like this." Bear shook his head, narrowing his hazel eyes on me. "What about you? You're the one that got shot. You okay with waiting?"

I shrugged, taking a sip of water. Up until now, I'd been quiet. I generally didn't add much to the conversation unless prompted. I'd sworn my loyalty to the MC, and whatever they decided usually had my best interests at heart. But Bear did have a point. Seeing Ru tied up and beaten in that basement had burned itself into my retinas, and I wanted blood. It didn't help knowing Benito was dead. It didn't help knowing I'd stood by while the MC enforcer, Doc, sliced off pieces of Pie until the shock killed him. A part of my soul died that day, and I'd never get over it.

So yeah, waiting sucked, but if we got what we were after when the time was right, it could be worth it.

"Patience is a virtue," I said instead.

He rolled his eyes and diverted his attention back to the dwindling crowd. "Whatever, man."

Thor finished his beer and stood, holding out his hand for me to shake. "All right, I'm outta here. Gotta run by the shop before I head home."

"I'm gonna head out, too." Bear got up and waved goodbye. "See ya tomorrow."

My focus went again to Ru, now leaning over the bar to give Lore a kiss on the cheek. I couldn't believe that motherfucker had the guts to show up here again. No cut this time, but a slice of irritating heat went through my body anyway, setting my nerves on fire. The memory of him sticking his tongue down her throat last night nearly drove me out of the booth and across the room to beat his face in.

"Saint." KC grabbed my shoulder and squeezed it. "You okay, brother?"

I took a sip of beer and nodded, forcing myself to unclench my jaw. "Of course."

"Really? Because it looks like you've been thinking of ways to murder our newest brother." KC raised an eyebrow and tapped ash from his cigarette into the plastic bowl between us. "You're not gonna do something stupid, are ya?"

I cut my attention to him and bit back my smile. KC had known about my relationship with Ru from the start, and he'd kept his mouth blissfully shut. He hadn't said anything when he caught us in the truck on Christmas Eve or in the eighteen months since then. Hell, he hadn't even chastised me when it ended and Ru's heart had obviously been broken. The look in his eye tonight said he had a thing or two on his mind.

"Never had a stupid thought in my life, KC." I took another drink and swallowed down my bitterness when Lore wrapped his arm around Ru and whispered something in her ear that made her giggle.

It's a fucking game. It's all a show. She wants you to react.

"I know what it feels like to be in love with a Washington girl."

"I'm not in love with her." I shifted in my seat and cleared my throat, taking another drink. The ways I loved Ru were innumerable. Undefinable, infinite, and unyielding. To say I was merely *in love* with her didn't encompass it. Never had, never would.

KC snorted out a disbelieving laugh and nodded. "Look, that's none of my business. But the wedding is in a few days. I don't want whatever this is to blow up right before—"

"That's not gonna happen."

"You sure?" KC took another long inhale.

"Yeah, brother. You have my word."

KC and Alba planned to tie the knot on a relationship that had started less than a year ago. I, of course, had every hesitation in the world about that, but who was I to tell them what to do? I couldn't even hang on to the one person I'd ever—*Enough.*

"She's still got it bad for you." KC stabbed out his cigarette and stood. "In case you were wondering." He clapped me on the shoulder and walked away.

I wasn't. It reminded me that I shared something with Ru I'd never shared with anyone before, and I could never touch it again.

Ru left with Lore, and after the night crew closed the place down, I went home to grab a change of clothes, forcing myself not to think about where she'd gone or what they were doing. Or what he was touching.

God fucking damn it, Saint.

WHEN I GOT to Aris's place, he was still awake, pounding away at the drywall in the basement. To save money and keep himself from drowning in whiskey, he did whatever renovations he could himself. No one liked hanging drywall, but the shit was pretty easy once you understood it.

"Hey," I shouted over the music, shoving my hands in my pockets as I took in how much the place had changed in just a few days.

"Hey!" Aris lifted his goggles and put down his nail gun, lowering the volume on his iPhone. "Thanks again for doing this."

"Yeah, no sweat." Two years ago, it wouldn't have been an issue. Ru wouldn't have cared if I was here or not. She woulda carried on with her life like I was her dad's annoying friend, and that woulda been it.

"You make up with Ruthie?"

I nodded, the lie coasting over my tongue as smooth as butter. "We're cool."

Yeah, I'm a fucking Saint all right.

"Good." Aris picked up a spare set of goggles and tossed them at me. "I could use your help."

I caught them in the center of my chest and nodded. "Sure. What do you need?"

He pointed at a stack of gray panels leaning up against the frame. "Grab one of those and bring it here."

Together, we finished the room he was working on. Like his daughter, Aris loved to talk, and once he got on a roll about something, he wouldn't stop until he'd told me everything he knew about it. It suited me fine because I liked to listen. I could listen to Ru for hours and hours until she wore herself out.

Aris reminded me of my older brother, Noah. He had liked to talk, too, and when we realized I was more introverted, he started doing the talking for both of us. If I were to do some deep psycho-analysis bullshit on myself, I might have said this resemblance was what drew me to Aris in the first place.

I never knew my folks. Noah and I had been raised in a Catholic orphanage just outside Chicago, and I figured if they never wanted me or my brother, they didn't deserve to know us, either. My brother died when I was twelve and he was fourteen. At the time, the archbishop in charge of the orphanage told me he had gotten sick and passed away in the hospital before I could see him. Grief-stricken and shell-shocked, I accepted the story with no thought.

After I grew up, I started working for the church. I wasn't about to give up pussy and join the fucking cult, but I was quiet and good at getting information out of people, so they put me in charge of investigating dioceses accused of stealing. A few years into my career, I ended up at the place where I'd been raised and discovered one of the priests, Father Darby, had killed Noah. The priest had been beating the hell out of my brother when he fell and hit his head on the corner of a desk. Luckily, he died quickly, but being an accident didn't stop the church from lying to me all those years. I hunted Father Darby down and blew his brains out.

With my whole life up in flames, I traveled around the country for a few years, looking for a place to put down roots. One cold January afternoon, I passed through Madison with no intention of staying long. I replied to a classified ad about one of the apartments Aris owned, and we hit it off during the tour. He introduced me to the Roses and convinced me to stay. Hell, Aris had even been the one to give me my nickname. Once I told them my story, he whistled, clapped me on the shoulder, and said, *"You're a fucking saint for not tearing him apart piece by piece."* The name stuck, and two years later, I patched in. We became brothers, and the dark memories of Noah, the ones only a few souls knew about, stopped riding my heart so hard.

Aris cracked open a beer and handed it to me, plopping down on the ground while he opened another one for himself. I sat next to him, leaning up against the freshly hung wall, sweat dripping down the sides of my face. I pulled on the lager and sighed, relishing the cool drink after the work we'd done.

"Alba asked me to walk her down the aisle." Aris sipped his beer and smiled.

"Really?" That warmed my cold, dead heart. "That's great, brother. I'm happy for you."

"You think Ru is gonna be upset I said yes?"

"No." I narrowed my gaze. "Why would she be upset?"

He shrugged. "For a long time, she was my only kid. My world was her. Now, she has to share that with someone else."

I understood his concern, but Ru didn't think like that. If anything, she might have taken to Alba as her sister better than Alba was taking to Aris as her father.

"I don't think you have to worry."

"Why?"

I cleared my throat. "Ru loves Alba. She'd want whatever would make her happy."

Aris nodded, bending his knees so his elbows hung over them. "I wish Penny were still here to see our girl get married."

I nodded and grabbed his shoulder in a show of solidarity. "She is, brother."

The sound of the front door closing upstairs caught my attention.

"Dad!" Ru called. "You awake?"

"Down here!" Aris shouted.

Her footsteps echoed on the stairs, and she paused at the threshold, raking her bright gaze over me. She tried to hide her reaction in front of her father, but I knew her body so fucking well: the quick flush in her cheeks, the way her eyes heated and quickly cooled, the sharp inhale. I took a drink of my beer and smiled, pleased with her reaction to the sight of me. Ru crossed her arms over her chest and ignored it, which only added to my smugness.

She's still got it bad for you.

I wished she didn't. I wished she'd move on with Lore, even if the thought itched like a scratch on a phantom limb.

"What time are you leaving tomorrow?"

The silhouette of her thin, loose blouse and the cutoff jeans high on her thighs mesmerized me. I traced the dragon tattoo on her thigh with my gaze, knowing it ended on her hip. When I fucked her from behind, my big hand covered the whole head. I saw something else peeking out from under her bra, a few dark marks under her breast that hadn't been there before.

She'd gotten new ink.

Jesus Christ, I wanted to know what it was.

"Right, Saint?" She snapped her attention to me, and for the second time today, she'd caught me eye-fucking her. She straightened like she knew what it was, but then Aris looked at me, and I locked that shit down real fucking quick.

Fuck, I wasn't paying attention.

"What are we talking about?"

"The bachelor party on Friday. You guys are still going to the Viper, right?"

"Yeah." I pursed my lips and nodded, remembering I'd agreed to that a few weeks ago.

"You're going to the Viper with KC, Bear, and their idiot friends?" Aris raised his eyebrows, taking another drink of his beer.

"Sure." I nodded.

"Fuck, you're brave." He stood and held a hand out to help me up. I took it, and he yanked me to my feet, turning to pull Ru into a hug. "The last time those fuckers dragged me out, I was hungover for a month." He'd sworn off tequila forever after that.

Aris gave Ru a kiss on the head. "I'm heading to bed. I won't see either of you before I leave, so I'm saying goodbye now. Have fun this weekend." He headed toward the stairs, but then stopped and turned back to face us, pointing his finger like a commanding patriarch. In his best serious dad voice, he said, "Don't do anything I wouldn't do." He held the expression for a whole five seconds before he clapped and laughed. "Ahhh, I'm fuckin' with ya. Love you."

Then he disappeared up the stairs, his footsteps descending toward the back of the house.

Ru pursed her lips, and I went to move around her, but she put a hand out to stop me when I passed, squeezing my wrist with her delicate fingers. She opened her mouth and looked up like she was going to say something, but instead she dropped her hand and glanced away. Which was honestly for the best. Whatever she had to say was better left unsaid. I went upstairs, carrying on with my night like there weren't a fucking million things like that between us.

4

SAINT

The nightmare came to me again. I stood over Father Darby's bleeding body, his arms tied to a chair behind his back, the blindfold soaked and stinking with his sweat. I'd been at him for hours.

"Please, don't. Please. Think of your soul. Think of your damnation." He'd pissed all over himself, and now that I had my gun's cool metal barrel pointed at his temple, he could barely get the words out without spitting like an infant. "There's still time to repent."

"Is that what you told my brother?" I moved the gun from his temple to his mouth, pushing it between his lips as they trembled. "Before you killed him?"

"It was an accident, I swear. I swear." He garbled the words around my weapon, but I'd heard enough. I pulled the trigger, and his brains exploded through the back of his head.

I woke up in a panic, gasping for air, and threw the covers off because it was hot as hell in the room. The greatest heat wave in the history of Madison County had descended upon us, and Aris's window unit wasn't cutting it. Sitting up, I reminded myself to go out tomorrow and get a bigger one, but a creak in the floorboards made me lift my head. I froze at the sight of Ru wearing nothing but one of my old T-shirts, sneaking out of my room.

"Ru?"

She winced and stopped, turning to face me. "Sorry. I heard you having a nightmare, so I came to wake you. But you're already awake, so..." She turned back toward the door. "I'll go."

The tension in my muscles melted, and I wanted to pull her into my arms to hug her, remembering at the last second why I couldn't do that. The only person who knew about the nightmares was Ru. I didn't get them that much anymore, but when I did, I shouted in my sleep.

"Thank you." I ran my hands over my face and reached for my cigarettes on the nightstand, pushing to my feet.

"You're welcome," came her small reply.

"You want one?" I held the pack out to her and nodded toward the porch, hating the glimmer of hope that flickered in my chest when she stopped and faced me, quietly shutting the bedroom door. She nodded and grabbed the pack, taking one between her lips as she followed me to the deck.

The humid night air hit me in the face when I slid the door open, choking me more than the cigarette did, but I breathed them both in deep before holding the lighter a few inches from Ru's face. She inhaled on her smoke, pulling it away as she narrowed her eyes. In the moonlight, they seemed so dark that they were almost the color of the ocean—deep and indigo and never-ending. She wrapped her free arm around her ribs and sighed.

"They're not getting any better?" It came out in a whisper, and I reminded myself Aris's room was close. The deck wrapped almost all the way around the house, and he'd only need to come outside to hear us.

"No." I leaned my elbows on the edge and flicked ash into the backyard. I'd always loved the view from their place. The trees and the small stream in the valley below gave the house a rustic feel, even if it was only an hour outside DC.

"Have you talked to someone?"

I sighed. "Yeah. Sure."

Alba subscribed to that psychotalk therapist bullshit, and maybe it had helped her, but it wouldn't do the same for me. I was too fucked-up, too traumatized, too much of a piece of shit for anyone to put back together. I'd killed a priest. I'd killed criminals. I'd stood idly by while grown men were ripped apart right in front of me. My hands weren't just bloody; I was covered in the shit, and the longer Ru hung around me, the more she'd be covered in it, too.

When she realized I was teasing, she shoved my shoulder and laughed, taking another drag on the cigarette. I smiled and let myself have this quiet moment with her. Alone out here, those heartbreaking ten months apart could have happened to someone else, and if I squinted hard enough, perhaps I could be someone else, someone good enough for her.

"I'm worried about you." She shook her head and frowned. "You live alone. You ride alone."

"I'm not alone." I nodded toward Aris's room. "I've got the Roses."

"That's not what I meant." She glared at me from the corner of her eye, but I recognized the look. Excitement sizzled down my spine because *this* was the Ru I'd known before we fucked it up. This was the Ru who'd lived to tease me and volunteered to run the charity drive every year, the one who had gotten trapped in the truck with me on Christmas Eve.

I hadn't seen her in a while, so I decided to be the old Saint. Ya know, just for shits and giggles. I narrowed my eyes and leaned toward her. "What'd you mean?"

"I mean—" She shrugged and glanced toward the lawn, coming to stand next to me so my bare upper arm ran the length of hers from shoulder to elbow. "We said we would move on."

"Ah." I nodded, taking another long drag on the cigarette.

"People are talking, Saint."

I shrugged. "People talk all the time." She gave me a skeptical look, and I cleared my throat, deciding to switch directions. "Is that what you're doing with Lore? Moving on?"

Ru smiled, and I memorized the curve of her mouth, recalling how much I loved to bite it. "I'm having fun."

"Fun." A sledgehammer hit me in the gut because that one word held so much weight between us. When we'd ended things, I told her she needed to go out and live her life. *Have fun.* I hadn't said it to be cruel, but she'd taken it to mean that the time we were together hadn't been enjoyable for me. In reality, they'd been the best ten months of my life. She couldn't know that, though. No one could. It was another one of those things I locked deep down inside my heart and never let anyone see.

"Yeah." She stabbed out the cigarette and turned to face me, her body so close, the heat radiated off her and warmed me. It made me itch to yank the shirt over her head and remind myself how fiery her skin was. "Isn't that what you wanted? To stand by and watch as a younger version of you whisked me off into the sunset?"

"Don't get it twisted, baby girl." I straightened and mirrored her pose, putting out my smoke, too. "I didn't say I wanted you to fuck other men."

"Then what am I supposed to do?" She stepped closer, her nipple piercings brushing up against the bottom of my chest through her shirt. "Sit around and wait for you to decide I'm old enough?"

"I didn't say that, either." I swallowed and resisted the urge to put some space between us. God, I missed her, and standing there on the deck in the dark, I wanted to touch every beautiful inch.

"No, you don't say much, do you?"

She traced a fingertip up the center of my stomach and over my pec to my shoulder, swirling around my tattoos like she used to when we were together. The touch zinged down the center of my body, headed straight for my balls, and a faint groan ripped out of my throat before I could stop it. I grabbed her wrist and yanked it away from me, and she snapped her big blue eyes to mine, tucking her bottom lip between her teeth when my cock jerked between us. "I can still do it, huh?"

Fuck.

"Turn you on with one touch?"

"No." She could turn me on with a slight breath and a lingering look.

"Yes." Ru pushed up on her toes, bringing our bodies in contact with each other from torso to pelvis and down to our knees. She touched my neck with her lips, a soft caress that made every muscle in my body tremble. She, too, shook like a leaf, and whether that was from the intimacy between us or the summer night's breeze, I didn't know. I didn't care.

Teeth nipped at my cropped beard, and my balls clenched, my head swimming. Out here in the moonlight, our voices hushed by the cicadas and crickets and frogs, the rest of the world seemed so far away. I could have her, maybe just this once, maybe just out here.

No. Stop this, the logical side of me said. *Aris is asleep two rooms away.*

I grabbed her shoulders and pushed her down, touching my forehead to hers. "We need some ground rules while I'm staying here."

Ru made a low giggling sound and shook her head, taking a step back to break the connection between us. In her absence, the humid air whooshed in and brought me back to my senses. I had good fucking reasons to stay away from Ru. One lonely night on the porch could not bring all that crumbling down.

"Okay. Let's hear them." She crossed her arms and pursed her lips in that bratty indignant way of hers. Fuck, how it made me want to tame her, to break her down to a quivering mess. I clenched my hands to keep my body still.

"Number one: no showing off."

That made her laugh harder, but I held firm. This had all started with her putting on a show, and Goddamn it, I was a human. I could only withstand so much.

"Okay, fine." She rolled her eyes. "What else?"

"Don't bring Junior around here. It's one thing to fuck him on your website, but I don't need to hear the two of you—"

"I don't fuck anyone on the internet but me," she said. The relief that sliced through my chest damn near toppled me, and I had to clench my hand on the wooden railing to keep myself upright. "But I'll ask the same of you."

"I haven't been with anyone else—" It came out before I could stop it. Jesus Christ, I shouldn't have said that.

"Why not?"

I cleared my throat. "That's none of your fucking business."

It wasn't. She didn't need to know the thought of anyone else repulsed me. That at night, when I was alone, the only person I thought of was her. The only person I wanted to curl myself around and drift off to sleep with was her. No one else could compare. Ever.

"Fine, rule number three." She gave me that deliciously cruel grin. "You can't touch me."

I swallowed, shifting my shoulders against the stab that went straight through my sternum. No touching her? *Ever*?

"I'm serious." She narrowed her gaze and held firm. "You keep your hands to yourself."

"Fine. Same goes for you."

She clenched her jaw but said, "Fine."

If she wanted to fight with fire, so be it.

"Rule number four, and I fucking mean this one." I closed the few inches between us and wrapped my hand around her throat, brushing my thumb against her pulse point. She tried to hide a shiver, but I felt it anyway, and I yanked her closer, leaning down so my teeth nipped along the curve of her ear. "My patience is wearing thin. Don't fucking tease me." I pulled away and stared down at her with a dominance that dared her to disobey. She liked to push my buttons, and this one would be tough for her. "You understand me, little sinner?"

I brushed the pad of my thumb over her lower lip, the sensation singing in my blood as I shoved it past her teeth to her tongue. She lapped at me and closed her lips around it to suck, just like I wanted. My cock gave a half-hearted throb, making my knees tingle. I zeroed in on the motion, memorizing how plump her lips were.

"Say you understand me."

"I understand you." She mumbled the words around my finger,

and when I let her go, her palms came to my chest to keep from tumbling forward.

"Good girl." I nodded and put a few feet between us, gesturing toward her door. "The rules start now. Go back to your room and don't test me again."

She did as I said, scampering inside and shutting the glass door behind her. My heart pounded, and I took a deep breath to try to soothe it because I knew one thing very clearly.

We shouldn't have done that.

Setting rules in the starlight, touching each other under the watchful eye of the galaxies, it crossed a line. Back when we were together, I had lived to give her rules.

And my beautiful brat had lived to break them.

5

SAINT

I committed a big sin when I went back to my room. My curiosity got the better of me. I'd seen Ru naked a thousand times. I could pick her out of a lineup by taste and scent alone, and maybe doing this crossed a boundary now that we weren't together anymore, but none of that mattered.

I sat in Aris's guest bed, propped up against the headboard, my phone glowing in the dark as I paid the monthly subscription fee to Alba's website.

My heart nearly stopped when I found her.

Sienna Sin.

Goddamn it.

The fucking tease had named herself to taunt me. Whenever we did a scene, her honorific to me was sir. Mine for her was sinner. The pride that shot down my spine had me adjusting myself and questioning my morals. But fuck it, I'd never had any.

I told myself I was doing this out of some kind of sick well-being check. I wanted to make sure she was safe, and that mighta been true if she had been any other girl. But this was Ru, and I was a masochist. Was I doing this because I was hoping to see her with someone else? Possibly. But she'd said the only one she fucked on the internet was herself, and when I scrolled through the first few pages of her site, I confirmed she hadn't lied.

All of it was solo.

Hating myself and knowing I would regret it, I clicked on the highest-rated one and ran a hand over my mouth, reminding myself I could look all I wanted, but I'd just set a rule not to touch.

"God, it feels so good." She ran her fingers over her clit and arched her back, big eyes focused on the camera. "I saved it all up for you. Only for you. Don't you want to come with me?" Ru pouted and rubbed harder, moaning louder, forcing herself into a climax. My cock gave a half a jerk but like Ru, my heart wasn't in it.

I'd seen her orgasm a thousand times. I'd made her come myself a thousand more. This was a performance. I looked at the logo on the top of the website.

Real people. Real orgasms.

I snorted a sardonic laugh and went to the next video, watching as she coached herself through that one, too. On and on, each video was pretend. Ru was a good actress, and she'd racked up a ton of followers based on that, but I really knew her, and my little sinner was lying.

I thought about it the rest of the night, even after I'd clicked my phone off and stared at the ceiling, and again when I jerked off in the shower the next morning with memories of her flowery feminine scent in my nose and her sweet strawberry taste in my mouth.

Then I stood in the freezing cold water with my forehead pressed up against the tile and prayed for forgiveness. I prayed for strength. I prayed for whatever I'd need to get through these next few days. Because now that I knew she was faking it, I wanted nothing more than to make her come on her filthy website for real.

Fuck.

I still wanted her, and I'd always want her, and this keeping her safe from afar bullshit was the stupidest idea I ever had.

After I dressed and headed downstairs, I pulled up short at the entrance to the kitchen. Ru sat on the island, wearing a low-cut tank top and a pair of cutoff shorts, her bare feet swinging back and forth while she ate a bowl of cereal and read something on her laptop.

She'd piled her hair on top of her head, bits sticking out in odd directions. The urge to position myself between her knees and scoot her closer to the edge swelled up inside of me, but I shoved it away. I could have done that a year ago. Now, I went to the coffeemaker on the opposite side of the kitchen instead.

"Morning," I said.

"Hey you." She seemed like she was in a good mood, and the sudden change in attitude made me suspicious. "Did you know that at any given moment, thirty million people around the world are watching porn?"

I blinked as I grabbed a mug and poured coffee into it, clearly needing more caffeine for this conversation.

"I mean, that's thirty million people a minute that could subscribe to Crimson." Ru whistled and shook her head. "Could you imagine the profits we'd bring in? The ad revenue alone would pay for our grandkids' college." I woulda let the slip go, but she cleared her throat and said, "I mean...my grandkids, obviously."

"Obviously." I tried not to smile at how adorable it was when she got flustered. Not much rattled Ru. I'd seen her stand up to bikers twice her size and beat them down with logic or whatever object she could find. Once or twice, I'd had to pull her off some asshole at the Beacon for getting too grabby with the girls.

But, fuck, the fact that one look from me could make her blush went to my head more than it should. I leaned back against the counter and drank my coffee. I liked it black, no sugar, no cream, something Ru once teased me about. *"Pitch and bitter,"* she used to say. *"Just like your soul."*

"I've been thinking about the Beacon. I have a more formalized plan for you." She smiled, taking another big bite of cereal. "If you're interested."

"Is this your sex club idea?"

"I'm talking membership fees, NDAs, the whole shebang." She swallowed and tilted the bowl over her mouth, drinking the leftover milk. It was such a Ru thing to do, and surprisingly, one of the things

I'd missed the most about her. "We'd make it anonymous and private. Give people a safe place to play with their secrets."

I thinned my lips and continued sipping my drink, disregarding the first fifteen things I thought to say.

When can we start renovations?

Would there be a private room just for us?

How many secrets could you and I keep in those walls?

I thought about her bringing up sex clubs yesterday, and I again wondered what she'd gotten up to while we were apart. The thought of her on Crimson didn't bother me; Ru was a beautiful woman, and if she could make easy money off that, more power to her. But the thought of who she might be going to sex clubs with and what she might be doing there had me swallowing down the scalding envy in the back of my throat.

Christ, Saint. Get a fucking grip.

"Anyway, I thought it would be fun if we rebranded that way. It could be cash only, which would allow the MC to scrub the same amount from the guns, if not more." She hopped off the counter so she could place her bowl in the sink.

Trying to settle the rage in my gut took work, but when I finally found the words, I said, "You think it's a good idea? You running a kink club with your ex?"

She laughed, and the light, carefree sound almost calmed me down. "No, silly. The MC is going to let me take it over."

I raised an eyebrow. "You sound pretty sure about that."

"When I bring it back to life, they won't have a choice." She threw her messenger bag over her shoulder and slipped on her aviators before nodding and grabbing her to-go coffee. "I'll see you later." Then she headed toward the front door and closed it behind her.

For the two weeks she'd been home, she had tiptoed around me. If we had to be together in front of other people, we put on a good show, but that's all it was—a misdirection so they didn't see behind the curtain. Backstage, we'd been playing this game for four years. She teased me, and I took it until I couldn't.

I'd told her to have fun, find someone her own age, and she dangled a younger version of me in my face to drive me to my breaking point. She was moving on with her life, and I got back my old relationship with Ru, the one before we fucked. That was what I wanted...right?

I cracked my neck and dumped what remained of my coffee in the sink, bitching to myself about how much of an idiot I could be. I closed my eyes and took a deep breath in through my nose, visualizing the air filling my lungs, cleansing me of the sickness in my soul. I exhaled slow...1...2...3...4. Then, I found my keys and my wallet, and I headed outside to my bike.

When I opened the door, Ru's two-door pickup still sat in the driveway. She cranked the engine, but it churned without turning over. I walked around to the driver's side and knocked on the window.

"You need some help?"

She shook her head. "No. Thanks. I'll call KC, and he'll tow it."

Yeah fucking right. Like I was going to leave her sitting there. I nodded toward my bike and put on my glasses. "Come on."

"No, really. It's—"

"I wasn't asking." I walked away, pleased when the door closed and her shoes echoed off the asphalt behind me. I handed the extra helmet to her and put mine on, lifting one leg over the seat and sticking the key in the ignition.

Ru looked down before wincing and glancing back up at me. "I've got a lot of errands to run today. I don't expect you to drive me everywhere."

I kicked the motorcycle to life to drown out the rest of her argument. Her features dropped in annoyance, but she relented, putting the helmet over her hair and climbing on behind me. She wrapped her legs around the outside of my hips and closed her arms over my stomach, reminding me how perfectly we fit together. A sense of fulfilling rightness settled in my bones that had no business being there.

I put the bike in first, and we took off.

"WHAT DO YOU MEAN A WEEK?" Ru put her hands on her hips and circled around the counter to Selene, balking at the computer screen.

After we swung by Rose Garage, Thor and KC had gone to Ru's house to tow her truck here so KC could run the diagnostic. She needed a new starter. While these things were common for new cars, Aris had been driving around Ru's Tacoma for ten years before he gave it to her, and it was used when he bought it.

"I can't get the part before then." Selene pointed to the date. "See?"

"Fuck." Ru rubbed her hands over her face. "I don't have time for this."

"Relax." Selene put her arm over her friend's shoulder. "You can borrow any number of beautifully restored pieces of shit in the back." She gestured to a wall of keys containing the beaters Thor had gotten at a cheap price and put back together. I grimaced at the thought of her rolling around in one of those death traps.

"No fucking way," I said. Both of them looked at me. "You can drive my truck until yours is fixed."

Ru narrowed her eyes. "Are you serious?"

Selene crossed her arms over her chest, eyeing me with her best big-sister glare. When Ru and I had first gotten together, we promised to keep it a secret. But Selene and Ru had been best friends their whole lives. Ru musta told her after it was over, and now Selene had changed her opinion of me in the wake of her friend's heartbreak.

"Sure. I'll get you the spare key this evening." I held up a hand to give her one caveat. "Just don't wreck it."

"Of course." Ru skipped around the desk and threw her arms over my shoulders in a hug. Her scent plumed around me, and I wanted to lean down to kiss her. Not even a whole twenty-four hours had passed, and she was already breaking the rules. But I couldn't stop her. "Thank you. I'll repay you somehow. I'll fix breakfast every morning you're at the house."

"The house?" Selene leaned over the counter and looked between us, her bright blue eyes suspicious.

"Yeah, Aris is making Saint stay there while he's on his trip."

"Uh-huh." Selene nodded. "You're okay with that?"

Ru shrugged. "Yeah. It's fine."

Selene shifted her gaze to me and picked up a tire iron, swinging it around in her hand as she moved toward the garage. "All right, you two. I have smut to read, so..." She pointed to the door with the long metal rod before clapping it into her other hand and narrowing her eyes. "I'll call you when the part comes in."

We said our goodbyes and got back on my bike, heading toward the studio Alba rented for her website. I took the long way through the mountains, enjoying the breeze in the shade and the views of the bright green scenery.

After learning about my brother, Aris had asked how I could still believe in God. I didn't have a great answer for him at the time, and even if I did, it wouldn't have anything to do with my reasons today. It was because of moments like this, when I had my girl on the back of my bike, the wind in my hair, and the finger of heaven painting the world around me. How could there *not* be divinity in that?

Ru had to stop by Crimson before we went to the Beacon, and when she asked me to pick her up in an hour, I squinted in confusion. "What the fuck are you doing that's going to take an hour?"

She clenched her jaw and tightened her fingers around her messenger bag, swinging a leg over the bike and taking off her helmet. "Thanks again for the ride."

Her reluctance to answer the question set a small flame in my gut as images of what I'd witnessed last night assaulted me. They'd been churning around in my guilty conscience ever since. I closed my eyes and sighed.

Am I really about to go through with this?

I couldn't stomach her doing this with anyone else, and the thought of her faking her way through another few rounds this morning made the animal inside me pace. I shut off the engine and kicked the stand out to climb off my bike.

"What are you doing?" She set her icy gaze on me.

I took off my helmet and hung it on the handlebars. "Going inside with you."

"Why?"

"Because I wanna see where you work, baby girl. Got a problem with it?"

She raised an eyebrow but didn't respond, just turned on her heel and led the way. Air conditioning hit me in the face as soon as I walked in, sobering me to how much the place had changed since they'd bought it last year. Alba and KC started in a one-room studio with a bed and some furniture. Now, they'd built out a whole production setup. The main foyer gave way to a corridor with doors running down either side. Offices sat off to the right, decorated in whites and pinks, giving the whole place a sleek feminine vibe.

The shit was impressive.

Alba straightened when we passed the break room, making eye contact with me as I followed Ru toward the back.

"Um, excuse me," she said, peering around the corner with a big grin. "You weren't going to say hi?" Her brilliant gaze looked from me to Ru and back again.

Ru forced a smile, her cheeks blushing like she'd been caught with her hand in the cookie jar. "Hi."

Alba pursed her lips. "It's good to see you, Saint."

"Likewise." I recognized the innuendo in her tone, and I gave her a stoic expression that let her suspect whatever she wanted.

"Do you need your own room or—"

"No," Ru answered for me. "He's not staying."

I shifted my attention to her, recalling the way she'd teased me last night by running her finger across my chest to get my attention. Well, she had it now, and I wasn't about to let it go.

"That's right," I said. "Ru's just giving me a tour."

"Is she?" Alba flashed a playful smile before turning back into the break room. "Have fun."

"It's not like that," Ru called after her, but the fact she had to make excuses for my presence stung. Once upon a time, we'd been attached at the hip, and I woulda been the first person she told about this. Now, the distance between us made her keep things to herself, and I didn't like that shit at all.

"Well, go on then." I linked my hands behind my back and stared down at my girl with an indignant glare.

Ru looked at me like she was trying to figure out what I was up to. Good luck, because I didn't even know myself. I just knew I loved having her wrapped around me on the back of my bike and I was too damned territorial to let her walk in here alone ever again. Or, God forbid, with Lore.

"What are you doing?" She shook her head. "I told you I had to run errands. I don't need a—"

"Babysitter. Yeah, I know." I took another step toward her, all the reasons why I needed to stay away suddenly falling out of my head, leaving a burning hot intensity. I wanted to see where she touched herself and why she was faking it. I wanted to make her come for real. "But since I'm here, I might as well take a look around. C'mon, sinner. Show me the ropes."

Then I walked around her stunned form and continued down the hallway, exploring on my own.

6

RU

Is he serious?

When we were together, I'd just started to get to know Alba, and I certainly hadn't started camming yet. There was no reason to think he'd ever be interested in doing this with me, and given he wasn't an exhibitionist, I stood there for a moment to debate what I should do.

It was the honorific that gave me the courage to keep going.

Sinner.

He'd called me baby girl since I met him. I couldn't even remember anymore where the nickname came from. No one in the MC batted an eye when he said it.

Sinner was something we used in kink space. Like sir, it told me Saint wanted to revive what we had. There was a part of me that wanted to slam the fucking door in his face, to put up a wall and say he was the one that drove me to it. He hadn't earned the right to this. But hell, I always was a sucker for punishment, and I wanted it too damn much.

When we walked into my favorite room, I ignored the stammering in my heart and the shaking in my knees. I managed to keep myself upright, swallowing my shame when the door shut behind him, trapping us alone together.

He turned the lock, and the sound reverberated through my skin. My lower belly clenched, but I'd never been one to back down from him, and in here, I wasn't Ru anymore. I shed that skin and became Sienna Sin. If he stuck around, he'd see that transformation. I'd give him any show he wanted.

"This is where I do my thing." I cleared my throat and spread my arms out to either side, going back to the flimsy excuse he'd used to follow me.

He looked around the space, dark eyes inspecting the camera equipment and lighting tents. "You edit your own videos?"

"We hired a professional." I watched him size up the toy wall, my breath catching when he paused in front of the ropes. Memories of nights long ago flashed through my mind. I could almost feel the burn of the threads digging into my wrists, his hot fingertips brushing my skin as he looped the knots. "Performers can do it themselves, or they can use our services for a fee." I ran a hand over the back of my neck, hoping he didn't notice the burn in my cheeks. "We're trying to stay as legit as possible while allowing our associates creative freedom."

Saint put his hands in his pockets and continued his stroll, stopping next to the company logo.

"Is that true?" He pointed to the slogan.

Real people. Real orgasms.

I grabbed my arms behind my back and nodded, doing my best not to fidget. Since I'd been home, Saint and I had been alone only a handful of times, and none of those interactions were particularly friendly. This felt different, like last night on the deck. He was being nice to me, and strangely, I had it in me to be nice to him, too.

"How can you be sure?"

I narrowed my eyes. "What do you mean?"

"If the performers are editing their own videos, how do you know their orgasms are real?"

"Oh." I nodded. "We have the right to take anything down that doesn't fit with our brand. But we don't have a problem with that." I stepped closer to the bathroom. I only had the space for an hour, and time was money. "Most of our performers are happy to turn out the real thing."

"Hmm." He didn't believe me, and as he set his full attention in my direction, I tensed my muscles to keep from shivering at the heat in his stare. "Are you"—I ignored the throb in my clit when he brushed a stray piece of hair behind my ear—"happy to turn out the real thing?"

He didn't need to know I faked my way through my videos, that the only time I got off was when I thought of him, and even then, it came with heartache because I'd never be able to have him again.

"Yeah, sure," I lied.

"Hmm." This noise questioned my answer. His eyes pierced through me like I was a peasant among a titan. *No, this look meant something more, like he knew I'd been faking it. How?*

"Did you watch my videos?"

He pulled his lips into a big grin. "Liar, liar, pants on fire." He took another step closer, the smell of his deodorant and woodsy cologne nearly bringing me to my knees. "Why are you faking it, Ru?"

My mouth opened, but nothing came out. I considered lying again, perhaps saying I had performance anxiety or other things on my mind. In the end, we'd promised the truth between us. "Because nothing does it for me anymore."

"You can't make yourself come?"

"No, I mean..." I closed my eyes, debating whether I should confess the whole thing. I wasn't ready for him to know how badly he'd affected me, so instead I said, "It's a lot to think about. Positioning and postures and new angles to keep the viewer entertained."

Okay, that isn't a total lie.

"Ah." He nodded. "You need direction."

The word hung between us, and I balled my hands into fists as the tension suffocated me. I'd tried to be strong, the version of me that had been heartbroken by his betrayal and angry at his apathy. Maybe I'd been able to do that for a while. But in that room, with this kinetic buzz in the inches between us, that Ru was long gone. In her place was his sinner, a mere mortal that prayed for whatever mercy he wanted to give.

He had ages of groveling to do, but it didn't matter. I wanted whatever he was about to say next with a ferocity I hadn't felt in months.

"Go get dressed," he continued. "Put on your mask. Then get on the bed."

The submissive in me wilted, ready to jump right back into this dynamic, but the brat in me fought it. He hadn't earned my obedience yet, especially after last night. "Isn't this against your rules?"

He crossed his arms over his chest, smirking at my back talk. We hadn't negotiated any new boundaries between us. He couldn't shove himself in here and start ordering me around the way he used to.

"Sure. Maybe Saint and Ru have rules between them." He grabbed a piece of my hair, pinching it between his fingers like he was trying to capture the feel of it forever. "Maybe Sienna and her director don't."

I took a deep breath and let it out through my nose, wanting to give in to this for all the wrong reasons. I wouldn't be his secret anymore, but this was *my* secret. Maybe we could have one more between us. Just the one. Just for old times' sake.

"No touching," I said, grasping for ways to keep this professional. "And you stay off camera." This was my show, my fanbase.

"Okay."

I paused, waiting for my conscience to take the steering wheel and tell me this was the worst thing I could do. When that didn't happen and he didn't back down, I said, "My safe word is blizzard," and grabbed my messenger bag to get ready in the bathroom. I didn't check to see his reaction, but it must have stung his pride. It was the same word we'd used when we were together.

I hadn't planned on Saint staying, and I definitely didn't account for him wanting to coach me through a scene. If I had, I might have planned a little better.

Am I an idiot for going along with this?

Probably, but every stupid urge in my body wouldn't back down. I needed his eyes on my skin again. I needed his voice in my ears. Perhaps there was a sadistic part of me that wanted to show him what he'd been missing.

I did my makeup and styled my hair, slipping into a bra and thong before attaching the garter belts to thigh-high tights. I tied the black mask onto my face, making sure to reapply my ruby-red lipstick before I went back to the main room.

My pulse pounded and my stomach swirled with butterflies as I ignored his stare. He'd grabbed a chair and sat on the other side of the room, far away from the camera on the tripod. I went to the iPad built into the wall and clicked a few buttons, turning on all the equipment in the room. I'd get multiple angles all at once and decide later which were the best ones to use.

When I finally gained the courage to look at him, I gasped. Control laced his expression, the dominant already awake in his eyes. His jaw ticked as he adjusted his hips in his seat, his legs spread wide, his hands resting casually on his thighs.

Good God.

He was so hot, even dressed in his jeans and dark T-shirt. But, he'd given me an instruction, and the minute I walked out of that bathroom, Ru had been locked away in a dark corner of my mind. His sinner took over. The only thing that existed between the two of us was this magnetic pull, this feeling that I'd been put on this earth to do whatever he said. I trusted him to take care of me, and only he could do that so completely.

I climbed on the bed and sat up on my knees, waiting for his next instruction.

"For the duration of the scene," he said, "I will refer to you as Sienna. You will refer to me as sir." He rose and went to the wall, retrieving a clit-suctioning toy and a vibrator before tossing them on the bed and sitting down again. When I moved to grab them, he tsked and I paused. "I didn't tell you to touch those."

I smiled and pulled my palms back to my thighs, waiting for him to give me a command. A tremble rocketed down my spine and into my legs, which shivered in a way they never had before. I couldn't believe he was actually here, doing this with me, and the erotic way he raked his gaze over my body made my skin burst into an inferno.

"From now on, your hands are my hands. You touch yourself because I want you to. Is that understood?"

Fuck. A hard throbbing lust hit me between the legs, and I clenched them shut to soothe the ache. Time stretched between us as I stared at him, relishing in the way his presence took this to an entirely new level. When it was just me, I couldn't focus enough to make this enjoyable. I tried to put on a good show, but it was *nothing* compared to having his demands in my head.

"I asked you a question."

"Yes, sir."

"Good." He wielded so much power in that one word, it stole my complete attention. My entire world focused on him and him alone, just like it used to. "You liked when I took you on your back, so lie down, Sienna."

The more he called me by my stage name, the more I could believe this was happening to someone else, that the rules between Ru and Saint had dissipated within these walls, and we could be different people. I spread out on the mattress with my back arched and my open knees facing him.

"Run your hands over your thighs. Unhook the garter belts."

His voice coated my skin like honey, and I rushed to obey, my fingers shaking and slipping over the cool metal clips as I unhooked them.

"Good girl."

Goddamn, that made me shake harder. I lived for his compliments. "Run your hands over your thighs. Spread your knees farther apart. There ya go."

Closing my eyes, I pretended my fingers were his, and I went back to a year ago, when we touched each other freely. Something like this would have been so vanilla compared to how he played my body then, but it was the most intimate thing I'd done in ages.

"Pull your bra down. I want to see your piercings."

I bit my bottom lip because the silver barbells had always turned him on, and when I freed my nipples, I resisted the urge to pinch them between my fingers. I loved when he bit them, when he rolled them between his teeth. Thinking about it now made me moan.

"You're such a good little sinner, aren't you?"

I nodded. "Yes, sir."

"Take off your panties. Slow. We have to tease the audience."

I did what he said, sliding the fabric down my legs and off my feet, leaving me in the thigh-high tights. He went silent, the static charge between us buzzing almost as loud as my heart. I leaned my head to the side so I could meet his gaze where he still sat in the same leisurely pose.

His expression almost stopped my heart, irises twinkling with desire and pupils dilated with lust. He wanted to revoke the no touching rule and climb into this bed with me so he could use his hands on my body for real. But I'd set that boundary because his fury fueled my own. His wanting made me want, and perhaps this is where I took my revenge on him for all these months because I held firm. I jutted my chin out and nailed him with a stern gaze.

"Sir? What should I do next?"

He cleared his throat and met my gaze, the tension between us vibrating like a palpable thing. "Touch that pretty pink clit."

My fingers connected with my most sensitive skin, and my hips surged off the bed. I was so wet and ready for this that the heat and slickness of my body surprised me. I wanted to rush it, to bring myself to climax right away, but Saint's voice cut through it all.

"Slow down, Sienna."

I panted, my blood hammering against my insides, making me desperate. But I steadied my strokes and moaned, wanting more, needing more.

"Grab the vibrator. Use it on your clit the way you like."

After I found it on the mattress, I turned it on to the medium setting, knowing I was too riled up already to start low. I stared into his eyes while I pressed the toy into the spots that sent sparks of pleasure up my body, and his gaze never left mine. He held me there the way he used to, captivated and mesmerized. "There you go. That feels good, doesn't it?"

"Yes, sir." God, so good, especially when he crossed his arms over his chest and studied me, the bulge in his pants indicating how badly this impacted him, too.

"Put the vibrator inside you. Grab the other one."

I obeyed, struggling to turn on the toy. My entire body shook like a scared kitten. I hadn't even trembled this hard the first time we were together, and the fact I had wanted this for so long made my shivers even more immediate. I pressed the toy to my clit and pushed the vibrator inside me, writhing against the sensations building in my body.

Everything about this experience made me wetter, hotter, more eager. Saint's presence and his commands and the way he looked at me turned me into the sexiest person in the world.

"Fuck yourself with the vibrator. Fuck yourself the way you want me to fuck you."

Ohh, the statement should have stopped me cold, but it didn't. I held his gaze, making sure he knew this was all for him. This show. This buildup. This climax.

It was his.

It had always been his.

The thought consumed me and I pushed the toy inside me harder, rougher. My muscles tensed, blinding, burning euphoria pulling me down into the abyss. I came with the agony of the thousand faked times before it, every disappointment since him evaporating in my soul, surging through my veins.

"Fuck, fuck, fuck." It went on and on, racking my body, twisting me into oblivion. Nothing had ever been so powerful or all-consuming.

I wanted to revel in it forever.

I never wanted it to stop.

Eventually, the hormones subsided, and I rubbed my face,

gasping for deep inhales to slow my racing heart. My muscles still quivered, and my hands shook as I brushed them back through my hair.

He punctuated his soft chuckle with a quiet, "Now, that wasn't so hard, was it?"

7

───────

SAINT

Ru gave me the middle finger, making me laugh.

"Now you're being a brat. I'll have to punish you for that."

She pushed up so she balanced her weight on her elbows, staring down her perfect body at me. Watching her come had been the highlight of my year so far, and even if I got up and walked out of here with the hardest cock in the world, I wouldn't have changed a thing.

Two days ago, I chastised myself for agreeing to house-sit while Aris went out of town. But c'mon, I knew it would end up here. Me, telling her what to do. Her, willingly complying. It had only taken one midnight conversation and a list of rules to reel us both back in.

Allowing the connection between us to flare to life again had the added benefit of unscrewing a valve to let out some of the pressure. Yeah, my cock throbbed in my jeans, but it was like old times again, back when we laughed easily and teased as hard as we fucked.

She dropped her gaze to my lap and licked her lips, drawing my attention to the motion. I knew what would have happened next if we were together. She would have gotten on her knees between my legs and opened her mouth like a good little slut, preparing herself for whatever I wanted to do to her next. And I would have slotted myself down her throat and fucked her face until I couldn't stand anymore, but we'd said no touching. I needed to stick to that for my sanity.

"See something you want?" My throat felt like sandpaper, my voice coming out hoarse and rough.

She bit her bottom lip and nodded. "What about you, sir?"

"This scene isn't about me." It had been about her from the beginning.

She sighed and sat up on her knees. "Couples do better. I'd split the pay with you fifty-fifty."

"I don't want your money." That wasn't why I did this, but at the sight of her pout, my dick reminded me of his say in the conversation, jolting under my jeans in a desperate plea for attention. I winced and adjusted my hips, grabbing the damn thing and shifting it around in my pants.

"Still, you got to watch me." She slumped to the side, holding herself up with one hand on the mattress next to her. She looked so beautiful like that, all curves and wild hair. I ached to run my hands through it again, maybe yank a handful back and capture a moan on my tongue. "It's only fair that you reciprocate."

What a fucking tease. I smiled and raised an eyebrow. "So desperate for my cock?"

"Insatiable."

I took a deep breath at the filthy images floating around in my head, running my palms over my face as I considered. It was one thing to watch her film a scene she intended to make public anyway. It was another to whip out my dick while she watched. That seemed like crossing a line.

But, like she said, fair was fair.

I reached for my button, undoing it before sliding down the zipper one slow link at a time. Ru liked the anticipation of the eventual release. Back when I took her freely, I loved to edge her until she couldn't think anymore. Part of me had considered doing it today, but that, too, crossed a boundary we hadn't negotiated between us.

Her gaze stayed glued to my hand as I shoved my jeans down my hips. Next went my boxers until my straining cock bounced out of the fabric, angry at having been neglected this long.

Ru moved to get up, her foot going to the ground like she intended to break the one rule between these versions of us. I held up a finger to stop her.

"You stay over there."

Her features fell, but she slumped back on the mattress, digging her fingers into the sheet while she watched with desire behind her eyes. I let my gaze roam over her more freely than I had when I was directing her. This time, I lingered on my favorite pieces—the dragon tattoo swirling up her leg, the dimples in her thighs where the tights dug into her skin, the way her tits fit my hands like they were made for me.

I stroked myself, remembering how her soft skin gave under my callused fingers, and when she stuck a hand between her legs again, I groaned before I could stop it. I grabbed the tip of my cock, slowing my pace before I exploded prematurely and embarrassed myself.

"You see what you do to me?" I told her, throwing my head back, clenching my eyes shut. I remembered sinking into her tight cunt, how warm and wet she could get, how she purred and shivered just for me. "You filthy fucking sinner."

My sinner.

My filthy girl.

My Ru.

"I always loved you like this," she said. "Completely unhinged. At the mercy of your worst impulses." She tucked her lip between her teeth, and I longed to bite her again.

God, I was so fucked because she kept saying the dirtiest things I'd ever heard her say, and for as much as it surprised me, it hit me right in my weak spot.

"I used to love when you fucked me like a wild beast." She giggled and sighed.

I fucked my fist faster, my heart pounding in my head, and when I came, I launched my hips off the chair like I'd been zapped in the ass. My orgasm hit me behind the eyes and in the center of my chest, yanking me down into its oblivion. I hadn't been with anyone since the last time we were together, and if that was the price I had to pay for this? I'd gladly it pay it over and over again.

My heart pounded, and my head swam. I saw stars behind my eyelids and struggled to catch my breath.

Jesus fucking Christ.

When I eventually came back, I opened my eyes and found Ru on the edge of her seat, playing with her clit, adoration pouring out of her in thick suffocating waves. If this had been a year ago, she woulda crawled into my lap. I woulda shoved my head between her legs and made her come on my beard for the next two hours. I woulda tied her down with those shitty ropes and apologized for every month we'd been apart.

But that wasn't the point of today, and that wasn't part of this scene.

"Don't look at me like that, sinner." I gave her a stern glare and raised an eyebrow while I cleaned myself off with the nearby wipes. "We step outside that room, our rules go back into play."

"Then I suppose we'll have to come here more often." She smiled and climbed off the bed so she could head toward the bathroom. "Won't we?"

Big fucking mistake. Playing with Ru had always been one of my most favorite ways to pass the time, and camming? Well, it should have been me from the start. If she was going to do this, really do it, then she needed to be with someone who would take care of her in every sense of the word. After what I'd woken in her two years ago, the only person that *could* do that was me.

"We'll see," I said. "This doesn't change anything. The same reasons we couldn't do this before are the same reasons we can't do it now."

Disappointment flickered behind her baby blues, but she forced a small smile and shut it down. "No one will know it's you." She closed the door to the bathroom before I could respond.

That wasn't what I was worried about.

ONLY A CERTAIN TYPE of person joined a motorcycle club. Most of us lived on the edge, the call of the open road ringing in our blood, the thrill of the next adrenaline rush just out of reach. That ride to the Beacon hit me differently than any ride before it. She held my waist tighter. The sun shined brighter. The world was calmer and more radiant than it had been in months. I woulda sworn the scene we did at Crimson relieved some of the tension between us, but emotionally, all the shit we'd bottled up was still there. When we got to the Beacon, Ru thanked me again for offering to let her drive my truck. As if I woulda done anything else.

"You really don't have to do that." She smiled and unlocked the front door, walking to the alarm to punch in the code.

"I know I don't."

"Then why are you?" She dropped her stuff on the bar, circling around to the other side so she could flick on the lights.

I paused, all the terrible reasons bubbling up in my mind. Because she was my girl, even if I didn't like it. Because her dad woulda wanted me to. Because I didn't want Lore driving her around instead. Eventually, I said, "Because I can."

She sighed and rolled her eyes. "Right."

My hackles rose at her tone. "What's that supposed to mean?"

Ru turned to face me, putting her hands out on the bar in either direction, eyeing me with suspicion. "Do you remember that night we got trapped in the snow?"

Every fucking day. It was the first time we'd ever hooked up, the first time I'd ever let myself admit I wanted her. "Yeah. Sure."

"I made you promise that whatever you told me, it would be the truth."

I didn't know where this conversation was headed, so I shoved my hands in my pockets, preparing myself for the grenade she was about to lob my way. "I remember."

"I thought that might make you open up, but all it did was make you more secretive."

"I'm not secretive." I just didn't like spilling my shit all over the place. The more people knew about me, the more they had to use against me and the more vulnerable I was. But maybe she had a point. Ru deserved to see that softer side of me. She'd earned the right to it with her sweat and come and tears.

"Then, tell me. Rapid-fire. The first thing that comes to your mind. Why'd you wait around for me on the porch the other night?"

Fuck. I realized the trap too late, and now I couldn't get out of her web.

"No, no," she said. "Don't clam up. Tell me."

"I wanted to make sure you got home safe."

"Why?"

"Because I care about you, Ru." I forced myself to stay firm, to not retreat when everything in my body wanted to get out of this conversation. "That's never gonna change."

She took a deep breath and let it out in slow defeat, giving me a soft smile and a quick nod. "I care about you, too." ·

"I know."

Ru leaned closer, her top falling open with just a teasing hint. "I'm not really with Lore."

"I know that, too."

Her features dropped, and she raised her eyebrows. "How could you possibly know that?"

I straightened and smiled, taking a step back, keeping my swagger cocky. "C'mon, Ru. We've been playing this game a long time now. It's still all for me." I held her gaze as her cheeks turned that delectable shade of rosy pink. "Isn't it?"

Her lips parted, and I focused on the shadow beyond her teeth, remembering how I used to lick my way inside and play with her tongue until she squirmed. Visions of what we'd done at Crimson not two hours ago echoed behind her eyes, and I knew I had her.

Yeah, I'm a sick fucker. It's all for me.

"That's what I thought." I chuckled to myself and took another step back, needing to put space between us before I grabbed her by the neck and bent her over the bar top. Winking, I turned to head toward the office upstairs. I had an entire day of leads to follow up on, and I couldn't afford the distraction.

As soon as I opened my email, I clicked on a message from my contact in DC on the inside of the Caputi operation. "The Emperor's New Groove," said the subject, but that was code. When I opened it, there was a picture of the sorceress from the Disney classic.

Gabriella was back in town. I opened the attachment and ran it through my decryption software, smiling when the shot showed Gabriella at her mansion in Georgetown, arguing with a clearly bored Leo.

Bingo.

Whatever they'd been doing in the Caribbean was over, and now, she'd come home to berate her only surviving nephew.

"Baby bear got into too much fun while Momma was away," my informant wrote.

That made sense. Leo Caputi was too concerned with pussy and drugs to give a damn about the family business. I wondered why Gabriella hadn't taken him out of the picture yet and figured it would probably be a blessing for him if she did. He seemed insecure and desperate to fill the void inside himself.

I ran through the next set of shots before picking up my phone to call Crow.

"Hey, brother," he said when he answered on the second ring.

"Hey." I pressed send on the forward button, sending this information out to the entire officer group. "The boys are back in town. I'm sending you an email right now."

Crow paused for a moment before sighing. "Good work. We'll talk more about this at church."

"I'll see if I can find out anything else, maybe get my asset to dig deeper."

"Don't get her killed," Crow said, his voice stern in that demanding, patriarchal way.

"Got it," I said. "She's smart. She knows what she's doing."

He grumbled something about her being important for other reasons before ending the call. I understood that, too. Even though this asset was close to the Caputis, as close as kin, they wouldn't think twice about dumping her in a ditch if they found out what she was really doing.

"Be careful," I wrote back. "Send me more when you can."

After I hit send, I said a silent prayer out into the ether for my friend, hoping she kept her mouth shut and her eyes on her six.

We opened a few hours later, and Ru said she'd upped spending on the social media promos. She musta done something right because business had picked up. Candy and the rest of the girls put on more shows than normal, and I had to hop behind the bar to help Ru serve drinks. By the end of the night, she'd doubled what we'd earned in total the four nights before.

I stood in the office as she counted it three times.

"Holy shit." She stuffed the money in the bank bag. "You mind if we drop this off at the clubhouse on the way home? I don't want it sitting here all night."

I nodded, and she tucked the plastic bundle in her messenger bag as I yanked open the door. Some of the girls were still huddled around the bar when we came down, drinking to how much they'd made.

"Hey, boss!" Candy waved. "Hey, Ru. Both of you. Come do a shot with us!"

"No, no." Ru shook her head. "I have to get to the clubhouse before it's too late."

"I'm driving." I held up my hand to refuse.

"C'mon!" Jasmine whined. She grabbed two glasses and flipped them over, filling them with whiskey before Ru could protest again. "Just one shot!"

Ru looked at me and sighed before walking over and grabbing the smaller of the two. She held it up and Jasmine took the other. Candy and Hilaria did the same, saluting to a night well earned.

"And to our fearless leader." Candy raised the glass toward me. "What would any of us do without you?"

"Cheers!" The girls took their shots, and Ru swallowed hers back, squinting her eyes shut with the sting of alcohol.

"Thanks everyone." Ru gasped and set the glass down. "Don't forget to lock up, okay?"

"Oh, we won't, sugar." Candy looked between Ru and me, her grin widening. "You two have fun."

Ru shook her head and chuckled. "He's giving me a ride. My truck broke down this morning."

"Uh-huh." Candy pursed her big red lips and raised a disbelieving eyebrow, but I didn't react, opting instead to push my way out into the hot summer night. Ru followed me, a big smile on her face as she approached. I couldn't stop eyeing her, remembering what we'd done at Crimson earlier, remembering the way she'd moaned and arched off the bed.

Fuck, I still wanted her.

She shook her head and sighed. "People are going to keep talking if you keep staring at me like that."

I opened my mouth to fight it. How was I supposed to avoid her? She captivated me no matter where we were, and given the choice between her and literally anyone else on this planet, she would win every Goddamned time.

But I couldn't bring myself to let anyone know that.

Because once they did, they'd figure out what a depraved, fucked-up monster I actually was. That I could look my best friend in the eye knowing the despicable things I'd done to his daughter.

And I didn't have any reason to dissuade them.

8

RU

The stink of old beer and fifty years of cigarette smoke hit me in the face when I walked into the clubhouse. Despite the garage doors being open, no amount of fresh air or bleach would scrub that patina off these walls. I'd grown up in the MC, and this place had long ago become my home away from home. It was the head of operations, and no matter what time of day or night, someone from the club protected it.

Tonight, Led Zeppelin blared out of the speakers and the sound of cracking pool balls broke up the various conversations. Selene stood by the bar, laughing with Alba and a few of the hang-arounds. Then, I focused on the woman standing next to her, sipping at a tumbler of clear liquid, likely tequila knowing Crow's youngest child, Verona. She wore Doc Martens and a short black skirt, the dark makeup around her eyes making her violet irises even more radiant. I hadn't seen her in four years, and I'd missed her terribly.

I decided to catch up with them later because I wanted to have a conversation with Coins, the MC's treasurer. He sat in the back corner with his laptop open, a few invoices out on the table in front of him. I plopped the bag of money down and put my hands on my hips. "Here ya go!"

He startled and looked up at me, tapping his cigar in the ashtray. "What the fuck is this?"

"That's the take home from tonight."

Coins looked down at the bundle, then back up at me. "You made this at the Beacon?"

I nodded. "I told you I could flip the place around. That's just the start."

Coins bit the end of his cigar and leaned back in the seat, narrowing his eyes as he considered me. I'd had enough of people underestimating me. I was raised in this club, I knew the Beacon like the back of my hand, and I had the ovaries to stand up for myself. If Saint wouldn't listen, I'd get the rest of the club on board first.

"If I keep this going for the next month, will you consider my request for an investment to renovate the place?"

"Jesus Christ, girl." Coins chuckled to himself and tapped ash into the tray. "You sound like your old man, you know that?"

"I'll take that as a compliment." I meant it. Dad had done wonders for this club. Sure, he wasn't perfect. He'd single-handedly contributed to the escalating blood feud between the MC and the Caputis, and he kept it from most of the MC for years. But I'd like to think that the good he'd done had far outweighed the bad. With my sound mind for business, I took the gifts I'd inherited and made them better.

"Look, I can't just hand over that kind of cash." Coins eyed me up and down, a proverbial grandfather developing a scheme with his favorite grandchild. "I'll talk to Crow and see what I can do."

"Really?" I nearly jumped out of my seat.

Coins groaned. "I'm already regretting this." Then he nodded to the rest of the room, gesturing to leave him alone. "Now, let me count this in peace, okay?"

He ripped the plastic open and grabbed the wad of cash while I grinned like a kinkster in a leather store and went to find my sister. She was at the bar with Selene, but Verona had gone over to the pool table with her brothers.

"I want it to be super low stress, okay?" Alba shook her head, taking a sip of beer and pushing her glasses higher on her face. "Let's just have a party with this tiny little thing in the middle."

"Tiny little thing?" Selene laughed. "Alba, you're becoming my sister."

"I'm already your sister." Alba rolled her eyes. "In all the ways that matter."

"This is a big day." Selene narrowed her eyes. "Aren't you more excited?"

"Of course." Alba glanced at me before looking back to her, a worried stare in her expression. She'd already talked to me about her concern weeks ago. I'd done my best to try to calm her, but to be fair, I'd been thinking the same thing. KC had killed Benito Caputi. Alba was Benito and Gabriella's granddaughter, a Caputi by blood, the one thing that mattered the most to them. If they were going to do something, the wedding would be a great place to make a statement. No one wanted to get hurt.

"I just don't want word getting out." Alba took another sip of beer. "I love KC, and I'd marry him no matter what. But—"

She didn't have to elaborate. We both understood.

"Okay, on the day of," Selene explained, "we'll get you ready. We take a limo here. Crow is doing the ceremony."

"And then we party," Alba cut in with a laugh.

"Of course we party." Selene clinked her beer against Alba's and took a drink.

Deep rumbles echoed from the driveway, bringing all of our attention out front. Thor led a pack of motorcycles, sitting huge on his custom-built Harley. Next to him was a man I didn't recognize. Long white hair nearly covered the Steel Roses Boston Chapter patch on his cut, and his weathered face spoke to how many years he'd spent riding in the sun. The rest of the Roses club filled in around him, and I looked to a tall, dark-haired guy in the back, swinging a long leg over his bike.

Lore.

I smiled, despite myself. Sure, we weren't together, but Lore and I were friends. His presence usually brought me joy. They'd gone to escort the Boston chapter into our clubhouse. Thor led their president to Crow, who had come out of the backroom as the noise descended.

"Titan, my old friend." Crow threw his arms out, embracing him with a giant hug.

"Crow, you old son of a bitch." Titan clapped him on the shoulders. "How ya been?"

"Seen better days." He gripped another man's hand and pulled him in for a hug. "We weren't expecting you guys until tomorrow."

Titan shrugged. "We got an early start."

"Good thing, too." Crow nodded toward the bar. "Just put a new keg on."

"Fuck yeah." Titan and his guys crowded the bar for drinks, but I closed in on Lore and gave him a hug.

"Welcome back."

He laughed when we broke apart. "I wasn't even gone that long."

"I still missed you."

"Hmm, right." He laughed, giving me a look that said he knew what I'd been up to in his absence.

I rolled my eyes and shook my head. "C'mon, I'll get you a beer." When I turned around, I straightened because Saint stood right behind me, leaning against the bar with an arrogant smirk on his face.

Uh-oh.

"Don't you have a report to give?" Saint raised an eyebrow, his grin suspiciously benevolent, and I tried to calm the mild panic in my chest.

Lore gave him a cocky smile. "Crow and Titan are catching up. I'll see the prez in a minute, brother."

Saint kept his features annoyingly calm while he regarded Lore. "You've been looking out for Ru these last couple months."

Lore shifted his shoulders and nodded. "Uh-huh."

"Thank you." Saint stood upright. I'd thought they were pretty close in height when I met Lore, but side by side, Saint had an inch or two on my buddy. "The club owes you one."

"No sweat, man." Lore threw an arm over my shoulder, and Saint zeroed in on it like a bull spotting a red flag. "Ru's a lot of fun."

"Right." Saint's grin tightened and his jaw hardened. "But now that she's home, she's got lots of Roses keeping an eye on her."

Lore didn't skip a beat. He shrugged and clapped Saint on the shoulder. "That's okay. I don't mind everyone knowing I got it bad for a girl like Ru." He kissed me on the cheek, and my heart raced, anticipating what Saint might do with the slight. Lore added, "Even if it's unrequited." He gasped and playfully grabbed at his chest, backing away as he went to slap hands with a few of the brothers from Boston.

To be fair, he knew what he was doing because Saint shook his head, tsked, and sipped his beer. "I like him." The words dripped with sarcasm.

I furrowed my brows and stepped closer. "Is that jealousy?"

Saint stared down at me, dark and perilous intentions dancing in his eyes. "Why would I be jealous over something that's already mine?"

The other Roses had gotten distracted by our friends from the north, and the hang-arounds sniffed along the perimeter, waiting for their opportunity to jump on the fresh meat. Selene had disappeared. KC and Alba had likely found a room in the back. No one paid any attention to little ole me and quiet, stoic Saint.

Just like old times.

"So, if I'm yours and you're mine"—I moved another inch closer, the smell of cologne and beer and *him* reeling me in—"why do you keep prolonging the inevitable? Do you think I'll turn twenty-four, twenty-five, thirty, and that'll make it any better?" My fingers crept across the bar top, stopping millimeters from his, so close the heat radiated off them.

He scowled and lowered his voice to a growl. "Don't tempt me, baby girl. That never ends well for you."

I shivered, echoes of his palm colliding with my ass shooting through my nerves. He parted his lips and watched as I rubbed my index finger over the letters just below his knuckles.

HOPE.

Such a reckless, stupid thing. What was hope in the end? A yearning for a love that may or may not happen? A longing for something that never was going to work? When Pandora fucked around and let out all the evils in the world, hope was the only thing left in that stupid box. Did that mean humans wouldn't perceive it as evil? Or did that mean that despite our best efforts, having it would lead us nowhere and bring us nothing?

All these years, I had hoped Saint would come around and here I stood, twenty-two with nothing to show for it. After the scene at Crimson this morning, perhaps I hoped for more than the same. Silly girl that I was, I'd forgotten that was never going to happen.

"Ru, come here!" Crow shouted from the tables in the back. "Talk to me about this plan for the Beacon." The moment broke between Saint and me, and I moved around him to explain my plans to the MC's president. His stare burned my back as I retreated.

WE STAYED at the clubhouse for a while after that. By two in the morning, most of the brothers had found girls to disappear with, and most of my sisters had gone home to sleep. For the last few hours, the clubhouse buzzed with music, beer pong, and the ramblings of drunk bikers celebrating.

Saint got pulled in to a game of Texas Hold'em with Thor and Coins, so I went to lie on the swing in the parking lot out front. Nursing a warm Natty Boh and trying not to feel sorry for myself, I stared at the glowing moon behind the night clouds. Boots stumbled in my direction, and the sound of crunching gravel preceded Hollywood's enormous head blocking my view. He slumped down on the swing at my feet, lifting them so they lay across his lap.

"Why are you sulking out here alone?" Hollywood grabbed my ankle in a show of solidarity and gave me his best James Dean grin. But the dark circles under his eyes and the crease between his eyebrows told a different tale. His older brother, Trojan, had died trying to protect me and Alba last August, leaving behind not just our family but also a grieving old lady, Marissa, who had taken off a few weeks after his funeral. "Why aren't you in there with your fuck buddy?"

Back when Saint and I had gotten stuck in the snow, KC and Hollywood had come to rescue us. They'd opened the door about three seconds after we got done hooking up, so the whole cab reeked of sweat and sex. Somehow, Hollywood had managed to keep his mouth shut all this time.

"He's not my fuck buddy." I sighed the words.

He furrowed his eyebrows. "Why not?"

I shrugged. "My dad, mostly."

He laughed and tilted the beer bottle over his head, taking a long gulp. "That'll do it."

"Why aren't you balls deep in some hang-around by now?"

This time, he shook his head and sighed wistfully. "Guess I don't have it in me tonight."

"What?" I balked. That didn't sound like Hollywood. "What do you mean?"

His sorrowful eyes and drawn features hinted at a sadness he so rarely showed to anyone. But I saw through that swagger to the scared, exhausted little boy underneath, the one he desperately tried to hide, the one clawing at him to forget about his brother and whatever happened to his parents. He had always buried himself in pussy because the thought of having to be him for one more second ached too damn much, even more now after everything. I saw it because I'd been there. Perhaps he understood this because he let himself be more vulnerable with me than anyone else.

"When Trojan died," he said, "there was a part of me that wanted to follow him. I didn't think I could do this on my own." He took another long pull on his drink. "At his funeral, I made a promise to do the living for both of us. For so long, he'd been the smart one, bailing me out of trouble, making sure I kept my shit on straight." He shook his head. "Now, I only got myself."

"He knew you liked to fuck around when he was alive, Hollywood."

He chuckled to himself. "Yeah, but not when my best girl is sitting out here, moping."

I laughed and kicked him playfully in the side. "Best girl, my ass."

Hollywood and I had a brother-sister relationship. He flirted occasionally, and tonight, he goaded me on because he wanted to make me feel better. We both knew it wasn't sexual, and I never got a vibe from him that it ever would be, not even sitting like this. We were family. That was it.

"You know." Hollywood leaned closer, raising an eyebrow. "If you went inside and crawled in his lap, you'd get exactly what you wanted."

"It's not about sex," I told him. "I could fuck him anytime."

Hollywood glanced back out toward the parking lot.

"It's about not hiding it. I want him to claim me. I want to wear his patch on my jacket."

"Jesus, Ru. Really?" Hollywood whistled. "I didn't know it was like that."

I sighed and sat up, swinging my legs down so I faced the front. "It's not, and it never will be."

"That's not what I saw that night in the truck."

I snapped my focus to him, searching for any sign of insincerity.

"He wants you, Ru. He's just conflicted about it." Hollywood laughed. "Hell, I would be, too. And I'm not even that close with Aris."

"Then you're both cowards."

"It's not cowardice." Hollywood took another long drink of his beer. "It's respect. Saint is grateful to the MC for taking him in and protecting him. Touching you is like...touching the holy grail." He made a sad noise low in his chest. "Besides, he probably thinks you deserve better. You do deserve better."

"What are you talking about?" I downed the rest of my beer and set the bottle in the gravel so I didn't have to hold it anymore. "I'm a Rose, same as you. If you're a piece of shit, I'm a piece of shit."

He laughed and threw an arm around me, hugging me close. "You got no idea how wrong you are."

He'd never admit as much, but I heard the agony in his tone. He'd been on a downward spiral since Trojan died and Marissa took off. She blamed him. She blamed me. She blamed the whole MC, and in the wake of her tragedy, she'd left the only family she had. Hollywood had taken the loss personally, even though it wasn't his fault. It wasn't anyone's fault but Benito Caputi's, and KC had avenged that death months ago.

"How come it never crossed a line between us, Ru?" Hollywood pressed his forehead to my temple. "How can I keep it straight with you, but not with anyone else?"

"Because you see me like a sister, and you don't wanna fuck your sister."

He pointed a finger at me and nodded. "So you're saying that if I wanna stop fucking around, I gotta treat everyone like a sibling."

I chuckled and nodded, clapping him on the shoulder. "You got it, buddy."

"Jee-sus Christ." He whistled dramatically and pushed to his feet, tripping slightly before righting himself. "I don't think I can do that, Ru. Who am I supposed to fuck?"

"Your right hand."

He blew out a disbelieving breath and headed toward the clubhouse. "Fuck that."

I giggled, thankful to have him in my life. Hell, I was grateful to have all these assholes in my life. I couldn't imagine what I'd be like if they weren't. Even Saint. I wouldn't trade the bad memories for the good, no matter what happened between us.

A while later, I woke to someone tapping me on the shoulder. I must have fallen asleep on the swing, so when I blinked up at Saint, he gave me the most tender smile I'd ever seen. He squatted down so he was level with me, his eyes kind and endearing.

"C'mon, baby girl. Let me get you home." He helped me to my feet and wrapped his cut over my shoulders when I curled into him for warmth, nuzzling my head under his chin the way I'd always done. I wanted his familiar arms around me, reassuring me I was safe, and when he relented, holding me tight, I moaned. He chuckled and nodded toward his bike, guiding me there with a steady grip on my shoulder.

I held on to him the entire way, my cheek pressed against his back, the smell of sweat and *him* enveloping me in the protective cocoon of his safety. When we got to my house, we silently walked inside, the same routine we'd been using for years. He opened the door for me, I went ahead, and he closed it behind him. I was too tired to do anything else, so I trudged through the living room and up the stairs to my bedroom. The sound of his boots on the hardwood echoed behind me, and when I stopped at my bedroom door, I turned to face him.

Muscle memory almost pushed me on my tiptoes to give him a kiss and tug him into my room. I stopped myself at the last second, a tender stab in my heart making me wince. Yeah, he'd coached me through an orgasm earlier today, but that was Sienna and her sir. This was Ru and Saint. We had rules and boundaries and a long troubled past keeping us apart.

"Good night," I whispered, gripping the doorknob behind me.

He grabbed my chin and forced me to look him in the eyes, but I didn't want him seeing how badly I ached for him, so I tried to jerk my head away.

He slid his palm to the back of my neck and yanked my mouth to his in a soft, tender kiss that crossed every single one of those pesky parameters he'd set last night. But oh...I felt it all the way down to my toes. I curled my fingers into the back of his soft hair and coasted upward, holding him closer, scratching his scalp to get more of him. Pressure built between my legs, and my heart pounded in my head.

Yes! Finally!

It didn't last long. Soon, he broke away and pressed his forehead against mine, the heat of his breath coasting down the side of my neck.

"Good night, sinner." He kissed the tip of my nose and backed away, heading down the hallway to the guest room before I could question it.

9

RU

I spent most of the night tossing and turning, wishing I could forget the way his lips felt against mine. Part of me wanted to get up, tiptoe across the house, and crawl into his bed. Another part wanted to forget it ever happened. He couldn't just barge his way into my life again, not after the way he'd so unceremoniously left it.

Grumbling and tossing onto my back, I stared at the ceiling and seethed with frustration. When I'd had enough, I rolled off the mattress and made my way to the shower to cool down. After I dressed, I sat at my desk and unlocked the bottom drawer, grabbing my laptop and the folder I'd used to collect anything useful.

It was club business, and the guys wouldn't like it if they found out I was sticking my nose where they thought it didn't belong. Since I'd been home, I'd been doing research on the Caputi family—who they were, who they hung around with, where they came from. Not that I thought I'd add anything useful to what the club already knew, but I couldn't do nothing.

I'd felt so helpless for so long after the abduction—fucking Nikki and fucking Pie and the whole Caputi lineage that had screwed us over. Alba and I had paid the price. I'd been beaten up, kidnapped, and tied to a cement wall in a basement by horrible monsters. Admittedly, it was other horrible monsters that had saved me, but that was a nuance I didn't want to face at four in the morning.

My focus was on Nikki McNally. She'd been raised in the MC, her mother being a hang-around and her father being any number of the brothers she'd slept with. I'd known her my whole life, and even if we were never close, the fact she'd sell me out to our enemies burned through my blood so hot it set me on fire anytime I let myself sink into it.

After Pie got caught, Nikki ran to the Caputis—specifically Leo. I pulled up the file on my laptop containing all the photos I could find of the two of them together, flicking through them for anything I'd missed, any sign of where they were or what they were up to. The photos had been taken in Miami, the Keys, the Caribbean, no extravagance spared. Nikki had been trailing along with him, her newborn in tow.

I flipped to the next page and read the information about Gabriella, Benito's widow. Not long after his death, she'd shown up to threaten me and Alba. So far, she hadn't done anything to make good on that. She, too, had been carrying on with her life, picking up where Benito left off. Leo had taken over the business in name, but she had taken it over in reality. All the old players now came to see her, and the guys that used to surround Benito now sat at her table.

That scared the shit out of me.

The MC and the Caputi mafia were two sides of the same coin. We chose our family, and they ran things based on bloodline. We thrived on chaos and the feral side of life; they wrote the definition of organized crime. It made sense that we'd be pitted against each other. But we had one thing in common—it took a lot to get the group's respect, even more if you were a woman.

Whatever Gabriella had done to earn the loyalty of these people was fucking terrifying. What more was she capable of doing to keep it?

I rubbed my hands over my face and sighed. Enough was enough for one day.

Saint was gone before I came downstairs, and I pretended like that didn't hurt. I drank my coffee, feeling the sting of his lips on mine again, and tried to focus. It was Alba's bachelorette party day, and even though I felt like hunting Saint down and making him explain his disappearance, I decided to let it go. Revenge was a dish best served cold, after all.

I wasn't sure how I felt about that amazing kiss, either. I had yearned to feel his lips against mine again, but only if it came with the whole package. I wouldn't sneak around anymore, no matter how much I had once loved this stupid game we played.

"Are you sure it's cool that I came at the last minute?" Verona asked, sipping her mimosa while her footbath bubbled.

"Of course," Alba said from her spot near the hallway. "The more the merrier." She didn't want anything big or stereotypical for her bachelorette party. She ran a cam business for a living. *I see enough titties and dicks in my day job.*" Which I understood. So we took her to the spa.

"I know I just met you and everything, but I really needed this." Verona sighed and downed the rest of the drink in two gulps. Coming from her, the words were comical. In high school, she'd always emanated this goth girl antisocial vibe, all angry stares and guarded, hissed responses. After graduation, she'd gone to college at a prestigious art school in New York City. It had taken an act of God to convince Crow to let her go. Maybe it was college or living on the Lower East Side, but now, she seemed a lot more mellow. Whatever it was made me more excited to get to know her again.

"God, me too." Selene shook her head and laughed, readjusting her robe. She and Alba were waiting for massages.

"I never thought KC would be the one to get married first." Verona gave Alba a sheepish smile. "Congratulations. He's a great guy."

She smiled and glanced down at her engagement ring. "Yeah, I didn't think I'd ever get married, either. When it works, it works."

Before anyone could respond, the hostess came out to take Alba and Selene to their rooms, leaving me alone with Verona while we got pedicures.

"So, what are you up to these days?" She raised a dark eyebrow.

"Busy." I smiled and sighed dramatically. "My life is all webcams and strip clubs."

Verona chuckled softly and regarded me with studious eyes. "I saw you and Hollywood out on the swing the other night. Are you two like…"

I barked out a laugh before I could stop it. "No. Never me and Hollywood."

"Oh, thank God." She laughed. "I thought I was going to have to remind you of all his *hold my beer* moments."

I shook my head. "No, he's like a brother."

"You'd be smart to keep it that way." She leaned her head against the seat, closing her eyes in relaxation.

"What about you?" I grinned and nudged her shoulder with mine, making her look at me. "Anyone in the big city with a broken heart?"

A forlorn expression flitted through her violet gaze, and she bit her bottom lip before locking down the emotion and forcing a smile. "No, there's no one."

That sounded like a lie, but I let it go. "Really?"

She sighed and leaned back in her seat. "It's okay. Men annoy me anyway."

"Do you like women?"

She pulled one side of her mouth into a smile. "Who doesn't?"

I laughed, remembering that Verona had always had a great sense of humor. "You were there for four years. You didn't meet anyone at school?"

She rolled her eyes. "School was worse. Everybody was a fucking nepotism snob."

My heart broke for her, and I reached out to grab her hand. "Why didn't you call me?"

She rubbed a finger over her eyebrow and forced a smile. "You had your own shit going on. You didn't need mine, too." She pulled her hand away and looked at the chipped nail polish options in her lap. "Whatever. It's over now."

The girl I'd known four years ago lived in the shadow of her three big brothers and her Goliath father. Because she was the president's daughter, she had the same problem as me in high school. No one wanted to touch her because of what might happen to their fingers when her family got wind of it. She used to mask all that insecurity behind a thick wall of anger and eyeshadow.

She seemed different now. She'd grown into her skin, maybe more confident in who she was. The four years away had done her some good. But there was something else there, too, something she didn't want me to know.

Verona let out a deep sigh before adding, "Hey, I've been looking for a part-time job."

"Really?"

She nodded. "Do you think I could work at the Beacon? I bartended in Queens for a while."

I narrowed my eyes at her because she didn't seem like the bartending type, but what the fuck did I know? I believed her if she said she'd done it before. To have help would be fantastic. To have *experienced* help, even better. And another MC princess? Christ, I couldn't hire her fast enough. "Yes. You have the job. Yes. A thousand times, yes."

She furrowed her eyebrows at my quick offer. "Don't get too excited. Won't Saint want a say?"

"You're hired." I laughed. "Come in tomorrow and I'll show you around."

"Really? Damn, okay. Thank you."

"I'm happy you're home," I told her. I hadn't realized how much I'd missed her, but now that she was here, a piece of my heart righted itself. When we were younger, Verona and I were friends. I remembered sleepovers at Crow's house, late nights spent painting each other's nails and making mud pies in the backyard (not necessarily in that order). High school and college had driven us apart, but I looked forward to mending whatever had happened since then.

"Don't get sappy on me." She rolled her eyes and chose a purplish-black color to put on her toenails. I picked out a bright sky blue. Then I smiled to myself because nothing could represent our personalities more exactly than those two options.

After we were glowing with relaxation, we headed back to my house for a sleepover—pizza, alcohol, and Damon Salvatore.

"Not even male strippers?" Selene whined for the twentieth time.

"No." I laughed and carried the takeout up the stairs of my porch, yanking open the storm door. "She didn't want any."

"For shame." Selene shook her head and laughed in that carefree way of hers, letting me know she was only *mostly* joking. I'd been friends with this girl my entire life, and if anyone were my sister by relationship, it would be her. Only five years older than me, she'd been looking out for me ever since I could remember, and now that we were grown, I couldn't imagine my life without her.

Alba and Verona sat in the living room, watching *Vampire Diaries*. Verona had stopped watching after season two, which was where it all picked up, in my opinion.

"See, this is why I didn't like this show. Elena's just cool with him being a vampire? Here, drink my blood; I'll sustain you?" Verona grabbed a handful of popcorn and stuffed it in her mouth, shaking her head as she chewed. "Ridiculous."

"Oh, we're just getting started." I laughed, sitting the pizza on the kitchen table before walking into the living room.

"Are you Team Stefan or Team Damon?" Verona asked.

"Neither. Team Uncle Mason." I held up a fist in a power move.

"Ru has a thing for older men," Selene said.

I snorted out a laugh. "You're one to talk."

She balked, dropping her jaw in outrage. "I'm not fucking anyone right now, thank you very much."

"At least I go after the things I want."

"I'm happy being single." Selene opened the pizza box and grabbed a slice, plopping it down on her plate.

"Who are you trying to convince?"

"Enough." She gave me a friendly bump with her hip. "Twat."

I crinkled my nose at the insult, remembering the first time she'd called me that. We were children and had just gotten into our first fight. I had shouted back the same word I muttered in that kitchen. "Cunt."

She laughed and sat, picking at a pepperoni to bite into, but I knew the truth. Selene had been in love with Thor most of her life, even if she'd never admit it. He'd been married to her aunt, which legally made him her uncle. And in a strange, fucked-up way, he'd been less a father figure and more of a role model. A much older best friend. Growing up, she'd get into big fights with her Aunt Gemma and run off to hide for days at a time. KC and I would search, but the only one who could find her and bring her back was her aunt's husband.

Whatever bond had been formed in those private moments had only gotten more intense as she'd gotten older. At twenty-eight, she still couldn't admit how much she wanted him, nor could he accept the fact he lusted after his dead wife's niece. Nothing had ever happened between them, not like Saint and me. After Gemma's death, guilt and shame had forced things to stay platonic, and there they both remained—frozen, terrified, and stubborn. She never dated, and neither did he, as far as I could tell.

Verona shook her head, bringing me back to the present. "So wait. You're single, I'm single, Ru's single, and we're just sitting around here for Alba's bachelorette night?" Her eyebrows shot up her forehead. "We should go out."

"Huzzah!" Selene held up her beer and cheered.

Alba sighed and picked up her phone, flashing five text messages from KC. "He wants us to come to the bar where they are."

"Your fiancé wants you to crash his bachelor party?" I laughed.

"That's so adorable I think I'm gonna puke." Selene pretended to vomit, which made me chuckle harder.

10

SAINT

The Roses had to keep KC's bachelor party low-key. Since Benito Caputi's disappearance last August and the shoot-out at the docks, Crow had been under investigation by the local PD. You bet your ass the rest of us were being watched as well.

We couldn't risk leaving the state unless it was important, so no Atlantic City or Vegas, and we couldn't get rowdy at a DC club. KC had opted for an old biker hangout on the outskirts of town called the Viper, some skunky dive bar with photos of half-naked women lining the men's bathroom like wallpaper. Some went as far back as the '70s.

People dressed in leather and shit-kickers filled the space, bodies dancing and grinding on the bar tops, others milling around and talking. What really made the place special, especially to KC, were the pictures of his parents on the wall in the main area (thankfully, not half naked.) They'd come here when they were his age, as had all the old Roses. The place stank of sin and rotten alcohol, but I'd admit, it was a sort of second home.

"I wanna thank you all for tonight," KC said, holding up his shot glass. He'd ordered a round of tequila. "Hollywood, you did good."

Hollywood smiled as Bear clapped him on the shoulder.

"To family," KC said, his bright blue eyes even more shimmery in the overhead light. "To the ones we lost and the ones we've yet to meet."

"Cheers!" Everyone held up their glasses, and I drank mine in one gulp, wincing as the burn slid down my throat. My thoughts went to Trojan, our fallen brother who had died to protect Ru and Alba. Tonight, we celebrated KC's upcoming nuptials, but we remembered those who had ensured we'd lived to see today.

I shot the shit with the guys for an hour before I found myself alone in the circular booth with Hollywood. KC had gone to the bathroom, Thor and Bear were at the bar getting another round, and everyone else had gone looking for tail. Hollywood parted his lips like he wanted to say something, but didn't know how to start.

"You got something on your mind, brother?" I took a sip of beer.

He scooted closer until we were a foot away from each other, the smell of his cologne hitting me in the face. "Yeah. What's going on with you and Ru?"

I stiffened, tightening my fingers around my glass. "Nothing's going on with me and Ru. Not anymore." If there was, Hollywood would be the last fucking person I'd tell. I was surprised he'd been able to keep my shit a secret this long.

"Uh-huh." He nodded, his lips thinning.

"Speak your piece or get out of my face."

"It's just... I'm seeing things clearer now." Hollywood leaned in. "Alba's got me thinking about going to therapy and shit."

"Jesus Christ." I pinched the bridge of my nose, the beginnings of a migraine brewing right between my eyes.

"If I had a girl like Ru, it wouldn't matter who her old man was. I'd fall to my knees at his feet and beg him to accept me."

I set my "fuck off" glare on him and took another long drink. Sure, it was easy for him to say that. He'd never taken a relationship seriously in his life, and if he did, it certainly wasn't with his best friend's much younger daughter.

"Hollywood?"

"Yeah?" His eyebrows rose up his head like he expected me to thank him.

Instead, I said, "Don't you have any number of random people to fuck off with?"

He laughed and nodded. "Look, KC told me it's none of my business." He pointed at me, narrowing his eyes again. "But you broke her heart, and you're still breaking it. None of those fuckers will say anything because, well"—he held up a hand and gestured to all of me—"you're scary as fuck with that silent stare thing. But listen to me when I say if you break her heart again, I'll bury you myself."

I took a deep breath, willing the rage in my belly to not bubble over. This little shit was a good eight years younger than me. I could knock his perfect fucking teeth out with hardly any effort. How Hollywood would that smile be, then? I swallowed that down and took a deep breath.

"What are you going to do when she moves in with Lore permanently?" Hollywood hissed in a teasing breath. "I heard they got *really* close in Mount Vernon. You ready to watch her live her life with one of your brothers?"

Ru insisted nothing had ever happened between the two of them, that they were just friends. But my relationship with Ru had been friendly once upon a time, too, and it would only take one night, one slip, one accident in the snow, to change everything.

"What are you trying to say, Hollywood?"

He let out a lighthearted chuckle, shook his head, and clapped me on the shoulder. "I'm saying get your fucking head out of your ass." He scooted to the edge of the booth and stood, adding a quick, "Preferably before I have to kick it," before walking away to join the others at the bar.

I sat with that, squeezing the glass so tight I thought I might break it. Sure, it chafed that I'd been put in my place by *Hollywood* of all fucking people. What hurt the most, what really made my heart pound in my chest, was the fact he was right. If it were reversed, if it had been *him* who had done to her what I did, I woulda already had his guts wrapped around his neck.

What made me so special? What made me any different? *Fucking nothing.*

I had broken her heart. Teasing her, *touching* her, kissing her in the dark, only to disappear in the brutal light of day, confused us both. God help me, I couldn't stop myself. Waking her up, taking her home, walking her to her room, it reminded me too much of how things used to be. I had my mouth on hers before I knew what hit me.

She was everywhere and everything. My whole Goddamned life. All the shit I'd ever been through had been leading me to her. No one else could say the same.

Aris would accept that, right?

Christ. Why did I care so much what he thought?

A glint of curly chestnut hair caught my attention from across the bar, and I focused on a dragon tattoo twisting up a long leg.

Ru.

She wore a black AC/DC halter top that tied behind the neck and the middle of her back, exposing all her silky skin in between. Her matching miniskirt barely covered her ass, making my cock twitch in anticipation of bending her over my bike at the end of the night. Alba stood on one side of her, pushing up to give KC a kiss, and Selene circled around to the other side of Bear, giving her cousin a hug. Lastly came Verona, dressed in her normal black fishnets and boots. Her long obsidian hair had been tied up, making her purple eyes seem even more radiant and rare.

What are they doing here?

I'd just been about to stand up and ask when Hollywood threw an arm over Ru's shoulder and guided her to the bar for shots. His threat echoed through my mind. *"Listen to me when I say if you break her heart again, I'll bury you myself."*

10-4, brother.

Loud and clear.

SHE IGNORED ME FOR AN HOUR. She didn't say hi or go out of her way to check in. Not that I blamed her. I'd ducked out on her this morning, so why should I expect any special treatment?

I lurked in the shadows of the booth and watched as my brothers made their rounds with the locals. The girls danced through the night, and I did my best to look anywhere but at her. I ignored the fresh tattoo on her rib cage that read, "Have fun," in a beautiful cursive. The need to know why she'd gotten it inked infected my gut.

Maybe it was a reminder.

Maybe it was a threat.

"You know, I'm proud of you, KC," Bear said, lifting the beer to his lips. "You got yourself a good woman. You got a good head on your shoulders." He grabbed his cousin by the shoulder and gave it a squeeze. "You're gonna make it."

"Thanks." KC pulled Bear into a half-hearted hug, and I laughed to myself, thankful that we had a team of sober prospects on standby to make sure everyone got home okay.

Across the way, my attention caught on Selene and Thor in a darkened corner, just the two of them. She leaned against the wall, staring up at him with those glacial eyes that matched her twin's, and he smiled down at her with a rosy tint to his cheeks. Any other time, I woulda looked away and minded my business.

But I struggled to remember the last time I'd seen Thor smile. He and Trojan had been close, and after his death, Thor had retreated deep inside himself. The bags under his eyes and the permanent crease between his brows hinted at sleepless nights pining for his fallen buddy. That shit tore us apart, so seeing him enjoy something again lifted my spirits, even if it was his niece.

Hollywood slid into the booth next to KC, quickly followed by a giggling Ru, who had her fingers linked in between his. Alba and V scooted in next to me, forcing me to move closer to Bear to make room. And then Hollywood grabbed the back of KC's neck and pulled their faces together, connecting their lips in a quick kiss.

KC startled and yanked away from him, shoving him and wiping at the back of his mouth. "What the fuck, man? So much tongue. I don't know where that thing's been."

The rest of the table erupted into laughter, and KC looked between them, shaking his head.

"I didn't think you'd actually do it!" Alba chuckled the hardest.

"Don't dare Hollywood to do anything, Sunshine." KC tapped ash from his cigarette into the crystal. "The fucker doesn't understand the word boundary. Just warn me next time." He playfully wiped at his mouth again, making a big show of swishing beer around to clean out the taste. "Fuck."

"Shut up, you loved it." Hollywood leaned in to try to kiss him again, but KC laughed and pushed his face away. "All right, my turn." Hollywood snatched a spare shot from the table and brought it to his mouth, swallowing it down before placing the empty glass in front of Ru. Next, he picked up the tequila bottle and filled it to the rim. "Ruthie, truth or dare."

The rebellious look in Hollywood's eyes banged a territorial bell in my chest. Considering the conversation we'd had earlier, I'd bet he had nothing but rotten ideas on the tip of his tongue.

Her defiant gaze cut to me before refocusing on him. "Dare."

"Oh, fuck." KC groaned at the same time Hollywood slammed his hand down on the table and shouted, "Woo! Fuck yeah."

"No stranger shit," Ru said.

"And nothing that will get her arrested," Alba cut in. "Please."

My heart hammered, and I closed my hands into fists on my thighs, anticipating the debauchery that was about to fly from Hollywood's lips.

"I dare you to get up on that bar over there and show these scraggly hags what you learned at the Beacon." He grabbed the shot and held it out to her, raising an eyebrow as he waited for her to consider.

She darted her eyes to mine, mischief flitting just behind them. I knew what she was thinking. If ever there were an opportunity to break rule number one, now was the time. I tried to send her the message with my stare: *No showing off.*

"What the fuck, Hollywood?" Bear said, rolling his eyes. "She's not gonna—"

"I'll do it." Ru grabbed the shot and swallowed it before hopping up on our table to get out of the booth without making her cohorts stand. Empty glasses and ashtrays shifted around as we struggled to keep it steady. She jumped down and sauntered up to the counter with the other half-naked women dancing and grinding on each other.

They helped her up, laughing and pawing all over her. She knew what she was doing, throwing her head back and giggling like that. She wanted a reaction out of me. This was all for show, but I sat through it. I clenched my fist so hard my knuckles turned white. Venom mixed in my blood, and I ground my molars together. When she yanked on the string holding her halter top up, I lost my fucking nerve. I couldn't control it anymore.

I didn't care that people paid to see her naked on the internet. I didn't want anyone else touching her, especially not the pieces of shit in this dive. Maybe it made me look jealous or protective or whatever the fuck. She was mine. *Mine.*

"Get up!" I shouted at Bear and KC. "Get the fuck up."

They hustled to move out of the way, and I launched to my feet, a predatory panic seizing every molecule in my blood. I shoved my way to the edge of the bar and glared up at her. "Ru, get down."

She pursed her lips and shook her head, rubbing her pierced nipples against the woman next to her and throwing her head back to sway to the music.

"Ru. Get the fuck down here." I slammed my hand on the bar, the loud *boom* audible over the blaring speaker. "Now." It was enough to make her snap to attention. I grabbed her legs and hauled her over my shoulder, carrying her through the crowd firefighter style. Bursting through the front doors, I stormed out into the humid night air with Ru giggling and digging her hands into my lower back to keep herself upright.

"You should see the look on your face," she stammered in between breaths.

My tolerance had reached its breaking point. I tossed her down in the grass beyond the tree line, the roar of the nocturnal insects echoing from farther in the forest. Somewhere between the bar and the woods, she'd lost her top completely, so I ripped my T-shirt over my head and yanked it on her, covering up those breasts I loved to bite.

"It's okay to want me, Saint." She leaned back in the grass, staring up at the midnight sky. The full moon shone bigger and brighter, delighting in its mockery of my pathetic display. It illuminated her like some night angel sent to give me a revelation.

"What the fuck do you think you're doing?" I snarled, taking out my frustration with myself on her. "Do you think this is a game?"

"No." She launched to her feet, jutting her chin out, a growl suddenly replacing the giddiness in her tone. "If this were a game, it would be fun. But nothing about this has ever been fun. Right, Saint?" She shoved my shoulders, making me take a step back. "None of it was fun for you. Not when I was sucking your dick dry. Not when you spent hours with your head between my legs." She shoved me again, this time nudging awake a side of me I'd been trying to keep dormant, a side that had been leashed when she ended things and hadn't been let off since. "Not when you told me how good I felt and how much you wanted to spend forever in my bed. No. Fun. At. All." She accentuated each word with a slam of her fists on my chest, and I let her pound at me. "I'm some stupid mistake that you keep whipping yourself for."

I grabbed her wrists to stop her, yanking her so she fell forward into me. "I never said that."

"Then tell me what you want because I'm starting to think I imagined everything." She stared through me, and I sighed, suddenly grateful to be concealed in the darkness. Perhaps I could be honest with her. Perhaps she wouldn't see how much this hurt. Christ, I prayed she didn't.

"The few months we spent together were the best in my life." I said the words low, keeping them just between us. I didn't want God to overhear. I didn't want *anyone* to overhear. "And the months we've been apart have nearly fucking killed me. If I could change anything about my past, I'd come to the Roses four years later, so at least I could say I met you when you were grown, and I wouldn't have to explain to anyone how badly it aches to want you and know I'm the reason I won't ever have you again." I shoved her away, but not hard enough to make her fall. Just enough to put distance between us.

My confession broke the final barrier, and whatever flimsy guard she had left around her heart fell to pieces. She launched herself at me, grabbing my neck and colliding our lips together hard and rough. She forced her tongue against mine, and sweet Jesus, I melted.

My arms went around her, holding her as close as I could get her, falling to her ass out of habit. *God,* she felt amazing, and as I kneaded, she spread her legs wider, moaning her signal for me to pick her up. I wasted no time arguing. My hands went to the backs of her thighs, lifting her so she could hook her ankles around the small of my back. I pushed her up against the closest tree as fire raged inside my gut, spiraling out of control and sinking down the back of my legs. My cock brushed against her clit, making her moan again, and this time, I inhaled the sound like I could breathe her in with it.

"Tell me what you want, sinner." I used her nickname, the one that told her I was in dominant headspace. If she wanted to play along, we could get back what we had. Sure, it was wrong in a thousand different ways, but Goddamn it, I was tired of pretending.

I needed this.

She needed this.

We were gonna fucking have it.

11

RU

"Tell me what you want, sinner." It came out as a whisper meant for me, making me run hot between my legs.

I had yearned for this for so long and now that it was here, I wanted to pinch myself to make sure it wasn't a dream. Saint really pinned me against a tree a few yards away from the parking lot. He'd really carried me out of there like a caveman in front of everyone. Now, he used my nickname like he wanted our dynamic back.

Yes, he'd broken my heart, and yes, he owed me an apology, but those were worries for future Ru. Present Ru had an itch, and Saint knew how to scratch it just right.

"Take what you want from me against this tree"—I swallowed because once I said the next word, there'd be no going back—"sir."

The last of Saint's patience snapped, and he let out a low growl, holding me up with one hand while he unbuckled his belt with the other. The *whoosh* of leather on denim sent a chill down my spine, and when he wrapped both my wrists together with it, I tensed my muscles to keep from shivering. He must have felt that because he laughed and pushed my hands above my head.

"Don't make a fucking sound," he murmured, looking over my shoulder to the bar beyond the tree line. Our friends were in there. If any of them came out to make sure I was safe, they wouldn't have to go far to see how *unsafe* we were being. The thrill of being caught only urged me on.

Normally, I would fight him, our dynamic making me wrestle until he earned my submission. But tonight, I needed him hard and urgent, and we didn't have time for anything else.

His zipper sounded next, and he speared his fingers between my thighs to find nothing. "You came to this shithole wearing nothing under this tiny scrap of fabric?"

I growled a laugh and kissed him, rolling my hips into his touch. He flexed the hand gripping my ass and dug his nails into me. It made me fucking feral, and I sank my teeth into his bottom lip, the coppery taste of his blood pooling on my tongue.

He gasped and yanked away, surprise in his eyes as he darted his tongue out to lick over the wound.

Yeah, he turned me into an animal, and that part of me had been caged for entirely too long. "It's all for you, Saint." I licked my lips, devouring the taste of him, swallowing it down. "Always."

A moment passed where I wondered if I'd gone too far too soon, but he positioned himself at my entrance and surged inside me, hard and deep, with no preamble. Maybe I should have stopped him for a condom, but I was on birth control and I hadn't been with anyone in months. Neither had he. I wrapped my arms around his neck as he buried his face near my ear, thrusting his cock inside me before pulling out and surging in again. The bark scratched my back through his shirt, but God, I didn't care.

He was hot and familiar in a strange foreign way. We'd connected like this a million times, but after all these months and the few people in between, it could have been our first again. He dug his teeth into my neck, claiming and marking. The pain mixed with the delicious agony between my legs and I groaned.

"Shh." Saint wrapped his hand over my mouth, pressing his forehead to mine. "I said don't make a sound. We wouldn't want anyone else to know how much you love being fucked under the moonlight."

I whimpered, another shake of my muscles cascading over me. He was so hot like this. Shadows made his face look more sinister and evil than it actually was, adding to the tattoos on his neck and torso and turning him into a demon, hellbent on taking my sweet virginal innocence. Except I wasn't any of those things, and I hadn't been in a long time. If Saint was a demon, I was his demoness. I was the queen in his den of iniquity, and together, we reveled in the filth.

"Harder, sir. Please." The words came out muffled from behind his hand, and maybe because I begged for it, he slowed his pace and moved his grip to my throat, squeezing my windpipe enough to remind me who was in charge. I didn't get to make demands in this headspace. *He* took what he wanted from *me*, and I liked it that way.

"Yeah?" he snarled against my ear, his hot breath coasting down that side of my body. My nipples hardened, aching to be against his skin, lamenting that he'd put his shirt on me to keep me covered. "You want to come on my cock?"

I whined an approving noise.

"You think you've been good enough for that, sinner?"

Uh-oh.

I hadn't. We had rules. We had boundaries. I'd broken three of them. He tightened his fist around my throat and picked up his pace, slamming into me deeper and more demanding. I matched him, and together we collided like thunder, loud and deafening, almost as piercing as my pulse pounding in my head.

My ecstasy rose, reaching a peak, and my muscles clenched, squeezing down on him. But if we were playing our old games, I needed permission to orgasm. In this headspace, he owned my body and my pleasure. I released at *his* mercy.

"I need to come, sir. Please."

Somewhere in the haze of my impending release, there were voices in the background.

"She couldn't have gone far," Selene said.

"She's with Saint. Leave her be." KC this time.

"I hope they're doing us all a favor and finally fucking it out, sweet Jesus." Hollywood laughed.

I let out a small giggle as the voices faded back inside, but Saint covered my mouth again, drilling into me, hitting the spot that drove me wild. I pulled at the leather belt around my wrists as my mind gave way to the euphoria. I couldn't hold out anymore. The rush of the whole thing pulled me under a tidal wave, and I curled into him, my cunt fisting his dick as the climax rolled through my body.

I tried not to make noise, but in the blurry glow of it all, I wasn't sure how quiet I'd actually been. The rush pulled me under its enormous weight, and the feel of him inside me while I came sent sparks of flame up my spine. My toes tingled, I dug my fingers into whatever they could find, and when I fell back to reality, I had turned to mush in Saint's hold. It was relatively tame compared to some of the shit we'd gotten into, but I'd waited for this for so long that subspace claimed me by surprise. My body numbed, and the world had faded around me. Everything hurt and nothing ever would again.

Saint found his own release with his nails digging into my neck and soft sighs against my shoulder. We stayed like that for a while, reveling in the comedown, basking in the light of the full moon. When he leaned back to look at me, the adoration in his eyes told me this hadn't been a mistake. Some part of me feared he'd regret it, but no. Saint was with me, here in the present.

"You came without permission." He raised an eyebrow.

"I know, but it was fun." I leaned in to lick the remaining blood off his bottom lip and gave him a lazy smile, lowering my feet to the ground. He winked and unhooked the belt from around my wrists, checking the circulation in my fingers.

"Are you okay?" He kissed each digit. "How's your back?"

"It's fine, Saint. It's all fine." That was the serotonin high talking. In the morning, I'd probably hurt, but those were also worries for future Ru, who had no place in present Ru's business. *Fuck off, future Ru.*

"Your place or mine?" he asked, rubbing his thumbs over the small pink indents on my arms, trying to soothe them away.

In all the months we'd hooked up last year, we could never do it at my house. Dad was always lurking. We'd gotten used to going to his, and in a lot of ways, it had become mine as well.

"Take me home, Saint."

THE NIGHT BREEZE whipped through my hair and Saint's smell enveloped me as I buried my nose between his shoulder blades. I wrapped my arms around his midsection and put my thighs on either side of his hips. If I didn't hold on tight, I'd go flying off the back, but I didn't have to worry. I was on *his* bike, holding *his* torso, breathing in *his* scent. I'd never let go again.

The vibrations from the motor rumbled through me, setting my nerves on fire, and by the time we made it to his three-bedroom rancher, I wanted him to fuck me right there in the driveway. Saint lived alone in the woods; no one would see. When I suggested it, he only laughed and climbed off the bike, leading me up onto his front porch by the fingertips.

The place hadn't changed in the months I'd been away. The sofa sat off to the right as soon as I entered, the dining room and kitchen directly in front of me. The hardwood floors still needed to be redone, and the dark cherry cabinets could still use a fresh coat of paint, but it smelled like him.

I took a moment to soak it in, the memories assaulting me. He'd fucked me on that breakfast island more times than I could count. I had a spot on the sofa where I liked to snuggle against him to watch movies. My favorite burner on the stove was the front left, even if he insisted the right was better.

"C'mon." He nodded toward a hallway that led to his bedroom.

I didn't argue, choosing instead to ride this through to the end, if only to see where that was. I thought he might tie me down to his bed and make my ass feel like my back, especially since I'd broken the rules tonight. But he didn't.

At his bathroom he flicked on the light, gesturing me inside. I paused at the entry, glancing up at him, a silent question in my eyes.

"We both smell like the Viper." He leaned down to give me a small kiss.

While the front of the house hadn't been renovated, Saint had upgraded the bathroom a few years ago. The tub sat elevated in the corner of the large space, with a walk-in shower on the other side. He'd installed twin sinks and a marble countertop under an enormous mirror stretching to the ceiling just as you walked in, something that had made me gasp the first time I saw it.

"And," he added, "I need to check your back."

"It's fine." I smiled and shucked his shirt over my head so I could check it out myself in my reflection. Big pink welts lined my skin, but they'd be scratches in the morning. "I've done worse breaking a glass at the Beacon."

Saint walked up behind me and wrapped his arms around my waist, leaning down to kiss my ear. "I made them. I clean them up." Then he swatted me on the ass and gestured toward the bathtub, leaving no room for argument.

Just as I turned to push my skirt down, I noticed something on the counter that made me pause. My old hairbrush with the scrunchy wrapped around it sat next to the sink, likely in the same spot I'd put it last time I'd been here. After how everything went down, I'd never come over to collect my things. Clearly, that didn't matter because he hadn't bothered to put them away.

I didn't say anything, but I took a few steps closer to the shower, noticing my pink shampoo and conditioner bottles in the same spot. My razor sat next to his, probably rusty and gross by now, and my loofah still hung on the drain like I hadn't even left, like nothing had changed at all.

A part of me wanted to be excited about that, but the other part worried about him. Why hadn't he taken a lover after it ended? It had been ten long months. If he didn't plan for us to get back together eventually, why hang on to any of my things?

It's obvious, dummy. How is he going to bring it over to your house without your dad seeing?

He could have just thrown it away or packed it into a box until the next time he saw me. But no, he'd left them out in plain sight, so he'd see them every day. I tried not to read too much into that as I dropped my miniskirt to my ankles, kicking out of my boots before kneeling over the tub to plug the drain. I turned the water on scalding, just how I liked it, and dipped my fingers in the water as it pooled at the bottom of the tub.

Saint hustled around the space, prepping antiseptic and Q-tips for after the bath, but I took the time to appreciate him. His tattoos curved over his skin, cascading down his muscles in a beautiful display of ink and masculinity. Yeah, the age difference between us was a lot. People would think we were messed up, him more so than me. But how could I have ever resisted him? Especially when his eyes glimmered at me like I might be the only person in the world.

It was intoxicating stuff, being looked at like that by a man so powerful. He'd killed people. He'd done despicable things to horrible villains. But in these quiet moments, he lived to take care of me with a tenderness that radiated out of him in debilitating waves.

When he caught me staring, he smiled and straightened, kicking off his boots before dropping his pants to the ground so he could step out of them. My gaze traveled down his torso to his cock, already half erect and just as delicious as the rest of him. The circular scar on his thigh was new, telling the story of when he'd been shot last August. I thought it added to his appeal.

"The beauty's in the imperfections," my dad always said.

Saint prowled toward me, coming to stand with a foot on either side of my hips, his hands on my shoulders, brushing my hair to one side.

"Do you think everyone is wondering where we are?" I asked, moaning as his thumbs dug into a knot in between my shoulders.

"I'm sure they know exactly where we are."

I swallowed, debating whether I should ask my next question. I'd made my position clear. I wouldn't be his secret anymore. If we were doing this, really doing this, then I wanted to be up front. "And you don't care?"

He sighed and stepped into the tub, the water now at calf level. He sank into it and waved two fingers at me, gesturing for me to get in between his legs. I did, easing my tender back against his chest and my hips between his thighs.

"I can't stay away from you, Ru." He kissed my shoulder, moving his lips up my neck to my ear. "I'm tired of trying."

"So, we tell everyone?"

"We tell everyone."

I rested my head on his shoulder, imagining for the thousandth time what my father would do when he found out. Maybe someone from tonight would tell him. I couldn't imagine Hollywood being able to keep his mouth shut for much longer. Part of me feared my dad would lash out, that in his emotional state post-Penny, he'd take it as a personal slight. The other part of me knew my father to be reasonable. He hadn't cared about my sexual exploits up until now, and the fact it was Saint shouldn't matter. We took care of each other. If Dad was going to be mad at Saint about anything, I bet it would be because of how inconsolable I'd been once we broke it off.

Either way, there were only a few more days until Alba's wedding. The focus deserved to be on her, and even if she urged me to tell him myself, maybe it was best to wait until the wedding was over. Selfishly, I didn't need the added stress from a pissed-off father of the bride on top of my other maid of honor duties.

"What do you think about telling my dad after the wedding?" I glanced up, running my hands over his thighs, familiarizing myself with his body again. "I don't want to cause chaos right before Alba's big day."

He nodded and kissed the side of my head. "Okay, baby girl."

I turned around in his lap, putting my knees on either side of his hips, cupping his jaw. I brought our foreheads together before asking, "Why'd you keep my things?"

Saint leaned back, eyes half closing as he considered my question.

"I liked the thought of you still coming around." He cleared his throat. "Even if you didn't."

Aww, fuck. That hurt because I'd done the same thing. I still slept in his T-shirts and preened for him alone.

"Tell me it's real this time." I forced him to meet my eyes as I searched for the truth in his. *Please don't pull the rug out from under me.*

He grabbed my hips and pulled me closer, a pang of lust hitting me between the legs. His cock joined the conversation, pulsing against me as he brought a hand to the back of my neck and tilted my head down to kiss me. My nipples rubbed over his hard chest, tightening around my piercings, and twin sparks of ecstasy rolled through me. I was still sore from the rough fucking he'd given me against the tree, but God help me, I wanted him again.

"It's been real all along, Ru." He shook his head. "I needed time to come to grips with it."

Not three days ago, he was telling me to keep my hands off him. Now he was on board? "What changed?"

"The damnedest thing." He laughed and leaned his head back against the tub. "It was Hollywood." *Hollywood?* I put my chin on his sternum so I could look up his long body as he continued. "He made me realize what I'd do to him if he ever tried to pull the shit I did with you."

I took a deep breath, not entirely pleased with the explanation. I'd been throwing reason and logic at him for nearly a year and a half now, and it was Hollywood that had convinced him otherwise? And not even with facts, with plain ole jealousy?

"In the end," Saint continued, "you're right. You're not gonna get to be two, three, ten years older and have it be any different." He ran his fingers through my hair, brushing it away from my face the same way he'd done for the entire eight years I'd known him. "I want you. So I'll have you, and we'll deal with the consequences."

Hearing him say that made my heart beat so hard, I thought it would fly out. I scooted up his body so I could kiss him again, the softness of his lips contrasting with his beard. It started slow and sweet at first, but his tongue pushed between my teeth, demanding to wrestle with mine. I let him, and the sensation of this intimacy calmed me in a way I hadn't been since last August.

I hadn't let my guard down in all this time. I couldn't. Yeah, Lore was a good body man, but I never felt one hundred percent protected around him. Trojan had been good security, too. That had only gotten him a bullet to the head. With Saint, I felt like nothing and no one could ever hurt me again. I couldn't say the same about anyone else. When he chuckled and pulled away, I whined and tried to reach out for him.

"It's late, baby girl, and I'm exhausted."

As if on cue, I yawned, trying like hell to suppress it because I wanted him to fuck me again before we went to sleep. But I couldn't argue with my body's physical betrayal, so I nodded and stood, grabbing a towel to wrap around my body before drying off enough to walk the rest of the way to Saint's room.

LIKE EVERYTHING ELSE, Saint's bedroom also had not changed.

His mattress sat on a raised platform at the far end near the window. At a quick glance, it looked innocuous, but he'd had it custom made by the same people who made the furniture for the BDSM sex club in Washington, DC. It had hidden compartments for his playtime secrets.

I hung the towel on the hook by the door and sprawled on his enormous comfy bed, letting out a deep sigh of contentment. The sheets smelled like him, a heady mix of whiskey and wind, and I never wanted to leave again. The mattress shifted behind me and two massive legs caged my thighs in, a giant palm landing on the center of my back as he held me down.

"Don't move," he said. The sound of a bottle being uncapped echoed through the place, and I winced when a cotton swab pressed against my small scratches. He delicately massaged antiseptic into them, taking his time to make sure he'd applied an adequate amount. I didn't mind. Hell, I could have lain there and let them have his way with me forever.

That didn't mean I wouldn't be a tease.

As soon as he put the cap back on, I arched my butt higher and hit his cock, making him let out a subtle groan.

"Careful, baby girl," he growled, leaning over me with a fist on either side of my rib cage. He slid his cock in between my ass cheeks, rubbing up against that spot he'd once taken freely. He had a lot more groveling to do before I'd agree to that again.

"Or what?" I lifted my hips higher and whimpered, which I knew would pull on his heartstrings. After all, Saint did nothing if not spoil the living shit out of me. He clenched my hair with a fist, yanking my head back. I winced against the pang in my skull, but the way he hissed next to my ear sent a shiver down my spine.

"You already owe me for the rules you broke tonight," he said. "You want to add more to your punishment?"

I laughed, but Saint didn't like that response. He leaned back to flip me over, spreading my legs again so he could slot in between them, hovering above my torso with his face inches from mine. The look in his eyes screamed dominance, strong and piercing, and if I kept going, he'd tie me to the headboard and torture me the rest of the night, if only to prove a point.

He reached between us, shifted his hips, and slid inside me slowly. His lips were millimeters away from mine, and his breaths became my breaths as I inhaled every inch of him. I arched into the touch, and he held me, my skin tingling as his lips caressed my face, my throat, my shoulders.

Saint and I had fucked thousands of times. Millions. I knew every inch of his body, and he knew mine. But we'd only done this a handful of times. He so rarely let me see this softer, sweeter side of him. And I knew what this was, especially when I came and he captured my moans with his teeth and his tongue.

Earlier in the woods, we had rekindled the dynamic between us: the one where he took and I freely gave. It was animalistic and feral, the baser instincts of matching beasts that had been separated too long.

This... This was different. This was emotional, and I wanted to hate him for doing it because he hadn't earned my returned affection yet. He'd broken my heart, and that would take more than one rough fuck and a bath to fix.

12

RU

"Hey, bubba," Dad said, delight in his voice. "How's everything going?"

"Things are good." I wiped down the bar at the Beacon and put him on speaker. "How are you? How's the run?"

"It's going great. Better than expected. I think we're about done making the deal."

"Awesome." I cleared my throat, running a hand over my face as I continued. If Dad had heard about me and Saint at the bachelorette party, he would have said something by now, but he sounded totally fine. "Alba's party was a hell of a time. So was KC's."

"Yeah, I heard." He laughed. "You guys ended up at the same place, huh?"

"Yeah." I told him about Hollywood daring me to dance on the bar. "I was tired, so Saint took me home, but after we left, some guys started harassing Verona and Hollywood went ballistic."

"Verona?" Dad laughed. "Jesus Christ. I bet she tore their faces off."

The image made me chuckle because it probably wasn't too far from the truth.

"Did you get my plan for the Beacon?" I said, changing the subject. I didn't want him asking too much about what Saint and I had gotten up to once he'd taken me home.

"I did." He sounded optimistic. "You came up with that on your own?"

"Yeah." I cleared my throat. "Why? Is it weird? It's weird, isn't it? A sex club in the middle of an airfield?"

"No, Ruthie," he said. "Listen, we'll talk more when I get back day after tomorrow. But I've been thinking. How would you feel about me signing the Beacon over to you?"

Warm enthusiasm lit up inside me. That had been my plan all along. On the other hand, I was only twenty-two. I didn't know if I was ready for that kind of responsibility. "You would do that?"

"You're excited about this, and I'm an old man." He sighed, sadness echoing in every decibel. "I'm tired. I had planned to do it one day anyway, but now seems like the right time."

"Jesus Christ, Dad."

"Think about it." He laughed. "I haven't talked to Saint, but I'll leave that to you." He chuckled to himself. "You two always had a way of understanding each other."

He was right. Saint and I had a bond few others could understand. When I was younger, he'd been the dream. More than that, he'd been a friend and a confidante. There was *nothing* I couldn't tell Saint, and once we'd become lovers, there was nothing we wouldn't do together. "I'll say something to him."

"Okay. I'll let you go. I just wanted to check in. Love you, bubs."

"Love you, too, Dad. Be careful getting home."

We hung up, and I went back to my opening duties, the music blasting overhead. A few minutes later, Saint and Crow came through the front door, talking to each other about an upcoming ride.

"When we get to the Delaware line," Crow said, "I'll turn around and come back."

"Whatever you say, Prez." Saint's gaze ran the length of me, but I recognized the heat behind it. He was pissed. For good reason, too. I'd been a very naughty little sinner. "I wish there was a way to get the pigs off your back."

Crow grabbed Saint's shoulder in reassurance and nodded. "Me too, brother." The president's attention fell to me, and he smiled, holding his arms out for me to give him a hug. I obliged, of course. I loved Crow like a second father. He was the alpha, the patriarch, the glue that held our fucked-up family together.

"How you doing, Ru?"

"Good, good." I ignored Saint's incinerating stare. "Glad you could make it."

"I gotta be honest." Crow shook his head and ran his hands through his long, dark hair. "I'm hesitant about this. I'm already in hot water with the local PD."

"I know." I nodded. "I've checked out the laws, and as long as it's membership based and we're not catering any *services* to the public, it's totally legal." Walking around the bar, I pointed to the back part of the building. "I want to set up private rooms back this way and a few themed rooms over here." I gestured to the space currently being used as junk storage for old props. "I've done the research." I went into the estimated figures, all the details Crow would be most interested in. "If you want, I can visit a few of the surrounding clubs and talk to the owners."

Crow hummed to himself. "This is a good idea, Ru."

I smiled. "Thanks."

"One problem." He turned to face me, narrowing his eyes. "How do you think your old man is gonna feel about his little girl running a sex club?"

"I talked to him a few minutes ago." I linked my hands together behind my back, preening for both of these knucklehead alphas. "He wanted to sign it over to me."

Crow raised his brows in surprise and excitement, but Saint snorted and rolled his eyes.

"Wow. Fantastic." Crow clapped his massive hands and turned to Saint. "You got a problem with that, brother?"

Saint clenched his jaw, but he shook his head and ran a palm through his dark hair. "No. No problem."

Crow eyed my pissed-off secret boyfriend for a humbling thirty seconds, the silence filling the space between us with his massive presence. Of everyone in the MC, Crow was the biggest and baddest. Despite being in his early fifties, he was in the prime of his manhood. When he set all that on Saint, my dominant cleared his throat and straightened his shoulders, trying to bite back his defensiveness.

"You on board with this?" Crow's voice came out calm and measured.

"Doesn't look like I've got much say in the matter. She's gonna do what she's gonna do." Saint shrugged. "I'm in if you are."

I tried not to let it bother me. I would have appreciated his support, but after what I did this morning, I understood his frustration. We'd bared our souls to each other last night, and then he'd *made love* to me, our fingers intertwined, our bodies and souls twisted together. When I woke up bright and early this morning, I'd gotten dressed and taken a cab home without a goodbye.

Maybe my quick dismissal was revenge for when he'd left me hanging yesterday, or maybe I was purposely testing him to get a reaction. Either would be accurate. I knew what he would do, and I planned to make him work for it. Besides, I'd submitted too easily last night, a selfish desire fueling me to give in. I loved to act like a brat, and he loved to tame me. I wanted that again.

Crow smiled, old eyes crinkling with age. "Okay, kid. You got the MC's investment. How much did you say you'll need?"

I gave him my estimate. "That's conservative. I still need to talk to a contractor and figure out how to cut our losses while we're under construction."

Crow nodded. "Talk to Coins when you know more."

"Will do."

He pulled me in for a hug and headed toward the bar, reaching over the edge to get three shot glasses and a bottle of whiskey. "Let's drink on it."

"It's eleven o'clock in the morning." I laughed, but followed him.

"Ah, bullshit." Crow chuckled to himself. "Your ole man says a deal ain't a deal until you drink."

Saint stayed quiet as he came to stand on the other side of Crow, and I ignored the tension pluming off him in suffocating clouds. Crow poured liquor in each glass, and I took mine to hold it up, clinking it against the other two.

"To the future," Crow said.

"To the future," I echoed and swallowed, wincing against the burn in my throat as I sat the glass down.

"Now that's done, the three of us need to have a talk."

I froze, glancing between Crow and Saint. "About?"

"About whatever the fuck is going on here." Crow put his hands on both of our shoulders, glancing between us.

"There's nothing—" I started, but he lifted a finger to his lips and the words died on my tongue.

"There's not a thing that goes on in my club that I don't know about. Not anymore." Crow tsked. "That being said, I expect you to tell Aris the second he gets back from his run."

"We're waiting until after the wedding," Saint said.

"I don't want to ruin anything for Alba and KC." I cleared my throat against the shakiness in my tone.

Crow nodded, understanding in his eyes. "After the wedding, then. Not that I don't approve." That sparked a flame of hope in my gut. If Crow was okay, maybe my father wouldn't react as harshly as Saint feared. "It's none of my business," he continued. "But Aris deserves to learn the truth from you."

Neither of us said anything as the shock twisted down the center of my chest.

"He's my vice president for a reason. If you don't tell him, I will." Crow patted both of our shoulders and looked between us. "I'll give you some advice. It won't be the relationship that kills him. It'll be the lying. The MC can't handle another shake up right now, you understand?"

I nodded and looked to the ground, the whiskey rising up the back of my throat while I tried to decide if the shame of being dishonest to my dad or scolded by Crow ached more.

"Good." He nodded and turned to head toward the front doors. "Come to the clubhouse later. I'll have Coins get the accounts ready." He looked between both of us before putting his aviators back on his face. "You two play nice now." Crow barked out a laugh and pushed through to the outside.

Then Saint set his angry glare on me.

13

SAINT

I'd woken up alone. The filthy brat seduced me, fucked me into a coma, and snuck out in the brutal light of day. I didn't like that shit, and in those brief moments before I checked Aris's security app and learned she went home, I'd panicked that she was *gone* gone...that some Caputi prick had found her, taken her, and done worse to her this time.

Maybe she thought I hadn't meant what I'd said last night, or maybe she thought this was still some stupid game. Either way, I needed to make sure we were on the same page.

I stared at her until she couldn't stand it anymore, until she squirmed and shrugged.

"What?" She pursed her lips. "I had to open this morning."

Still, I stayed silent because she hated that the most. The longer it went on, the more she'd talk to fill the empty space, just like her old man.

"Why are you so upset?" Ru cleared her throat and took a step closer, mirroring my pose on the other side, hands outstretched in front of her, eyes echoing with mischief and defiance. "Does it hurt to wake up to an empty house after being kissed so thoroughly the night before?"

I straightened and lifted my chin, staring down my nose at her. I understood what this was. She was screwing with me. I'd left her yesterday morning after kissing her in the hallway the night before. She *wanted* me to react.

"What would you rather me do?" Ru pursed her lips and walked around the bar, dragging her fingertips down the wood as she came closer. "Wake you up with my lips around your dick the way I used to? You haven't groveled enough for that."

I ignored the pulse in my balls at the mental image that caused, and when she got close enough, I wrapped my hand around her throat and yanked her closer, my snarl inches from her face.

"You've been a bad girl, Ru." The need to bury myself inside her scalded its way through my nerves, poking the dominant side of me awake. All the evil things I ever wanted to do to her flicked through my mind, and I couldn't decide which one to act out first. We had two hours before anyone else got here, and even if she had a few things to do before we opened, I couldn't resist the urge to use these private moments for devious things.

"Does it hurt?" She pouted. "Can I kiss it better?"

She was such a fucking tease. She knew exactly how to get me in the right mindset for the things she wanted. Before I went there, I had a bone to pick between us.

"If we do this," I said, using a serious voice to let her know I meant business, "no more running away. I'm all in, Ru." I looked between her eyes, searching for insecurity. I didn't find any. Ru wanted to tempt the beast inside me, and now she had his full fucking attention.

The little brat.

"We need new rules." I took a deep breath, willing the monster in my gut to settle down. "The first one is no leaving in the morning without saying goodbye."

She nodded. "Number two: I have the same hard limits as before."

"Me too."

No needles, scat-play, or pet-play. Everything else was on the table.

"My safe word is blizzard." She cleared her throat, her voice trembling as she spoke.

10-4.

"Number three." I grabbed her chin between my thumb and forefinger, forcing her to look me in the eye as I continued. "I still don't share. You understand? Not even for your website—"

"Saint," she cut in. "Please."

"Please, what?" I whispered against her lips, and her body shook, giving me exactly what I wanted. "Tell me what you want." I lived to hear her pretty mouth say dirty words; it made me hard as a fucking rock.

"You were right," she moaned, pushing her pelvis against me, seeking a friction only I could provide. My hand twitched around her jaw. "I've been so bad, and I need to be put in my place so much it hurts."

"Uh-huh. I know. It hurts for me, too."

"Tell me what to do." She murmured the words slowly against my lips.

I gripped a handful of hair, yanking her head back. She hissed and winced, but she loved it, especially when I leaned in and gave her very specific instructions. We had time to play, and now that we both knew the rules and the boundaries, I wanted to make our dynamic official again. She had been *bad, bad, bad,* and Lord help me, I had a steady hand to set her right.

When I finished detailing my scene, she stepped away with a devious grin and linked her hands behind her back, walking toward the private rooms with a distinctive skip in her step. I took a few moments alone to get a grip. My heart pounded, and my hands shook as I rubbed them over my face, trying to ignore this overwhelming pressure in the pit of my gut that shouted, *Don't fuck this up.* It hadn't been there last time we were together, but now I knew I wouldn't survive her loss again. If that meant risking Aris because of it, I'd have to be prepared for that.

The reason burned in the back of my mind as I counted to twenty and let the darkness out. We were about to go into the scene. I needed to be the dom she'd come to know and love. I was surprised by how easily I assumed that role again.

Like riding a bike.

When I finally made my way to the blue room, I found her exactly how I'd asked—on her knees wearing nothing but what she had on under her clothes, a lacy thong and matching bra, her hair in a wild, curly mane around her head.

Sweet Jesus.

I scanned the length of her gorgeous body, my lower belly clenching and my cock jerking as I moved closer, coming to stand in front of her. She looked up at me and licked her lips, and I zeroed in on that perfect pink muscle. In this indigo light, her eyes glowed an even brighter shade of ice, and I ran my knuckles down her cheeks, brushing a stray curl back behind her ear before cupping her jaw. Her lips parted, and I traced the bottom one with my thumb, her skin so velvety soft against my callused finger. How we contrasted in the perfect way.

"Up on the platform." I nodded to the small stage on my right, stepping away to sit on the sofa. She obeyed, biting her bottom lip as she climbed up and grabbed the pole, swinging around it with playfulness shining in her eyes. "You wanted to give me a show." I held up a hand. "Go on."

She swung around it one more time with her legs hooked in front of her, landing on her knees and slinking toward me in a sexy cat crawl. Ru rotated her feet around so she sat on the edge of the stage and spread her ankles, testing my restraint when she clawed up her thighs and teased at her lacy panties. I resisted the urge to shift my hips when she ghosted over her pussy and stood, walking toward me so she could lean over and tease me with her full, heavy tits in my face.

I traced the curve of them, entranced with the way they hung in front of her, her perfect nipples so fucking bitable behind the flimsy scrap of fabric holding them in. She dug her hands into my shoulders and planted her legs on either side of my hips, rubbing her cunt right up against my stiffening cock. I'd been half hard when I came back here. It wouldn't take much to get me raging. She smelled amazing, like sugar and whiskey and *woman,* and I buried my nose in her neck to inhale her deeper. I dug my nails into the sofa cushion and hung my elbows off the back, struggling to keep them there.

No touching the merchandise.

Even though Ru was mine in every sense. Once we told her father, I'd put my name in her skin and hers in mine. Make it all official and shit.

Aw, fuck.

I locked thoughts like that down because they had no place here. I knew what we'd done last night hadn't been a scene. It had been my heart reconnecting with hers. I *made love* to her, and it was one of the best orgasms of my pitiful life. What did it say that every single experience on that list had happened with her?

Knock that shit off, too.

Ru writhed on top of me, rolling her beautiful pussy over my cock, but *fuck,* I had to stop that because if I let her go on, this would end too early, and I had plans for her.

"Careful." I gripped her hips to move her down my leg, settling her on my thigh. "I wanna watch you come first."

Her confused scowl nearly made me crack. "Sir?"

"Go on." I nodded toward her. "Get yourself off."

She thinned her lips and put her hands on my pelvis, rolling against my thigh, throwing her head back. Good God, I was a sick fuck because the moan that fell out of her mouth made me feel like a king.

"Yeah, that's it. That feels good, doesn't it?" I ran my hands over the length of her, cupping her flimsy bra and the swells of flesh spilling over the sides. I focused on her neck next, this long, beautiful throat that I loved to fuck.

"Yes, sir." She bucked against me harder, and I sat back against the couch, enjoying my view. Was there anything more entertaining than watching Ru get off? In my thirty-seven years, nothing had ever come close. The way her mouth formed that perfect O hypnotized me, and every curve of her body enticed me to lick. I remembered when she'd bitten my lip last night and my cock swelled even more. My sexy brat, my violent MC princess.

She made a mewling sound and rubbed against me so hard and fast I worried she might hurt herself. She kept going, and I kept watching, and when she hit a crescendo, I dug my thumb into her clit to add pressure. She squealed, trying to close her legs around mine, but I held them open.

"Let me see." I looked at the spot she'd made on my jeans, the giant wet area that would require me to change before the shift officially started. "Look at this mess." I tsked and she bit her bottom lip, giving me an innocent stare. "Clean it up."

She nodded and dropped to the floor between my knees, keeping eye contact with me while her perfect tongue darted out to lick at the spot. I watched, brushing hair out of her face, the power in her obedience damn near overwhelming. This was all good and everything, but I had ached to feel that tongue somewhere else.

"That's a good girl." She preened at the praise, and perhaps she knew my body better than I did, because she didn't need any instruction. She inched higher, going to my belt, jingling the metal as she undid it. I let her, shifting my hips when she yanked the denim down. My cock bounced out from under my boxers, and I buried my hand in her hair when she dragged her fiery tongue along the length of it. Electric jolts of pleasure shot down my legs and up my spine, and my head fell back on the couch, my composure momentarily gone.

I had dreamed about this mouth for months, and now that she licked over the most sensitive parts of me, I had to remind myself I was awake. She was here, and we were doing this.

For real this time.

Fuck, she knew how to work me.

"That's it. Suck me just like that." She squeezed the base with both hands and latched on at the tip, and I swear the heavens parted.

Ru *unmade* me.

The thought nearly tipped me over the edge, and at the last second, I pulled her away. We'd only just gotten started, and I wanted to be inside her before I came.

"You're still my dirty little sinner, aren't you?" I snarled the words in her ear, twisting us around so she bent over the couch, her knees on the cushion, her arms draped across the back. I sank to the floor behind her, tugging her thong down to her knees so I could squeeze her ass while I took in the view.

"You're so perfect."

"Please, sir." She wiggled in my grip.

It amused me as much as it wasn't allowed, and that reminded me of all the rules she'd broken and how pissed I'd been when I woke up alone this morning. I raised my hand high and slammed it down on that fleshy ass, the sound that ricocheted off the walls pleasing me in so many ways.

She gasped and squirmed away, but I wrapped my arm around her thighs to hold her still.

"Don't move again," I said, spanking her harder this time. "You tested my patience, sinner, and you left me hanging after fucking me so good last night. You take your punishment."

I punctuated that with a flick of my tongue over her cunt, and sweet hell, the way she arched back against my face made me groan. She tasted the same way I remembered, so Goddamned addicting, and when I spanked her a third time, I pulled my mouth away with a loud *pop,* standing behind her. My cock in my hand, I dragged the tip along her opening, teasing both of us with the forbidden rapture that lie one thrust away.

But...this had been an intense scene resulting from a fight. I wanted to check in on her to make sure we were still okay.

"Say yes."

She looked over her shoulder and met my gaze before tilting her chin up, mischief echoing behind her eyes. "Beg."

Fuck...the control freak in me didn't like her insolence, but the sick fucker that liked to tame her reared up at the opportunity to put her in her place.

I fisted a handful of her wild hair and arched her head back so she looked up at me. "Such a smart mouth on you, but I'm the one that makes the demands." I wrapped my hand under her chin and kissed her forehead. "Now, tell me to fuck you and say it real nice so I consider doing it."

"You think you deserve that?" She gave me a wicked grin. "Better convince me. Sir."

I tightened my hold, and her wince slowly became a moan. I'd never ignore a submissive's request during a scene, especially if she was persistent about it. "You want me to say please before I take what's mine?" I let out a slow, evil laugh. "Why the fuck would I do that?"

She grinned. "Because you set me free, and I refuse to be captured again." Then she reached up to run her thumb under my lower lip the way I'd done to her last night. "Not until I hear this fucked-up mouth say some real pretty words."

That set me off. That had been almost the exact thing I'd said to her the first time we'd hooked up. To hear those words now set a rebellious flame in my gut. I wanted to push back, but I could tell Ru wasn't just screwing with me.

The brat wanted the fight, the struggle and the suffering and the inevitable defeat that came with it. Ru yearned to give in; she just didn't want the shame of being responsible for our deviance. I could consensually force her, and we'd done scenes like that before. That wasn't what this was about. She wanted to play, sure, but there was also an undercurrent of truth, and that intrigued me more. I'd never been sure about our relationship the way I was sure about it now, and she needed to know that.

"Pretty words?" I ran my hand down her spine and leaned over her, bringing my lips to her ear. "Is that what my little sinner wants?"

She nodded and bit her bottom lip, attempting and succeeding in being the most adorable thing I'd ever seen.

"How about this?" I wrapped my fingers around her jaw and guided her face toward me, digging my other hand into her hip. "Your pussy is Heaven here on earth and if you don't let me fuck you right now, I'm going to spend the entire night edging you until you cry and scream for mercy." I gave her a tender kiss on her shoulder, full of every bit of love I had for her. "Please. I need you. Only you. Only forever you."

She trembled as a response, conceding defeat. "Fuck me, sir."

I sank home hard, shoving her forward. Heat enveloped me and a hot shiver snaked up my spine while I her still, taking my fill of her sweet cunt.

"No one can replace you." I bit the space between her neck and her shoulder, and she hissed, clawing her nails into my thighs. "No one." The beast inside me roared at the mark, and I couldn't contain him anymore. I pushed her down, put a hand in the center of her back, and pinned her in place while I took what I came to claim. "Don't you ever try to replace me again."

I rutted against her, deep and demanding, spanking and scratching and growling to release all these months of my frustration. Ru met me thrust for thrust, giving as hard as I gave.

"I need to come, sir. Please."

"Go on then," I said, and when her pussy clamped down on me, her climax vibrating through her body, mine exploded. The shame of our filthy encounter dissipated for one mind numbingly brilliant moment, and in that bliss, we were untouchable.

Nothing and no one could tear us apart again.

Especially not me.

14

SAINT

"Have you ever been tied up and whipped with a gag in your mouth?" Hollywood downed the shot and gave Ru a silly grin.

"Actually, yes." She laughed and wiped down the counter in front of him, but I glared over my shoulder.

We were slammed again tonight, so I had to jump behind the bar to help. With only twenty minutes left until last call, she started on closing duties while I handled the remaining customers and closed out their tabs.

Hollywood sat up straighter, his eyebrows shooting up his forehead. "When? With who?"

Ru giggled before saying, "A lady never tells."

I ignored both of them in favor of checking on Verona, who was currently serving drinks to a group of college-aged guys dressed in polos and boat shoes. They stank of privilege and old money, but she held her own.

"How's she doing?" Hollywood ran his gaze over Verona while she placed the beers on the table and went to the group of older businessmen on the other side.

"It's not her first rodeo." Ru shrugged and cleaned the empty glasses that had piled up next to the sink.

Yeah, until Crow finds out she's working here and then we're all screwed. I kept that to myself because Verona's relationship with her father was her own shit. I had enough of my own. I clicked a few buttons on the machine so it printed out the receipt before handing it to the customer at the end of the bar.

"Why are you asking?" Ru returned her attention to Hollywood.

"Just watching out for Bear's little sister." He finished his beer and stood, heading toward the bathrooms. Ru shot me a knowing look, but I shook my head and sighed, knowing full damn well that whatever was going on there wasn't my business, either.

By the time we closed the Beacon and headed to the clubhouse, almost the entire MC had arrived for church. Nearly forty bikes sat in the parking lot, all except the one I feared seeing the most. Aris still hadn't returned from his run, which both pained me and soothed me at the same time. I missed my buddy, even if I worried about what he would do when he found out about me and Ru.

The last time the two of us had walked through these doors, no one batted an eye. Everyone had taken our friendship at face value. Maybe it was a little too close for comfort, but no one would ever ask, only assume.

Now, all eyes turned to us, judgment in their stares, curiosity and unanswered speculation lingering in their trailing whispers. Did they wanna see me do a fucking trick? Or should I pin her down right here in the middle of the common area and prove their worst ideas were true?

I didn't verbally say anything, but I didn't need to. I'd always been a silent savage, and everyone in this place knew it.

"All right," our road captain, Slip, called from the meeting room. Tall and bald, Slip had once been a pilot. Now, he flew, drove, or sailed anything with an engine, and I meant anything. "Come on, you fucking heathens. We've got business to talk about."

While Aris was out of town, Slip filled in for the VP duties. As road captain, he technically should have been the one doing the run, but Aris had made a bid for a reprieve. He wanted to get away. I didn't want to let him go alone, but he'd told me my time was better served investigating the Caputis and taking care of Ru. Fuck me for being a sick bastard, but I agreed with him. I found KC, Bear, and Hollywood in the far corner and walked to stand next to them, crossing my arms over my chest while the rest of the brothers filed in.

"How you doing?" KC asked, a twist in his lips.

"Just fine, brother." I gave him a nod.

"Heard V had to fight off some asshole at the Viper the other night." Bear raised an eyebrow, shifting his incredulous gaze to Hollywood. "You settled it?"

He sighed and shoved at Bear's shoulder, giving him a playful laugh. "Just another night out with the Montgomerys."

I chuckled while KC and Bear, both Montgomerys through their fathers, narrowed their sights on their friend.

"What the hell is that supposed to mean?" KC said, pretending to be offended.

"Yeah, you got something against my baby sister?" Bear inhaled on his cigarette before stabbing it out.

"Fuck no." Hollywood shook his head, adamant in his sincerity. "Nothing going on with your sister."

Bear scrunched his eyebrows together, but before he could question it, Slip banged his rings on the table bearing the Steel Roses emblem and announced, "Okay, you assholes. Listen up."

Crow sat at the head of the table with Slip on his right in Aris's place. Thor sat on the left, and Coins took his spot next to Slip. Once the massive barn doors shut, separating this area from the front, we all went silent.

"Thanks, Slip." Crow said, officially opening the session. "Thank you all for coming. We've got some news. Gabriella Caputi was seen in DC yesterday." Crow put the picture down on the table and stood, gesturing to the rest in a folder. "The entire family's back in town." He pulled out another of Nikki next, and KC tensed next to me. I didn't know all their history, but there was a lot of it. Even though he was marrying his soulmate in a few days, he had spent over a decade with Nikki before that.

"Convenient," Bear said. "Easier to kill."

A few of the brothers hooped and clapped, but Crow shook his head and sighed. "Nah, they're up to something."

"They're always up to something," Slip said.

"We need to be strategic," Crow said. "Defensive."

"My wedding," KC added, crossing his arms over his chest. "If I were going to do something, I'd do it then. I already outed myself as the one who killed Benito. Everyone who was there that night saw it."

"We've beefed up security," Thor said. "The Boston chapter's here. We've got the Jersey and Ohio chapters coming in to run patrol."

"Let's talk about the days leading up to it," Crow said. "No unexpected surprises."

A few of the guys laughed. "No unexpected surprises at a wedding, Prez?" Coins chuckled harder. "Clearly you don't remember yours."

"I was blackout drunk the night before, so not very well." Crow ran his hands back through his hair. "All right, look. We've lost enough brothers this year. I'm not trying to lose any more, especially not at my nephew's big day."

"What about after that?" Slip asked. "What about when the wedding's over and the dust settles?"

"We need to find out what they're up to." Crow shook his head. "We can't plan anything until we know that."

"Gabriella promised vengeance," I said. "She promised to come after me and KC. All signs point to that being the case."

"Not that I'm happy about it, but technically, she promised to go after Ru and Alba." The MC's enforcer, Doc, raised a dark eyebrow. Once upon a time, he'd been a doctor by trade. He'd shown up here with his little sister, Fingers, a few years ago. He'd gotten his nickname because there were two sides to that scary son of a bitch, the Jekyll we saw on a daily basis and the Hyde he only let out on our enemies.

"Over my dead fucking body," KC muttered, and I clapped him on the shoulder because I agreed.

"If we do nothing, we're sitting ducks," Bear said.

"And if we start a war, we lose more people." Crow's tone made it clear the discussion wasn't up for more negotiation. "I'm not willing to risk that. Are you?" He turned back to the broader group. "Is anyone?"

I looked around at these motherfuckers who had taken me in when I had nowhere else to go. I was friends with most of them, and for some, I'd lay down my life. Fuck, I'd even kill for Lore, and that was saying something.

Speaking of...*where the hell is that fucker?*

I scanned the crowd for him, but when I didn't see him, I refocused my attention on the issue at hand. For now, I sided with Crow, but I didn't know for how much longer. I didn't like people threatening what was mine, and if Gabriella darkened any of our doorsteps again, I'd shoot her lights out, consequences be damned.

"Aris will be back tomorrow," Crow continued. "He's working on securing our partnership with the cartel."

He was?

He didn't tell me that. He'd told me he had to make a run to pick up before the wedding. Just a normal thing, no big deal. Now, he's negotiating deals with the cartel?

What the fuck?

Coins summarized the budget for the remainder of the year and when he mentioned the renovations to the Beacon, everyone got excited. Apparently, Ru was on to something, which didn't surprise me at all because she was the smartest person I knew. Smarter than her old man.

"And lastly, the run tomorrow." Slip looked at me and Thor. "You two know the route and the pickup."

I nodded, and Thor agreed. Honestly, of the people I normally went with, I preferred Thor. Like me, he was quiet and didn't say anything unless he absolutely had to. After today, I could use some alone time.

"Try to be back early enough to help out with the decorations, huh?" KC added. "Or Sunshine will get upset, and I don't like when she gets upset."

"That's because you're whipped!" someone shouted over the crowd.

"You're Goddamned right," KC said, yanking down his shirt to reveal the Sunshine tattoo on his collarbone. "Proud of it."

"All right, you fuckers," Crow said. "You're dismissed but before y'all go"—he put his hands up and pointed at KC—"this is the last session before one of our brothers gets hitched."

Everyone clapped, and Hollywood grabbed KC by the back of the neck, shaking him around. KC grinned like a kid that had gotten nothing but chocolate for Christmas.

"You know what that means."

The club surrounded him, all this found family closing in on one of their chosen brothers, and Hollywood ripped KC's cut off his shoulders, dragging it down his arms.

"Okay! Okay!" he shouted through laughs. "You can have it. Shit."

Hollywood whipped it from his body and held it over his head like a trophy.

"Here it is, brothers. The cut of a single man." He walked through the crowd, KC chuckling and shaking his head behind him. Bear pushed him over to the table for what we all knew was going to happen.

In my heart, I regretted that Aris wasn't here to enjoy it. He was about to be KC's father-in-law. Shit, he'd known the boy his whole life. But club business was club business, and whatever bullshit with the cartel that had pulled him away was too important.

"Be gentle with her," KC said, but Hollywood only laughed as he hopped up on the table, holding the scrap of leather up. Bear jumped up next, and both hoisted KC by the arms so he stood between them.

"Is KC single?" Hollywood continued, putting on a big show of pounding on his chest and pumping up the crowd.

"No!" I said with everyone as Bear wrapped an arm around KC's shoulders and jostled him back and forth.

"Does he ride with a woman on his back?" Hollywood threw his hand in the air.

"He does!" we shouted.

"Does KC deserve this cut?"

"No!" It was the last chant before Bear grabbed a knife and sliced KC's name tag off the main piece. One of the old ladies would strip the rest and sew them onto his new cut, one that proudly proclaimed him as "Property of Sunshine," the same way as the other married brothers' cuts. He'd get it at his wedding per the ritual.

"As KC's best man," Bear chimed in, "and his cousin, I wanted to say how proud I am. You got a good one, buddy. I know you two will be happy."

They hugged as Hollywood let out a wolfish howl and shouted, "Let's do some fucking shots," before hopping off the table and heading toward the door leading out front.

I was overjoyed for KC. Alba made him more fulfilled than I'd ever seen him, and who was I to tell anyone how soon was too soon to get married? Even if they'd met less than a year ago.

As I met Ru's eyes across the room where she sat talking to Selene and Alba, I realized the opposite could also be true. I'd waited entirely too long to do anything about this thing with her, and as Hollywood said, it was time to pull my head out of my ass.

15

——————

SAINT

I woke up the next morning curled around Ru in my enormous bed. Of all the things I'd ever owned, this singular piece of furniture was my prized possession. I'd bought it as an ambitious young man, new to the kink lifestyle. Even if I didn't play as much today as I once did, nothing thrilled me more than tying Ru down to it and doing deplorable things to her tight body.

Today, I had a run. I planned to drop her off at the clubhouse on my way out of town so she could help her sister set up for the wedding tomorrow, but I took a moment to watch her sleep. The way her forehead sloped down to become her nose and eventually her mouth fascinated me, and her mane of wild hair tangling around her face made me want to brush it back just so I could run my fingers through it.

I didn't want to leave. I'd spend the rest of my life in this bed with her if I could.

"It's creepy when you do that," she said before opening her eyes and smiling. "Why are you watching me?"

I hummed a laugh and kissed her, hugging her tighter to me. "I'm always watching you."

"Not making it any less creepy."

"If a man ain't a little creepy about his girl, he don't want her enough."

"I like when you call me your girl." She smiled and sat up, swinging her legs off the side of the mattress.

"You've always been my girl," I said, the words ringing true in my gut.

Her grin widened, and she stood to head to the bathroom. For just a moment, I let the panic sink in, the undeniable truth of our chaotic and dangerous existence. She'd already been abducted once, and every day I got closer to the Caputis was another day they could take her from me again. This war with them was escalating, and one of these days, the tension between our families was gonna snap.

Christ, Saint. Get your shit together.

Reminding myself to enjoy these simple moments with her, I followed her to the bathroom, wicked ideas filling my head about what I could do to her ass in the shower before the day started.

About an hour later, we headed to the clubhouse. She had more decorations to put up, and I went to find Thor. Unlike Hollywood, he would let me have my peace. He didn't gossip and had no interest in my romantic life as long as it didn't interfere with club business.

"You ready?" he asked, bringing his bike to life.

I nodded.

"Stay on my six." He kicked it into gear and took off.

It was a short drive today, just a trip up to the Pennsylvania border and back to make a drop and pick up the money. While we rode, I focused on the wind in my hair and the sun on my skin, trying not to think about the tightness in my chest this morning, the overwhelming concern that we hadn't seen our bloodiest days yet.

I thought back to when she'd been taken the first time, how those hours had ticked by like millennia, each minute bringing the possibility the Caputis would kill her and leave me with nothing but my vengeance and a corpse. Thor had rallied a bunch of us together to rescue her, and thankfully, we'd gotten to her and Alba in time.

What about next time? And the time after that?

Would this war ever end? I couldn't be with her every second of every day, and compared to shit like this, the thought of spilling my guts Aris shoulda been the least of my problems. When every minute could be a person's last, the opinions of others didn't mean a damn.

Thoughts like that made it easier to face the inevitability of telling him. I could sit him down, make him take a shot or two, and explain how much she meant to me. How much I wanted to take care of her. How much she took care of me without even knowing she did. How much the thought of losing her terrified me. He'd understand. He'd have to.

After all, wasn't he the patron fucking saint of forbidden romances? He'd fallen in love with the enemy's daughter, absconded with her in the middle of the night, knocked her up, and kept her hidden for twenty years. I shoulda told him from the jump. But shouldas and wouldas never solved a damned thing.

Thor and I made it to the drop on time. We had done this route before, so when we arrived to an empty lot, my hackles rose and a strange foreboding went through my stomach.

Something's off.

The Canadians were supposed to be here by now. They were supposed to have come into town yesterday.

I cut off my engine and glanced at Thor, who wore the same expression of alarm as was rolling around in my gut.

"Maybe they're running a few minutes late," I suggested.

"Not likely." Thor shook his head and looked around. "This doesn't feel right."

Yeah, no shit. Just me and him sitting in an empty lot in the middle of nowhere PA. It smelled like a trap.

"What do you wanna do?"

As sergeant of arms, Thor outranked me in the MC. If he said bounce, I'd roll. He pulled out his phone, clicked a button, and brought it to his ear.

"Hey, Slip. No one's here." A pause. I couldn't hear what Slip said over the locusts and cicadas in the woods around us. "Yeah." Another pause. "Okay. Let me know." He hung up and looked at me with a shrug. "Slip's going to give our contact a call."

"We wait?"

"We wait." He nodded and climbed off his bike, leaning it on the kickstand so he could stretch his legs. I did the same, relishing the feel of blood circulating through my lower half again. I kept my hand on my gun, anxious for the other shoe to drop. This was a new partnership, one we'd formed about a year ago to off-load the arms we bought from the IRA. So far, it had been a lucrative deal, but it only took one mistake to make me suspicious, and not showing up at the agreed-upon time and place sent my paranoia through the roof.

Ten minutes turned into fifteen with no word from Slip.

"If they don't show up in five, we split," Thor said. I agreed.

The crunch of tires brought my head up, and I turned to the parking lot entry, where a black Cadillac pulled in to the spot next to us. This wasn't the Canadians, and my stomach dropped. I grabbed my gun, unholstering it and holding it down at my side, but Thor held up a hand, urging caution.

The back door opened and a man dressed in a suit with shiny shoes climbed out, holding his hands up.

"Don't shoot. Don't shoot. I'm only a messenger." He laughed nervously and glanced between us. "I'm Bob McCallahan, Esquire. How ya doing?"

"Where's Arnie?" Thor took a step toward him, but a giant man in a black T-shirt climbed out of the passenger seat, his arms crossed over his chest.

"Yeah, Arnie isn't coming." Bob rubbed a hand over the back of his head. "He sent me instead."

My eyes narrowed, index finger hovering over the trigger.

"I have a message for the Steel Roses?" He gestured to both of us. "Judging by the bikes and the leather, I assume that's you two, huh?"

"What's the message?" I asked.

"Uh." He reached into one of his pockets, but that made me twitchy, so I held my gun higher. "It's a piece of paper. Relax." He held it up to prove it, opening it so he could read. "The deal's off. They got a better offer somewhere else."

Suspicion rankled foul over my head and down my spine. *Some-*

where else? There was nowhere else. The IRA would only deal with a few parties on the East Coast, and we were the major player this far north. Who the fuck else could compete?

"Somewhere else, huh?" Thor snorted out a laugh through his nose. "Okay."

"They said, uh…no hard feelings, right?" Bob looked between us again. "It's just business."

"Business." Thor nodded, pursing his lips. "Right. Well, listen, you tell Arnie that in Rose territory, a man delivers his own news. Only a coward piece of shit sends a messenger."

Bob chuckled to himself, glancing at his bodyguard before looking at Thor. "Yeah, I'll be sure to tell him you send your regards."

Thor nodded as Bob climbed back into the car. Beefcake followed, and the Cadillac took off, but I looked at my brother. The rage that flickered behind his gaze told me we were thinking the same thing.

Only one group had the means and the motivation to cut us off at the knees like this. Only one group would be ambitious enough to make a deal with the Canadians that beat the one we already had. Only one group would have the intel to know about this trade in the first place.

"Uh-huh." Thor hummed as he got on the back of his bike and kicked it to life. I did the same, anxiety seizing my chest as puzzle pieces started molding together in my mind.

Gabriella Caputi had lost her favorite nephew and husband within weeks of each other. Then she learned the daughter she'd thought died twenty years ago had faked her own death to live in enemy territory, birthing a child with an enemy prince. If I were her, I'd want blood. I'd wanna tear the heads off every mother-fucker that had wronged me, despite what my family had done to deserve it.

This blood feud pre-dated almost everyone who remained to fight it except for Gabriella. She had been around since the start. She wasn't impatient like her husband or reckless like her remaining nephew. No, Gabriella was strategic, and if this was what I suspected it could be, it was the first in a long line of partnerships that would suddenly find patronage elsewhere.

Slip and Crow stood outside the clubhouse when we made it back, twin looks of concern on their faces.

"What the fuck?" Thor asked after parking his bike. He kicked his leg over the side and stormed up to them. "Is this what I think it is?"

Slip took a deep breath, and Crow cleared his throat. "We heard from Aris. Gabriella Caputi's been a busy bitch."

I didn't have any doubt. This must have been what she was up to down south. Whatever she'd done, she'd been extra careful to cover her trail because this took me by surprise, and I had ears on the inside.

"We'll talk more when Aris returns." Crow clapped me on the shoulder. "Don't worry about the Canadians. There's no shortage of scumbags that need weapons in this world."

I didn't doubt that either, but it still itched the wrong way.

"What if we still have a rat?" I looked between Crow and Thor, whose collective job was to keep the MC and its women safe.

"It's Nikki." Slip crossed his arms over his chest and raised an eyebrow at Crow. "We shoulda taken care of her as soon as she had that baby."

"And do what? Kill a woman we once called friend?" Crow growled.

"She wasn't much of a friend," Thor said. "Especially now that she keeps running her mouth."

"Lore's been gone a few days," I said. "He's the newest member. It could be him."

Three sets of eyes shifted to me, and Thor shook his head. "I checked him out before he came here. He's clean."

"He stops coming around and suddenly the Caputis know our business?" I shrugged.

"What are you trying to say?" Crow raised an eyebrow and put his hands on his hips.

Slip ran a palm over the back of his head. "He wasn't at church yesterday."

"I haven't seen him since the ride to greet the Boston chapter," Thor added.

As much as it fueled a jealous rage in my belly, I squared my shoulders and said, "I'll have Ru reach out to him." I hated the next part, but it was my fault that it was true. "They're close."

Thor gave me a sympathetic glance and nodded. "Let me know what she says."

"Will do." Speaking of Ru made me remember I had something to sort out with her, too. "It's been a long ride. I need a drink."

I need Ru.

Adrenaline running through my veins and fire in my spirit, I pulled my phone out and shot her a text.

"We got plenty of those inside, brother." Crow threw an arm over my shoulder and pulled me in close while we walked. "Take a breath. We're good on muscle. We're gonna be okay."

I nodded and tried to take his words to heart. Crow had always been a good leader, and there was a reason I'd sworn my loyalty to him in the first place. Cautious and patient, he'd been waiting for a declaration of war from Gabriella before doing anything rash. As of now, we were at a stalemate. But the anticipation had made most of us twitchy, especially me and KC. They'd come for our girls before. They would come for them again. Gabriella had all but assured it.

I need Ru. Now.

My fingers itched for her skin, panicked and desperate to have her in my arms again, just to make sure she was safe and unharmed and mine.

"Yeah, thanks, Prez." I took off toward the back of the property, where I'd told her to meet me.

16

RU

A warm glow twisted in my stomach at the memory of Saint's words this morning.

"You've always been my girl."

I smiled and bit my bottom lip, my cheeks burning and my ass stinging from what happened after that in the shower. He'd bent me over the sink, spanked me for leaving his bed without permission (hardly a punishable offense), and bit me so hard that I'd probably still have a mark at the wedding tomorrow.

I didn't care. My stupid heart already belonged to him and it probably would forever. The logical part of my brain, the part that had to play mother to myself, warned caution. I wanted to believe Saint when he told me he was in this completely, and a huge piece of me had forgiven him for what happened last time, but we still had to tell my dad and deal with the fallout.

Over the last year and a half, I'd imagined the ways my father could react to the news so many times I was certain that I'd be prepared for any possibility. If he got angry, I'd remind him of the secrets he'd kept from me for my entire life. I'd remind him of the sex-positive environment he'd raised me in, that where I stuck my twat was the least of anyone's concerns. He couldn't shame me while also proclaiming my life to be my own.

Like always, Crow had been right. We shouldn't have carried on lying to him this long. Even then, I couldn't imagine him getting upset once I'd explained that I wanted to be certain about it before we made it public.

Something just felt off, like the other shoe had yet to drop, and when it did, it was going to be a doozy. I just didn't know what I was missing.

"You look conflicted," Verona said, looking up at me from the ground with her hands on her hips.

We'd come to the clubhouse to help get things set up, and with the rehearsal tonight and last-minute errands, there wouldn't be much time before the wedding tomorrow to put the final pieces in place. I stood on a stool, hanging white ribbons from the rafters.

"I'm thinking." I put the final piece into place and stepped down, wrapping an arm over her shoulder.

"About?"

I shook my head and lied. "It's all coming together. Alba's getting married. KC's gonna be my real big brother."

Verona bit her bottom lip and blinked at me, looking unsure. "Do you think we could talk later? Just you and me?"

Confused, I nodded. "Yeah. Of course. You okay?"

"Yeah. Totally. Don't be weird." She nodded and walked over to help Selene hang the fake flowers, but I kept my gaze on her a moment longer, trying to decipher what could be going on. She'd left the bachelor party with Hollywood, but it was reluctantly. She'd always hated him, taking every opportunity to knock the beautiful brother down a peg or two. By that point in the night, Bear had already left with some girl, and Hollywood thought it was his duty to watch out for his buddy's sister.

"Anyone else woulda done the same thing," he'd said.

The way KC told it, Verona had swung at the asshole first, and Hollywood only jumped in to pull her off the guy, kicking and screaming.

I looked at him on the other side of the club, getting the kegs in place behind the bar. He joked with Bear and KC, making both of them laugh and burn bright red with whatever naughty thing he'd said.

My phone buzzed in my back pocket, and I pulled it out to see a text from Saint. He'd been on a run the whole day, and even if I was still unsure about where this was headed, I always missed him when we were apart.

Saint: *Go to the sheds.*

Me: *Why?*

He didn't respond, but a girlish lust hit me between the legs as I put my phone back and glanced around at the bodies in the room. Doc, Coins, and Picasso stood in the back, drinking beers and deliberating the best way to put together the arch. KC, Bear, and Hollywood were distracted by the beer. Selene and Verona worked on the banners on the opposite side.

I took a few steps toward the hallway, darting my eyes from side to side to make sure no one saw me. When the coast was clear, I turned and headed out the back door. The best way to keep a secret was to pretend like there wasn't one, so I fiddled with my phone while I walked.

Nothing to see here. Nothing to see here.

Trudging through the back lot, I went toward the five barn-style enclosures in the field. Who the hell knew what was in all these things? They'd become a catchall for storage. Old tools, spare motorcycle parts, paint that probably had lead in it. I walked down the middle, glancing in between the buildings, furrowing my eyebrows when I didn't see anyone. I turned in a circle.

Where the—

A hand wrapped around my mouth and an arm tugged my waist up against a hard body. I startled at first, about to headbutt my attacker.

"Don't make a sound." Saint's growl echoed down the right side of my torso, and I relaxed, loving the feel of his rough hands on my skin.

He dragged me through the door of the smallest shed, kicking it closed behind him before pressing me up against it. The stale, humid air coated my cheeks, and I gasped, trying to breathe around his massive hand. Sweat beaded on my brow, but he didn't mind. He pressed his forehead to my temple and grinned.

"I've been aching for you all day." Our lips collided, and I melted, wrapping my arms around his neck to pull him in closer. The kiss turned greedy and demanding, his tongue surging inside my mouth. He bit my bottom lip between his teeth, yanking it back with a snarl so hard it hurt. When he finally let it go, I tasted metal...*blood.*

My cunt clenched at the sight of crimson on his lips, and he licked it clean with a smug look in his eyes. He cupped my jaw, brushing his thumb over the wound, smearing blood down the side of my chin. It throbbed and ached, but that turned me on even more.

"I'm addicted to the taste of you." He said the words so low, I could barely hear them, and he stepped closer to me, rubbing his cock against my pelvis in a display of obvious masculine desire. I loved how much he wanted me. "I can't go a whole day without it."

I raised an eyebrow. "Right here?"

He nodded. "Right here."

I swallowed because we were less than a hundred yards from the clubhouse. Anyone could come out here, searching for supplies or looking for a place to smoke. Even if most people suspected something was going on, overhearing us would confirm it.

But...fuck it. If I was going to ride on the back of his bike, people would learn soon enough.

"Okay."

He smiled and bit my earlobe, sending chills down that side of my body. God, how I always yearned for him, too. "Don't make a noise. If you do, I'll stop until you cool off and start again."

"We don't have that much time."

My protests meant nothing. I'd already given him the go-ahead, so he twisted my arms behind my back, forcing me to hold my elbows, and then he sank down my body.

There was no sight more overwhelming than Saint on his knees. A man this powerful bowing to me? Jesus Christ, I could come just from the thought alone. He undid my shorts with his tattooed fingers, shucking them down to the ground with my thong. But he didn't let me step out of them.

"No," he said when I raised a foot. "I like the thought of you restrained and unable to run away."

I laughed because no one would run away from this.

Oops! That made a sound, and he'd specifically told me not to. He bit the inside of my thigh so hard that I wilted and hissed in a breath, the bright red marks neon against my skin.

"You wanna know what I've been thinking about?" Dark eyes peered up my body, and I cleared my throat, nodding for him to continue. "Getting your pussy so puffy and swollen, you can't sit right on the way home."

I squirmed and tried to clench my thighs together to alleviate the throb. He held my knees apart and stared at my sensitive flesh, fascination flitting behind his gaze. Christ, it was like he'd never seen a naked woman before. Or maybe that he'd never seen *me* naked before.

"Oh, you like that, huh?" He chuckled softly to himself and leaned in, spearing his tongue through my flesh. I couldn't help the shiver, the sensation echoing through my veins. He knew how to work me, where to lick, where to suck. When his bearded lips latched on to my clit, I almost fell apart.

That was what he wanted, of course. That was what got him off. He liked to *unmake* me, to turn me into a pile of mush, knowing he was the one who did it. There had been nights when he'd tied me up and wouldn't let me come for hours. When he said he wanted me unable to sit right, I knew we wouldn't leave this shed until he'd accomplished it.

"I've been thinking about making you come in my mouth, so I smell it on my beard for the rest of the night." He sucked harder, humming so the vibrations radiated up my cunt and down my legs. How did he expect me to be able to stand through this? My knees were already shouting to give out.

"I wanna rub my rings on your little clit so I can taste you whenever I want." He traced the cool metal back and forth across my pussy. Then he looked up at me to make a big show of dragging his tongue across all four of them.

I whimpered. I couldn't help it. I was so turned on, agitated, and *intoxicated* by this man. He knew what he did to me because his smile lit up his entire face. I'd known him eight years, and I'd never seen anyone make him grin like that before.

He went back to work, sucking me long and hard, bobbing his head back and forth and twirling his tongue around the tip. No one else I'd ever slept with had done that to me, and the fact it was Saint had me throwing my head back against the wooden wall. A loud *thump* went through the small space, and I'd probably have a bump later, but I didn't care.

Saint let me go with a pop and slapped my pussy so hard I wilted and sucked in sticky air.

"You're doing a piss-poor job of being quiet."

I almost told him I was sorry, reeling the words back down my throat before I said them.

He helped me step out of my shorts with one leg so he could perch my knee over his shoulder. He attacked again, drawing on my skin harder, sending so much blood to that area I could barely think.

"Oh yeah." Saint rubbed his fingers over me, grin growing wider. "Look at this pretty cunt, getting so swollen." He went back to work, lips smacking and slurping, the sounds almost as vulgar as the act itself. I tensed, the crescendo rising in me. I wouldn't last much longer.

"Are you about to come? You can speak."

"Yes, sir. Please," I whispered.

"You better come on my face, you filthy little slut." He dove in harder, deeper, eating me with a passion, like he really had ached for me all day. My climax took me hard, rushing through my body. My hands turned into fists and my legs trembled, but Saint held me up with his big hands while I rode my wave of pleasure.

When I came back to reality, he was still on his knees, licking softly at me, watching me like I was his favorite show.

"You fucking rock me."

I chuckled softly to myself. "You're the one who made me come."

"I love eating your pussy. You have no idea how much." He pushed to his feet and kissed me, tasting like me and him combined.

My favorite flavor.

I started to drop to my knees, going for his belt, but he pulled me back up.

"There's no way I'm making it through that." He laughed and twisted me around, pressing my face against the panel. "I have to get inside you before I fucking bust."

I was so hot, dripping sweat and come all over the place, but I didn't care because when my man slid inside me, the rest of my worries floated away. His cock fit me like a glove; we were perfect for each other. I'd known it all along.

Sure, the age difference made people uncomfortable. What would a thirty-seven-year-old man want with a twenty-two-year-old woman and vice versa? We were supposed to be in different stages of our lives, going after different things. In the end, no. We were both after intimacy, and there was no one on this earth I trusted with my body more than Saint. There never would be.

He massaged my clit with one hand and wrapped the other around my throat as he drove into me. I matched him thrust for thrust, pushing back as much as he shoved forward. He ravaged me, burying himself so far inside he was in my marrow.

I love him.

I love him.

I love him.

He'd broken my heart, and he'd never do enough groveling in the world to make up for that. But that didn't matter. Because I loved him. I always would.

A second orgasm took me on the edge of that thought, and even though I didn't ask for permission this time, Saint let me have it.

He grunted and groaned and whispered, "Fuck yeah. Your pussy is so tight. Make me come. Make me come." All of those deliciously depraved things made my climax go on, and eventually, he reached his own, emptying inside me with deep grunts, turning me on again.

In the aftermath, the room stank of sawdust and sex. I could barely catch my breath. Saint's hands shook as he held me close, but the world had been set right. I was back to being his slutty little sinner, and he was back to being my savage saint.

Giggling and blushing, we righted ourselves. I pulled my shorts up, and Saint made a big show of licking me off his fingers.

"You taste like cinnamon and strawberries." He grinned and leaned in to kiss me, sucking the rest of the blood off my lip.

"You taste like sex." I likewise made a show of licking him off my mouth.

He pulled me close and touched our foreheads, his mood sobering. "I need you to do something for the club."

I didn't like the expression in his eyes. It reminded me we had dangerous lives and our enemies wouldn't think twice about taking them from us. "Okay. What is it?"

"When's the last time you heard from Lore?"

I narrowed my eyes as I tried to remember. In the rush of the wedding and getting things started with the Beacon, it had been a few days. "Maybe a week."

"He didn't show up for church yesterday. No one knows where he is."

That sent alarm through my chest and into my stomach. Lore wasn't the type to drop off the face of the planet. I pulled out my phone and sent him a text asking him to call me as soon as he could. It delivered, which meant his phone was on wherever it was, but when I tried to call it, it went to voice mail.

"I'm sure he's just out on a ride or something." Lore wouldn't abandon the club, not like this, not without saying goodbye to me. "He's tough. No one's taking him out without drawing attention."

"Hmm." That noise meant Saint wasn't so sure.

I wanted to believe it was nothing serious, but I made a note to swing by his house tomorrow if he didn't show up for the wedding.

For now, I refocused my attention on Saint and leaned in to give him one more kiss before nodding toward the door.

We burst through the entry like teenagers, not a damned care in the world.

Only to come face to face with my father.

17

RU

"Dad." It came out like a screech, and I froze, sensing Saint stiffen behind me. My stomach dropped to my ankles, and sweet Jesus, my heart pounded behind my ribs, my cheeks burning.

"Hey bubs. I was looking for you." He pulled me into a big hug and kissed my head.

How much had he heard? How long had he been out here?

I still had Saint's come dripping down the side of my leg, the taste of my blood on my tongue. Had he cleaned me up enough? I felt like I had everything we'd done written on my forehead.

"Hey, buddy." Dad looked behind me to Saint, and if he suspected anything, he didn't show it. His mouth cracked into a smile. "What are you two doing back here?"

"We were looking for rope," I blurted out. "To hang the banners." Saint turned his attention to me, but I ignored his searing stare. We'd agreed to wait until after the wedding to tell Dad. That was only one more day. Now wasn't the time.

"Oh." He scrunched his eyebrows together. "I think Selene figured it out."

"Oh." I cleared my throat and forced a smile. "Good. Great. Awesome."

An awkward silence fell between the three of us, and the tension grew suffocating. Poor Dad didn't even know why, but he sensed it. He flicked his icy-blue gaze between the two of us.

"Are you two still pissed at each other or something?"

"No," both Saint and I said at the same time. Mine came out more forcibly than his, but the urgency in it must have taken Dad by surprise. The confusion on his face deepened.

"Where's the rope?"

"What?" Saint asked.

"You said you were looking for rope. Where is it?"

"There wasn't any in there." Saint put his hands in his pockets. "I'm gonna go check the purple shed."

Dad nodded, and I turned toward the clubhouse. "I'll go see if Selene still needs it." I didn't wait for him to ask any more questions. I beat feet toward the door like my ass was on fire, scrubbing my hands over my face.

My dad and I had a strange relationship. He'd raised me as a single father, and since he had me so young, in lot of ways, we'd grown up together. My age may be twenty-two, but I'd been my dad's best friend and he mine since I could talk. There wasn't much we kept from each other, and the long months of sneaking around with Saint had started to wear on me.

Alba found me as soon as I got inside, wrapping an arm around my elbow to whisper, "Aris is back."

"I know. He came looking for me."

She searched my eyes, echoes of concern mixing with amusement in hers. "You should tell him."

"I will after your wedding."

She sighed. "Stop worrying about everyone else for a moment. You're not gonna ruin anything by being honest."

If he got pissed enough, he would throw a tantrum that could take days to get over. I didn't want him agitated when he had to be there for my sister. So, I shoved all the feelings I had for Saint down and went on with the great show like I always had.

After the rehearsal was done, Dad headed home to get the house ready for Alba and Selene to spend the night. We'd decided to have a sleepover so KC didn't see the bride before the wedding. He whined about the whole thing, but she insisted, saying, "We've had our fair share of bad luck, wouldn't you agree? Why tempt fate?" KC had relented pretty quickly after that.

Saint, on the other hand, refused to go back to his house. KC dropped Selene and Alba off in his truck, but Saint drove me on the back of his bike. I hugged him close the entire ride, my cheek pressed against his shoulder blades like this might have been be the last ride I ever took with him. I inhaled the scent of his leather cut, letting the warmth of his body soothe this ache in my soul.

Dad had beaten us there, so when we climbed off the bike and walked up the wooden porch steps, he was already sitting on the swing with a tumbler of whiskey in his hands.

"You driving her everywhere now?" he asked, raising an eyebrow at Saint. I swallowed down my panic because he'd had all night to voice his suspicions and hadn't said anything. By now, I was certain he hadn't heard us in the sheds, but the tone in his voice sent my pulse skyrocketing anyway.

"You told me to protect her," Saint said.

"Hmm."

"Where are Selene and Alba?" I glanced inside the door, but the kitchen was dark so I couldn't see anything.

"Selene's in the shower, and Alba's already asleep."

"What?" My heart dropped. I'd had plans of girl talk and binge-watching trash television, but I understood. It had been an exhausting day for all of us.

Dad nodded to the table next to the swing, picking up a glass and handing it to Saint. "Have a drink with me. Both of you." He pointed to the empty chair perpendicular to the swing, gesturing me to it. "It's a nice night."

"Actually, I'm tired, too. I'll probably just follow Alba."

"Shh." He shoved the third whiskey glass into my hand. "C'mon. Just one drink with your old man."

Despite every bone in my body telling me to get away from this situation, I sat and took a sip, relishing the smooth slide down the back of my throat. This was the good stuff, the expensive stuff.

"Is this the twenty year?" Saint stuck his nose down in the glass and took a long inhale.

Dad nodded.

"What's the occasion?" I took another sip.

"You two," he said. I whipped my head up, my heart hammering, my gaze going to Saint. He went on admiring the liquor like nothing was wrong.

Play it cool, Ru. Play it cool.

"You both mean so much to me." Dad put a hand on Saint's shoulder, giving him a reaffirming pat. "My best brother and my best daughter."

I laughed, recognizing the slur in his words. The twenty year must've hit him harder than the cheap shit did. He was already tipsy.

"You can't say that anymore," I teased. "You have two daughters."

"She's my best daughter, too." He chuckled, making Saint perk up his head. "I like your plan for the Beacon, Ru." Dad gave me another assuring nod. "You should do it. You both should do it. Take it over. Turn it around."

"What about you?" I took a slow sip. It went down smooth and delicious, although much too strong for my tastes. "What are you going to do?"

He sighed. "Retire."

"Well, you know what they say about idle hands, so you can't get lazy as fuck, okay?" Saint nudged Dad's shoulder and sipped, giving the spirit an appreciative hum of approval. It was the same sound he made when he went down on me, and the thought sent a shiver straight up my spine. I took another sip to hide my smile.

"Nah, man." Dad shook his head and set his unfocused gaze on me, giving me a goofy drunken grin. "Life's too short to work your life away."

Saint narrowed his gaze on my father before shifting it to me. I read the expression: Should we be worried?

"Are you getting all emo on us?" I raised an amused eyebrow at my dad. "Isn't that my job?"

"Hah!" He barked out a laugh and shook his head. "No. Life's just...different, I guess. Losing Penny put a lot of things in a new light."

I didn't know what to say about Penny, so I took another drink and looked out to the forest surrounding the house. My parents never worked well together. I didn't even have any good memories of them. It didn't make me upset to know Dad had loved Alba's mother, Penny. But it did piss me off that he'd spent our whole lives keeping us from each other. Alba was only two years older than me. We could have been close. We deserved that, and he'd robbed us of it. While I wasn't sure what I would have done in the same situation, I envied the version of me that grew up with a sister, that knew Penny as my mother and not the piece of shit rotting away in jail. I understood why they did what they did, but in my darkest moments, I'd admit I hated my father for it.

Deciding enough was enough for the night, I finished my whiskey in one gulp, set the tumbler on the table, and pushed to my feet.

"I'm exhausted," I said, and I meant it in more way than one. "I'm going to bed."

When I walked in front of them to go inside, Dad grabbed my wrist to stop me, and I glanced down at him to question what he wanted.

"I'm proud of you, Ruthie." He stared up at me with an unfocused version of my own eyes. "No matter what you do. You know that, right?"

"Yeah, Dad. Of course." I leaned down to give him a kiss on the forehead. "Good night. I love you."

"I love you, bubba." He let me go, and I got the sense it meant more than a simple send-off to bed, as if by telling me he was proud of me, he was officially releasing me to do my own bidding in life. We didn't have many secrets between the two of us, less now that I knew about Alba.

I wanted to say something right then and there. It felt like the right time.

I opened my mouth to tell him, but Saint cut me off with a quick, "Good night, baby girl."

Yeah. After the wedding is better.

"Good night."

SAINT WASN'T the only one that had trouble sleeping. Sometimes, the nightmares wouldn't go away. I'd be in that basement again with Benito's ugly mug in my face, his pistol pounding into my cheek over and over again. Or worse, I'd be tied to the stairs while they went to work on Alba, screams in my lungs, pleas for them to stop on my lips. No matter what I said, it did no good.

I needed to get out of this basement. I needed to kill Benito and Gabriella and every last one of them that wanted my family dead. I woke up sweaty and muttering in my sleep, but this time Saint already sat on the side of my bed, brushing my hair out of my face.

"You're okay," he whispered, leaning in to kiss my forehead and the tip of my nose. "You're okay."

I grabbed his wrists and heaved out a sob, tears streaming down my cheeks as I gave in to the haunting ache in the pit of my gut. I'd been trying to ignore it since August, but I didn't have the strength anymore. Between Crimson and the Beacon and Alba's wedding and now this thing with Saint, I'd hit my breaking point.

"Shh," he whispered, crawling into my bed next to me, sprawling his big body along mine. I curled into his torso, resting my head on his chest. God, he felt so good next to me, so strong and sturdy, like nothing would ever hurt me again. His steady heartbeat calmed me and brought me back to myself. "You're okay."

I draped my arm over his stomach, holding on to him for dear life, like letting go would mean I'd tumble back into my hellscape, alone and afraid.

"How long have you been having them?" He brushed the hair out of my face, lazily running his fingers through my thick, curly strands.

"Since it happened."

He didn't respond to that, and when I glanced up at him, his jaw ticked and heat flamed in his eyes.

"What?"

"You coulda said something." He shook his head. "I wouldn't have let you sleep alone."

"I don't need you to fight every battle for me, Saint."

He pressed his lips to my temple again. "If I can, I will."

The depths of his love for me nearly broke my heart. Perhaps I wanted to wrap myself in his adoration, or perhaps I needed to feel something other than the gaping hole in my gut left over from my nightmare, but I pushed up on my knees and swung a leg over his hips. I dug my fingers into his stomach and he groaned, readjusting himself so his pelvis was square under mine.

"What are you doing?" It came out low, almost too low for me to hear.

I leaned over him and grabbed his wrists, holding them in place above his head. "Don't move," I whispered. "Don't make a noise."

He sighed and shook his head. "Ru, we can't."

"Why?"

He made a breathy noise that meant, *Really?* My dad was across the hall. Alba and Selene were in the rooms on either side of us. We were surrounded by people who might overhear. But it was late, and they were passed out, and it wasn't the first time I'd silently fucked someone in my room. "You think I didn't sneak boys up here when I was in high school?"

Saint took a long measured breath in and let it out on a low growl. "I want names and addresses."

I laughed and leaned down to kiss him before I tugged off my old T-shirt so I could put a pierced nipple in his mouth. He took it between his lips and sucked, sending a jolt of passion down to my clit. Unable to resist, I rubbed against his cock, which twitched itself into the conversation.

Normally, Saint loved being the dominant, and I loved being his submissive. I did whatever he said, and I lived for the naughty scenarios he created.

But sometimes, I needed the control. Sometimes, I wanted to be on top, using his body for my own purposes, sucking him hard and leaving him sweating. I wanted to hold a hand over his mouth while he came down my throat in pained pants and throaty gasps. Tonight, I needed to ride him so hard I forgot about everything else.

I slid down his body until my mouth lined up with his cock, and I tugged his boxers so it sprang free. God, he was so beautiful. I licked it from root to tip, gripping the base with a familiarity that had come from the months I'd spent doing this to him. He loved to have his balls played with, and when I focused my attention on them, he groaned and threw his head back.

"Shh." I licked back up his staff, pride and amusement in my grin. I lived to make him a mess, knowing only I could do it. He'd had dozens of lovers before me, but none after me. It shouldn't, but that went to my head.

I could turn him on with a touch. He was so addicted to me that he had to lure me to the sheds behind the clubhouse in the middle of the day to eat me out. When I swirled my tongue around his cock a certain way, his legs shook. I could have spent all night worshipping him like this. It was one of my favorite things to do. But I'd set out on a mission, and I needed him in the worst way.

Straddling his hips, I positioned him at my entrance to slide home all the way down at once. He gasped and sat up, wrapping his arms around my waist, slipping a nipple into his mouth. Saint adored my tits, especially because they were pierced, and when he bit at them like an animal, I writhed harder against him.

"I love this," I whispered, wrapping my arms around his neck. He put his hands on my hips and helped me rock against him, staring up at me with every star in the sky in his eyes. "I never want to stop."

"Me neither," he murmured, brushing hair out of my face. "You're my favorite person, Ru. I mean that."

I smiled and leaned down to kiss him, slowly taking what I wanted. What had started out as me using my boyfriend to ground me in reality became me making love to him as softly and sweetly as he'd done to me the other night. I brushed my fingers down his face and delicately kissed each part of it.

"I love you, Saint." I leaned back to look him in the eyes while I said it. "I've loved you since the first time I met you. I think you've always known that."

He froze for a moment, his face turning into that stoic facade of cold calmness that frustrated me so much. I'd spent eight years breaking down that barrier, so seeing it after my confession of unyielding love almost broke my heart again.

"I know, baby girl."

For one terrifying second, I thought he was going to Han Solo me —leaving me hanging with an "I know" like I was supposed to interpret the "I love you" for myself. Then, his features softened, and he twisted us so he was on top, holding himself up with his forearms on either side of my ribs, his forehead pressed against mine.

"I love you, too. My sun and my moon set with you. Everything in my life revolves around your happiness, and it always has." He kissed me, soft and sweet, more tender than perhaps he'd ever been with me. "I won't ever keep you a secret again. I swear it. I shouldn't have done it to begin with."

"I love you," I whispered again.

"I love you," he repeated, and even though he'd said it to me since I met him, it never held as much significance as it did then. My soul nearly burst. Tears burned my eyes even though my climax seized me as soon as he picked up his pace. Agonizing, stabbing ecstasy burst through my body, and I melted into it. I had given him all of myself, and he returned the gift with the same.

For the first time in our relationship, Saint had told me the truth with his entire heart on his sleeve. He let me in, and I never wanted to let it go again. After he came, he rolled off me and got up to get a washcloth, coming back to wipe me clean and take care of me. Then, he pulled me into his arms, and with the full weight of his love in my heart, I fell fast asleep.

18

SAINT

Maybe it was the wedding fever in the air, or maybe it was the fact Ru had looked so relieved when I told her I loved her, but I needed to do something to prove it. I'd spent so long thinking she deserved better than me, not considering the fact Ru deserved better *from* me. She wanted to be the woman on the back of my bike. More than that, she was proud to be that woman, so I figured I needed to do a better job of being proud to be her man.

That started with making my intentions known to everyone.

"Morning," Selene said, standing next to the stove while she pushed eggs around in a frying pan with a spatula.

"Morning." I ignored the knowing side look she gave me and joined Aris at the breakfast table where he read the newspaper and sipped at his own steaming cup of coffee.

"How'd you sleep, brother?" He looked up, expecting a genuine response.

"Just fine."

"That's what I like to hear."

"It's wedding daaayyy," Ru sang as she rushed into the kitchen and kissed her father on the cheek. Alba came after her, wearing a white tank top that said, *Future Mrs. Montgomery.* Her hair was wrapped up in big curlers, sticking out on all sides of her head. If I had to guess, I'd say Ru and Alba had been up since 6 a.m. installing them.

"It's wedding day." Alba repeated the song and kissed Aris's other cheek before throwing her arms around Selene and pulling her into a tight hug.

"Congratulations." Selene hugged her future sister-in-law before dumping the eggs out on a plate and bringing them over to the table. "I know I'm supposed to give you some shit about being in love with my stupid little brother, but honestly, he's a great guy. You two deserve each other."

That made Alba grin harder, her eyes welling with tears. "Damn it, Sel."

"I'm happy for you both. Truly." Ru gave both of them a hug, and they giggled, wiping at their eyes as they broke away.

"Hell yeah," Aris said. "I can't wait for grandbabies."

Alba laughed and shook her head. "Well, you've got a couple years for that, Aris."

"Thanks, Selene. This smells amazing," I said as I waited for everyone else to dig in first.

"Yeah, you're welcome." She said it like she didn't mean it, but her expression softened when Aris shifted his attention to her. She shook her head and sipped at her coffee, shrugging off his confusion.

"Don't forget to pick up the flowers," Alba said, grabbing her purse from the counter. "They have to be there by eleven."

"Got it," Aris said, jotting it down in his cellphone.

"And the balloons, too." Ru picked up her keys from the counter and slung a heavy backpack over her shoulder. "We're heading there now to get everything set up."

"I've got the dress in my car," Selene said, draining her coffee in one gulp. Then she stood, put the mug by the sink, and followed Alba and Ru to the back door.

My heart hammered when Ru came closer, and for a moment, I almost grabbed the back of her neck to pull her in for a kiss before remembering who was there and where the fuck I was to stop myself.

Ru leaned in to give me a quick peck on the cheek, the way she'd done all her life, and continued out the door with Selene and Alba. "Goodbye!" they shouted to both of us as they left. A few moments later, the sound of my truck rumbled down the driveway.

"Thank you for letting her borrow your pickup until hers is fixed."

I shrugged. "No problem."

He cleared his throat and lifted his coffee to his lips. "How were things while I was gone?"

"Good." I nodded. "She's got the Beacon making money again. We're about to start renovations."

Aris nodded. "That's great, buddy. Thank you." He grabbed my shoulder. "It's good to know I've always got you watching out for what's mine while I'm not here." He tightened his grip.

I narrowed my eyes, my breakfast souring in my stomach. If this were six months ago, I wouldn't have thought twice about it. Now, I didn't know how to act. I ignored my internal alarm bells and changed the subject. "How was the run?"

He nodded. "Good. Got some intel on the Caputis."

I didn't say anything, choosing instead to wait for him to continue.

"They made a deal with Killian McMurphy."

I sighed and pinched the bridge of my nose. That motherfucker had been running pretty much anything he got his hands on longer than I'd been alive. Guns. Drugs. Sex. He'd been born in Jersey but ran to Cuba after the DEA took down his closest ally here in the States. He hadn't stopped doing deals; he just made people come to him now.

"That's why they were down south for so long." Another long sip of his coffee. "That's why the Canadians backed out of their trade with us. They made a new one with the Caputis."

"Trying to starve us out."

"Uh-huh." Aris nodded. "I thought this business with the cartel would give us the advantage. But we lost that when they swiped the Canadians."

"So, what now?"

He snorted a laugh and shrugged. "Well, we've got a wedding

today and then..." Aris grinned. "We take what's ours." He squeezed my shoulder again and stood, heading upstairs to get ready for the day.

Trying not to read too much into his reply, I did the same.

WEDDING CEREMONIES ALWAYS CONFUSED ME.

Who the fuck would want to be the center of attention for an entire day? Not only that, but Goddamn, they were expensive. Alba and KC had been as cheap as they could be, hoping to save up money for a honeymoon, but the thing still cost them nearly a grand in food, booze, and decorations. What a way to waste a thousand dollars.

Aris cried when he walked Alba down the aisle, which made the other macho motherfuckers in the audience shed a tear. Even a grump like me could admit the sight of KC's huge smile when Alba appeared in her wedding dress nearly cracked my salty veneer.

The clubhouse was crammed with bodies, most of the surrounding chapters having come in full force for protection. The collective SRMC had a unanimous philosophy: to fuck with one of us was to fuck with all of us. They didn't take lightly to Trojan's death, and now that they knew the Caputis were back in town, they'd come to keep us safe so we could focus on celebrating.

Despite being on edge about what our enemies might or might not do, we partied at the reception like true Roses. Pollux and his band played live music, and Picasso's old lady ran a catering business, so she supplied barbecue and the best cornbread I'd ever had.

The beer overflowed and the company remained superior, but Ru was so busy being the maid of honor, I barely got any alone time with her. I sat at an empty table, sipping whiskey and watching my family celebrate. Crow, Aris, and Bear sat at a table across the way, laughing and smoking cigars. Coins, Switch, and Castor played cards a few feet away.

My attention caught on a dark corner at the far end of the club's property where Selene leaned back against the fence with her arms crossed over her chest. Thor stood next to her, one hand on the chain link, leaning in while he whispered something in her ear. She grinned and rolled her eyes, shaking her head at whatever he said.

Weddings had a way of bringing that romantic side out in people, and perhaps that confused me most of all. What was it about the electricity of an "I Do" that got people so hot and bothered? Eventually, Selene stood up straight and walked away while he stared at her retreating form, narrowing his grey eyes.

I redirected my focus to Ru on the dance floor, her arms wrapped around Hollywood's neck while they slowly swayed to a cover of "Fix You" by Coldplay. Verona shuffled through the crowd to the couple and said something to Hollywood that made him turn around and leave with her, abandoning Ru by herself. I took a deep breath and stood to walk over, deciding we'd waited long enough.

She watched me approach, the excitement on her face mixing with apprehension.

"Dance with me," I said, holding out a hand.

She glanced around, checking to see who might be watching, looking for Aris. "Everyone will see."

"I don't care." Impatience boiling my blood, I wrapped a hand around her waist and tugged her in close, the scent of her perfume pluming around me: woman and sugar and pure undiluted temptation. I grabbed one of her palms and put the other on my shoulder, smoothing my fingers down the base of her spine as the song switched to an acoustic version of "Never Tear Us Apart" by INXS. I snorted out a laugh to myself.

How fucking appropriate.

"You look so hot in that dress. I can't wait to tear it off you," I said with a laugh.

"You tear my pretty dress and you'll pay for it."

Her brattiness amused me. "Oh, little sinner. I'll do whatever I want, and you'll like it, won't you?"

She pursed her lips, looking up at me with that haze in her eyes again, the one that meant she thought I hung all the Goddamned stars in the sky. A woman only had one thing on her mind when she gazed at someone like that, and I read my girl's thoughts loud and clear. She wanted me buried deep inside her, growling pretty words meant only for her. It got me so fucking hot that I almost claimed her mouth right here in front of everyone.

Maybe she read my intentions in my eyes because she pulled away and said, "Not yet," before nodding toward the parking lot, darkened in the distance. "Meet me in your truck in ten minutes."

She smiled and walked off the dance floor, waving at someone she recognized in the distance. I tracked her the whole time, retreating into the crowd myself. My hands in my pockets, I stalked the perimeter of the party, glancing around to make sure no one paid me any attention. Especially not Aris, who was still drinking and laughing at the same table with our brothers.

For someone who'd lost the love of his life not eight months ago, Aris hid his grief surprisingly well. No one else knew he had to drink himself to sleep every night to keep the dreams away. No one else knew he masked his pain with fake smiles, working until he couldn't move. The only reason I did was because Noah had been the same way: hiding the abuse behind charm and charisma, reading until all hours of the night to disassociate. If anyone looked too close, they'd see the cracks in Aris's soul, and sooner or later, he was gonna split wide open.

I headed toward my truck, parked at the far edge of the property under a giant maple tree. It was dark so no one would see us, and when I found her already waiting for me next to it, my heart throbbed, anticipation growing in my stomach.

"How much do you love me, baby girl?"

She smiled and hummed a noise, opening the back door to the cab. "We'll see."

Fuck yeah.

I climbed inside, scooting over so she could get in after me. As soon as the door shut, I grabbed the back of her neck and tugged her close, devouring her mouth, forcing my tongue between her teeth.

She moaned and climbed on top of my lap, tugging her dress up so she could get her knees on either side of my hips.

"We don't have much time," she said. "Dad will notice we're gone."

I circled her windpipe with my fingers and traced my thumb over her pulse point, mesmerizing the glint echoing in her eyes. She was a dream, the most amazing woman I'd ever known.

How appropriate for us to be in the back of my truck where it all started.

"Let him notice." I licked her neck, scrambling to unbuckle my belt and get my zipper down. "I'm done hiding." Resolution shifted in my heart. After the wedding was over, tomorrow if we could, we'd sit him down and confess the whole thing. We'd explain how much we loved each other and that we hoped he'd understand. If he didn't, that wasn't going to stop us.

Her grin brightened my whole world, and she slid her panties to the side so she could impale herself on me. God, she was so warm and tight and amazing. Fuck, I loved the way she felt when I was inside her.

"Yeah, baby girl." I moaned, throwing my head back, digging my hands into her hips. She held on to my shoulders, rocking her pelvis against mine, and shocks of pure bliss radiated down my legs and up my spine.

I wanted to do better for her, to be the man she deserved, to not waste another damn second being her secret. It had to be now. I couldn't wait any longer. I reached into my pocket and pulled out the ring I'd bought, red diamonds in the shape of a rose.

"I got you a gift," I said, holding the box open between us. "I never want to wake up next to anyone else. You wanted a public declaration. Here it is. Put my ring on your finger and call yourself mine."

Her jaw dropped. "Saint, is that..."

"It's whatever you want it to be." I kissed her slowly. "You want me to marry you? I will. You want to take it slow? I will. I don't want you to ever forget how much you mean to me. No one else will either."

"You don't think this is fast?"

"I've known you eight years. We've been fucking around for the last year and a half." I brushed hair behind her ear. "You match me in ways that"—I laughed and rolled my hips up so I slowly fucked her again—"I never thought anyone would. We have the same kinks. No one has ever gotten me off the way you do." I pulled her forehead to mine, inhaling her exhales. "Say you'll be mine. Wear my patch. Put my name in your skin. I love you, Ru."

19

RU

He wasn't asking me to marry him, but I didn't want him to. This was a gift, a declaration of his love for me. All I'd ever wanted was to be with Saint forever, to belong to him in all the ways that mattered. The fourteen-year-old girl inside me was *literally* screaming with excitement.

I held my ring finger up and he slid the cool metal over my knuckle while I tried not to shake. He brought it to his lips and kissed it, glancing up at me with a vulnerability in his eyes I'd never seen before.

I was young. There was no denying that, but I'd wanted Saint since I met him.

"I love you," I said, throwing my arms around his neck so I could claim his mouth again. I rolled into him, hitting the pleasure points inside my cunt. Goddamn it, but he was right. We fit like we were made to be together. Nothing else mattered. "Thank you."

He trailed his lips along my neck while twisting his fingers around the straps of my dress to tug them down, revealing my breasts. He claimed them, too. Biting and kneading and...*oh*...He flicked his tongue over my piercing, and my clit throbbed.

I was close...so fucking close.

He wrapped a hand around my throat, clenching the way I liked, and yanked my face toward him, drilling into me harder, faster, deeper.

"You're my good girl, aren't you?"

I nodded.

"Say it."

"I'm your good girl," I whimpered, my pussy muscles gripping him so tight. Everything in me clenched. "I love your cock, sir. I love everything about the way you fuck me." I went on and on, spewing the most depraved things I could think of because he liked that the best. He loved to watch my mouth say filthy words. He loved biting them off my lips even more.

I came with every molecule in my body, the fact that we'd made this show of commitment to each other propelling my euphoria into a different dimension. We couldn't keep this a secret any longer. We'd have to tell Dad tomorrow, damn the consequences. But in the back of the truck, just him and me in the place where we started, I was in heaven. Nothing could break that illusion.

It could have been an hour; it could have been a decade. Eventually, we'd had enough of each other, enough to get out of the truck and go back to the wedding. I held the ring up to stare down at it while we walked, transfixed by the sparkles in the moonlight.

"I love it," I told him, rubbing my thumb over his knuckles with my other hand. His eyes crinkled when he returned my grin. I traced the lines on his forehead and the gray in his hair with my gaze, thinking how much I loved everything about him. If we had just stayed in that moment, my world wouldn't have come crashing down. If I could have lived in that precious second forever, I would have. But when we crested the small hill by the clubhouse, I froze. Where music had once blared out into the night, there were now screams and cries of panic.

"Is he dead?" someone said. "Is he?"

Dead?

Concern lanced my heart as I ran toward the gate, but I already knew. There was one person that hadn't returned my texts or calls, one person I thought would always be able to take care of himself, no matter what. A group of people gathered around a figure writhing on the ground.

"Where's Doc?" Alba cried.

"Let me through." Selene shoved bodies aside, disappearing into the crowd.

My dad grabbed my arm.

"Where the hell were you two?" His tone smacked with every patriarchal impulse he had, stern and strict and furious. He yanked me into a hug and wrapped an arm around my head, giving it a kiss before letting me go.

"What happened?" I tried to look over the crowd, but I couldn't get a good view.

"It's Lore. He's hurt bad."

My stomach bottomed out. Everything in me went cold. I backed away from Dad, the world narrowing down to one primary focus: get to Lore. I pushed past him, elbowing my way through the bodies until I broke through the center.

There he was. My friend. My protector. The one that had gotten me through the worst breakup of my life. Blood pooled around his head, but I couldn't tell where it was coming from. He groaned and spat up blood as my knees bowed, forcing me to kneel beside him. Vibrating with emotion and adrenaline, my hands shook as I tried to find a place to touch him that wouldn't hurt him more.

"Lore," I murmured. "It's Ru. Can you hear me?" I looked at Selene, who gingerly poked and prodded at his torso to assess the damage. "Is he conscious?"

"Ru," came the pained croak. He lifted his hand toward me, and I took it, giving it a soft squeeze as I realized the blood was coming from his face. Both eyelids were swollen shut, but the one on the right looked sunken in...like his entire eye was missing behind the skin. I shuddered, praying that wasn't true.

"It's me," I said. "It's Ru."

He coughed and groaned in agony. Doc appeared, followed by a shocked Crow and Aris.

"All right," Crow said, waving his hands at people. "Give them some space. Back up. Go inside."

"Ru," Dad said, squatting down next to me to wrap an arm over my shoulder. "C'mon. Let Doc look at him."

"Ru," Lore moaned again, and I leaned down to give him a kiss on the forehead.

"You're gonna be okay, Lore," I whispered.

But just as I pulled away, he murmured a quiet, "They thought I was Saint."

I stared at his decimated face while Doc and Crow lifted him onto a stretcher, hoping I hadn't heard what I thought I did. But the words sliced through me, a physical blade that sent a million tiny splinters under my skin and into my brain.

"They thought I was Saint."

That meant this was the Caputis' work. They must have seen him hanging out with me, and Christ, they'd torn him to pieces. The weight of my involvement in this settled in my stomach like acid, and all the alcohol from tonight climbed up the back of my throat. I was gonna throw up.

"My son!" came a pained cry from the crowd, sobering me and making me feel worse. Titan, Lore's father, pushed through the dispersing bikers. "Who the fuck did this? Who did this?" He shouted it into the night, but it didn't take a genius to figure out the answer.

"They thought I was Saint."

The words made me shiver, coating my blood in ice, and as Selene and Doc disappeared into the clubhouse with our wounded brother, I found Saint standing at the edge of the crowd, his arms crossed over his chest. I needed to tell him. We needed to talk about what this meant for his safety, but I didn't get a chance.

He wrapped his arms around me and pulled me into a tight hug, kissing the top of my head like it didn't matter who saw.

"Saint, listen."

My dad cut in. "Where the hell were you?" His voice was calm and unsettling, a tone generally reserved for when I walked a thin line. If I didn't tread lightly, I'd tumble over the side and fall to my untimely demise.

"We were over by his truck." At least it was sort of the truth.

"I checked the parking lot. You weren't there." Dad's blue eyes flitted back and forth between us, raising an eyebrow when they finally landed on me. "Ruth? Honesty, please."

I cleared my throat and took a step away from Saint. "Dad, this isn't the right time for this conversation."

That was the worst thing I could have said.

"What the fuck is that supposed to mean?" He put his hands on his hips, his jaw squaring, pink patches snaking up his neck. He'd had a lot to drink, and now that the liquor had mixed with his panic and his temper, we were about to get the worst side of him. "Saint? Buddy? What's going on?"

Saint swallowed and took a deep breath. "Ru's right. The three of us need to talk, but tonight's not the night."

"One of you better start talking right now." He got loud, drawing the attention of the few people remaining in the crowd. "Do you know how terrified I was? The guy assigned to look after my daughter shows up beat to shit, and she's missing?" A short pause before he added, "Again."

I understood that. When I'd been abducted last August, his whole world had come crashing down. The twelve hours I'd been gone had nearly traumatized him as much as me. For those few moments between Lore's appearance and mine, Dad must have thought the worst.

"We were fucking, okay?" I whispered, trying to keep my voice low. "Saint and I have been together for a while."

"Jesus Christ," Saint murmured to himself, running his hands over his face and back through his hair.

"What?" Dad took a step closer, leaning in like he didn't hear me correctly. "What the fuck did you just say?"

"I said"—I got boisterous, angrier, matching his emotions with my own—"we were fucking. We're in love. We're together."

A few gasps from the audience brought me back to reality, one in which I'd declared to the entire world that I'd been screwing my father's best friend. Dad didn't say anything, and I took a deep breath to slow my racing heart, my glare burning into him, daring him to respond.

I didn't realize how angry I'd been with him until that moment. He'd had a child he never told me about. He'd had an affair with the daughter of the club's enemy. He'd had a whole other life that he'd kept a secret for decades. How could he be mad at me for this? It seemed tiny in comparison, which only outraged me further. I clenched my jaw, balling my hands into fists at my sides.

Dad turned toward Saint. "Is this true?"

Saint didn't lower his gaze, just straightened his shoulders. No answer *was* his answer.

"How long?" His tone left no room for argument, and I looked around at the people that had slowed down to watch us. Dad glanced between us, his jaw hanging open, seemingly unable to comprehend what we were saying.

"Since that Christmas we got stuck in the snow," I murmured, keeping my voice low. "Can't we please just—"

"You've been lying to me for two years?" he bellowed, startling me back a few inches. Dad's piercing stare met mine, anger and betrayal echoing through them. Crow had been right. It wasn't the two of us together that hurt him; it had been keeping it from him that did the most damage.

"It's complicated," Saint said. "We didn't want to make Alba's wedding about us."

"Oh, such a selfless guy you are, *Saint*." Dad laced that last word with sarcasm, as if he couldn't possibly live up to his nickname now, knowing what we all did.

"Aris, brother, we'll talk about this in the morning." Saint put his hands on Dad's shoulders, trying to get him to see reason, but he shrugged him off and took a step back, clenching his mouth shut.

"Brother." Dad laughed in a cruel, mocking way only we Washingtons could, and I knew what was coming next. For all the love and sunshine he emanated when he was sober, he could be a prick after a couple drinks. "You lie to all your brothers? Huh? Did you lie to Noah?"

That hit a nerve, and Saint grimaced as the words landed somewhere around his heart. And while he would allow the insult due to some demented form of honor among thieves, I wouldn't stand for such a low blow.

"Dad!" I shouted, trying to get his focus back on me.

His gaze cut to mine, betrayal and shame marring his piercing eyes. "What did I ever do to you to make you think you couldn't tell me this?"

I understood how he'd be hurt by what I'd done, but a surge of fury rose up in me so hot and bright, I couldn't contain it. I'd been enraged at him for keeping Alba and Penny from me, for living a whole other life, for not trusting me with his secrets.

What did HE do?

I shoved his chest, my fingers balled into fists and fiery tears stinging my eyes as I said, "You get to keep your secrets, but I'm not allowed to have mine? You get to have a child and a lover and everyone else has to be honest with you?" I pushed him again, putting more into it, making him hang his head and take a step back. "Fuck you."

The allegation hung between us, heavy and potent with the months I had bottled it up. Maybe I should have told him earlier. Maybe keeping it to myself had only made the situation worse. Maybe I was just another flawed human trying to do their best.

"Yeah. You're right, Ruthie," he finally said, nodding. Wiping at his red-rimmed eyes, he turned and walked away.

All the fire ran out of me at the sight of his retreating form. I wanted him to stay and fight it out with me. I'd been gearing up for this since he told me about my secret sister. Now, I felt like an angry asshole with nowhere to direct all my energy.

"Dad, wait," I called after him, but Saint grabbed my arm to stop me.

"Let him cool down," he said, turning to a few prospects nearby. "Go after him, would you?" They nodded and took off. I furrowed my eyebrows as he stepped in closer, putting his forehead to mine. "He'll be okay."

I nodded. "I know."

He needed time, and I just hoped he didn't kill himself in the process.

DAD TOOK OFF. No explanation. No plans of where he'd go. Just gone. What hurt the most was that he'd been drinking whiskey all damn night. Who the hell knew how toasted he was or if he could even operate a motorcycle. I could have killed him for it.

When I found out about Penny and Alba, I'd been pissed but understanding. He kept it from me for their safety, for mine, and I didn't begrudge him for the way he lived his life. I knew my father. He needed time to compose his thoughts, to sort through the clutter in his head to figure out how he wanted to respond.

Saint kissed me in front of everyone, and for the first time in my life, I didn't care what they thought. We had bigger problems. Those Caputi bastards had taken one of Lore's eyes, just plucked it right out of his head like it was nothing, leaving a note in his pocket that said, *A wedding gift for Benito's murderer. Minus an eye for what he saw.*

It was my fault. They thought he was Saint because of how much time we'd spent together. Hell, hadn't I picked him to go to Mount Vernon with me because of how much he looked like my boyfriend? Now he'd been caught and tortured, and it was my fault.

"This is because of me," I said.

"What?" Saint stared at me like he didn't hear what I'd said.

"What the fuck does that mean?" Crow raised an eyebrow, his hands on his hips, menacing in his overwhelming power.

I took a deep breath. "They thought he was Saint."

Crow sighed and Slip looked at the brother next to me, growling a deep, "You need to keep an eye on your six."

Saint nodded. "Got it."

"There's more," I said. "I've been doing research on Nikki."

"You've been doing what?" Saint cut his dark gaze to me, hardening his jaw as he waited for an answer.

"Goddamn it, Ruth Washington." Crow ran his hands back through his hair, pacing away from me.

"How much research?" Saint squeezed my hand harder, refusing to let me break away from him.

"She's up to something," I said. "Nikki's not going to go away without a fight. We need to—"

"*We* are not doing anything," Slip interrupted. "*You* are a twenty-two-year-old girl." He gestured to himself and the rest of the club. "*We* are the Steel Roses. You need to stay in your lane, you understand?"

I swallowed down my pride because there was some truth to that, but I wasn't a girl, not anymore. And technically, Nikki wasn't a Rose. If anyone had a right to go after her, it was the other women she'd betrayed. This wasn't really the Roses' lane, either.

"I wasn't going to do anything," I said. "Not without bringing it to the club first."

"This isn't a game," Crow said, keeping his voice calm as he gave me a stern father-figure stare. I had the decency to lower my eyes to the ground, acknowledging how foolish I'd been.

I let the shaming burn seep in before I nodded. "You're right. I know."

"Good." His tone left no room for argument. He looked at Saint. "Take her home."

Fucking ouch.

I ignored Saint's glare as we walked down to his truck in the parking lot. Verona and Hollywood stood at the tailgate, huddled close together, whispering in hushed tones.

"You're both still here?" I asked.

"Yeah, Ruthie," Hollywood said. "You mind if we hitch a ride?"

Verona gave me a sympathetic look and pulled me into a hug, reeking of whiskey and sweat. She'd obviously had a great time up until I ruined the whole thing. "Don't listen to Aris. He'll come around." Her words came out slurred and barely strung together.

"Jesus, V." I shook my head. "How drunk are you?"

She laughed and lost her balance, stumbling into me. "It's a good thing we live so close. Thank you for being a good friend." She giggled harder as I caught her and set her back on her feet.

"All right, c'mon." Hollywood wrapped his arm over her shoulder and helped her toward the back seat.

"Get off me, you big stupid lug." She shrugged him away, but he went right back to helping her despite her reluctance.

Saint drove, and Hollywood and Verona took the back seat. They both were staying with Bear, and his house was only a few minutes away from Saint's. Now that we were mostly alone, I remembered Verona asking to talk to me at the rehearsal. With everything going on, I never followed up with her.

Is she okay?

"I'm surprised I didn't have to pull you off any douche plus-ones tonight." Hollywood lit a cigarette and shook his head.

Verona scoffed and snatched the smoke right out of his hand, inhaling it deep. "I'm surprised you're not balls deep in your next STI diagnosis."

Hollywood let out a deep chuckle and lit another one for himself. "Why would I do that and miss this perfect moment here with you?"

I scrutinized the glimmer in his eyes as he looked at his best friend's little sister while she snarled at him. If any two people in the world were opposites of each other, it was them. She hissed, and he smiled wider. She swiped at him with her sharp verbal claws, and he reflected it back with his enigmatic levity and charm.

When he caught me staring, he froze. "What?"

I shrugged. "Nothing, I guess."

He balked. "What's that supposed to mean?"

"I guess I'm also surprised you ended up solo."

Hollywood rolled his big, beautiful eyes and shook his head. "I'm making sure V gets home safe without those jackasses from Jersey pawing all over her."

"Not that I needed him to do that." She shot him a nasty look.

"Yeah," Saint added. "Didn't you know? Hollywood's an altruist now."

"Har har." Hollywood shoved the back of his seat and gave him the finger. "Fuck off, dick."

Saint put his hand on my thigh, tracing his thumb over my leg with a sense of ownership that calmed me.

"Congratulations on coming out, though." Hollywood snickered to himself.

"Yeah, good job." Verona chuckled. "Who cares who you fuck anyway? At least he's not some stalker piece of shit."

Before I could unpack any of what she'd said, blue and red lights up ahead caught my attention. Two squad cars blocked the road, their sirens off but flashers going.

"Shit," I murmured, tensing at the sight of cops. I didn't trust them, never had. There was one thing every outlaw had in common, and it didn't matter what type of crime they preferred: cops were assholes.

"It'll be okay," Saint said. "Stay calm."

"Good evening," the officer on his side said. He was short and white, with a bald head and biceps that stretched his uniform. Meanwhile, the tanned guy on my side had a black '70s porn-stache and a silent, intimidating stare.

"Evening," Saint said.

Porn-stache shined his flashlight in the windows, beaming me right in the face and making my headache a thousand times worse.

"Where you coming from?" Biceps said.

"A wedding." Saint kept his voice level and his hands on the steering wheel. He was armed. There were at least three guns in the truck that I knew about. Hollywood had a piece, and if Verona was Crow's daughter, certainly she had one, too. We'd all been drinking, even Saint, though he was sober by now. Still, this could go very wrong quickly.

"Whereabouts?" Biceps shifted his attention from me to V and Hollywood before tonguing his chew around under his lip and spitting on the ground.

Disgusting.

"Up the road." Saint cleared his throat. "Is there a problem?"

"We're looking for some bad guys who might be up to no good." Biceps looked from him to me and back again. "Ring any bells?"

It didn't take a rocket scientist to figure out who Hollywood and Saint were. Even if they weren't wearing their cuts, they were big and tattooed and had that don't-fuck-with-me aura that screamed *bad, bad, bad.* Around here, only a Rose fit that bill.

Saint shook his head. "Can't say it does."

Biceps nodded, stern eyes going to Porn-stache through the window. A heartbeat passed before he said, "Step out of the vehicle."

"What? Why?" Saint gripped the wheel tighter.

"Because I told you to." Biceps stood to the side so he could open the door.

"I'm not stepping out of shit." Saint grew louder, more argumentative.

"If you keep resisting, this is gonna get harder for you."

"I know my rights. You have no cause to—"

Two *pops* rang out, and Biceps's head exploded, bits of brain, bone, and blood hitting both Saint and me in the face. Startled, I wiped my cheek, thinking it wasn't real. *That didn't just happen...did it?* Biceps's torso dropped to the ground, and I glanced at Porn-stache. He made eye contact with me for one horrifying second before another *pop-pop-pop* made me jump and he collapsed.

More warm bits hit me in the face.

I blinked.

My stomach rolled as the truth set in.

I have a man's brain. On my face.

"Fuck!" Saint shouted.

"Go, man!" Hollywood clapped him on the shoulder. "Go!"

Saint shifted the gear into drive, slamming his foot on the pedal. The truck crashed into the cop cars, but not enough to break through. He reversed and tried again. The truck rammed into the vehicles, but it still wasn't enough.

This time, he reversed and kept going, whipping the truck around. My world spun, gravity yanking me in all directions, and the minute we faced the opposite direction, my heart stopped beating altogether.

There, in the center of the street, stood five men in dark suits, two of them holding up guns aimed at us.

Caputis.

I met wide, startled blue eyes in the passenger seat of one of the cars, recognition hitting me in the gut, but I didn't have time to process what I saw before gunshots came at us again.

"Drive. Drive. Drive." Hollywood grabbed his gun from the holster on his side, cocking it and rolling down his window to fire, dropping two of the guys shooting at us. Saint veered off into the median to go around their parked cars as more shots came at us, shattering the front window.

Verona screamed, and Saint went limp, the truck swerving to the right, the steering wheel going wild. Shock burned through my veins as I grabbed it to keep us from crashing, but Saint's foot was stuck on the gas, and his head hung between his shoulders, dripping blood.

"Saint," I shouted. He didn't move. "Saint!"

Another *pop* rang out and a blinding sting pinched my shoulder, bursting through my back like a sledgehammer.

"Ah! Fuck!" I touched it, and my hand came away crimson and wet, but it didn't matter because I'd lost control of the truck. Just as I looked up, we slammed into a tree.

The airbags popped. The seat belt dug into my hips and chest.

Then...all was calm. Deafening silence filled the air while the dust settled. For one peaceful moment, I thought I'd died. Perhaps I even wished I had because, with the next heartbeat, agony exploded in my head and down my spine to my legs. In the crash, a piece of the steering wheel had hit me in the face, breaking my nose. My shoulder pounded, my face screamed, and my gut told me I'd witnessed something horrible that my brain simply hadn't caught up to yet.

I'd been shot. Actually shot.

Gingerly touching the wound, I winced when it spurted more blood. Pain radiated through my skull, warm, sticky blood dripping over my lips and down my neck. I wasn't even sure how much of it was mine.

Saint.

I glanced up, trying to focus on his face. It blurred, and I blinked, attempting to get my arms to work, needing to touch him to see if he was still alive, but all I could do was lie there. Moans came from the back, and I forced myself upright, grimacing as the movement burned every nerve ending I had.

"Saint." My voice scraped like rough sandpaper, and I managed to reach out to grip his chin, tilting his head up. An angry gash traced across his forehead, and it bled so badly I couldn't tell how deep it was.

Is he dead? Is he alive?

Rustling outside got my attention.

"Did you get them?" asked a familiar, high-pitched voice.

"I think so," came a deep response.

How do I know that person?

"Fuck." Verona whimpered.

"Shh, shut up." I opened the glove compartment with my left hand. I couldn't move my right, but I had to do something. Saint was probably dead, and from what I could tell, Hollywood had ducked over Verona to protect her. Now, he lay unconscious and motionless, and she was too drunk before the crash to know what the fuck was going on now. The only one with their head on straight enough to shoot a gun was me. "Don't make a noise."

I wasn't about to get abducted again, and I'd never been one to go down without a fight. I grabbed the 9mm with my non-shooting hand, doing my best to cock it and flip off the safety. The footsteps came closer.

"Hollywood?" Verona's voice cracked as she sobbed. "Ru… Ru, I think Hollywood's dead."

"Shut the fuck up, V."

"Do you hear that?" the familiar female voice said. "They're still alive."

"Good, it'll give you a chance to prove your loyalty."

My finger hovered over the trigger. The panic in my veins turned to rage. I was going to blow this fucker's head clean off. Swallowing down the blood from my broken nose, I leaned back in my seat and watched through the shattered mirror as the guy on my side came closer. He crept outside of the truck like a monster in a fairy tale, a ghostly pale smile on his ugly face.

My pulse pounded in my head, slow and dull, amplifying the headache and the fogginess to the point where I wanted to vomit. My whole body hurt, and the way blood leaked over my right side made me think the bullet had nicked an artery.

I didn't have much longer.

I was bleeding out.

I knew it.

It would be so easy to give in, especially when I closed my eyes and leaned back in the seat. I couldn't feel my legs anymore, and my brain throbbed like a spurting wound. I thought I'd died earlier, but now it was actually happening. This was it, and if I was gonna die anyway, I was damned sure taking one or both of these fuckers with me.

The assassin on my side stopped outside my window, reaching his hand in the broken window to brush a piece of hair off my forehead. The tenderness in the movement surprised me. He was sent to kill me, after all.

"This one's alive," he said.

I opened my eyes and fired two shots to the guy's head. He collapsed to the ground.

Then, I aimed it at the female on the driver's side, reaching my arm across Saint's corpse. I recognized the voice and maybe the blond hair, but my vision was too far gone now for me to see her face. She dropped the gun and held up her hands, taking a step back.

"I'm sorry," she said before scurrying out into the road like her ass was on fire.

Exhausted, I dropped the gun in Saint's lap, my eyelids the weight of anvils. The ringing in my ears sent spots through my eyes. My vision clouded into darkness. The ache in my head suddenly dissipated.

And then...the world went dark.

20

SAINT

Fire ricocheted through my brain, forcing my eyes open. I was in the truck. Verona sobbed hysterically in the back seat.

"Please help us," she said. "Please send someone. I don't know where we are."

"Route 16," I grumbled. "Just after the Callahan bridge."

Verona repeated it, and I touched the ache in my head. I couldn't see out of my right eye, and that part of my face hurt so badly that I couldn't tell what had been hit.

Ru.

The thought slapped me hard and my heart clenched. When I glanced to my right, I saw her slumped over in her seat, a gun in her hand across my lap.

"Ru," I grumbled, blinking and shaking my head to see straight. I grabbed her shoulders, coughing up airbag dust as I nudged her. "Ru. Wake up." When I looked for her pulse on her neck, it beat so slowly, I almost couldn't feel it. "Jesus Christ. No. Please, Ru."

God, she was covered in blood. *Where's it coming from? Where? Where?* I couldn't tell, and my own slid down the side of my face so thick I couldn't wipe it off fast enough to see what the hell was going on.

Sirens blared in the distance; the paramedics were close.

"Here!" Verona shouted, opening the truck door so she could roll out onto the ground. She grunted and screamed out in pain, clutching her stomach. Then, she stayed on her hands and knees, shouting for the EMTs as they came closer. "Here! Here! Goddamn it! Over here!"

I focused on my girl. "No, God. Please. Please, don't do this to me." Ru didn't move, and my heart shattered. *Fuck.* I couldn't lose her. I absolutely could not lose her, not when I'd just gotten her back.

The passenger door opened, and a paramedic leaned in, assessing the damage, checking her for signs of life.

"Save her," I croaked. "Save her, please."

"Sir," said a feminine voice from my left. "Sir, please. I need to check you."

"No." I pushed her hands away. "Help her. She needs it more."

"My buddy, Calvin, is over there. He's gonna help her. Okay? He's the best on our team." She grabbed my temples and pushed my head back against the seat so she could wrap a neck brace around my throat. "Please let me help you, okay? What's your name?"

I met her stern, calm gaze and my soul shattered. "I can't lose her."

"I know," the EMT said. "We're gonna help her, but I need to help you, okay? Will you let me?"

I must have sputtered an incoherent agreement because everything after that was a blur of medical bullshit and her telling me not to move my head. Another guy came over and helped her get me on a stretcher. Then they loaded me into the back of the ambulance. EMTs circled me, asking me questions about who I was and what happened, but I only wanted to know about Ru.

"Where are we going?" I groaned. "Are you taking us to the same place?"

Despite my pleas, they redirected the focus back to me, the paramedic pressing against my forehead so hard it sent angry spikes through my skull and down my spine. I hurt everywhere. This would be what I deserved for all the wrongs I'd done, for all the blood I'd spilled, for lying to my friend, my brother. For falling in love with Ru and wanting to keep her for myself.

I would lose her, and it would be my fault.

When I found the fuckers that did this, when I tracked them down, I'd make them suffer. They wouldn't get the same compassion I'd shown Father Darby. Whoever came after us tonight would know the most savage side of me, and they'd pray for salvation long before I'd grant it.

"Two centimeters to the left, and you'd be a dead man," Doctor Kelley said.

If Ru doesn't make it out of surgery, I'd wish I was.

I ignored that terrifying thought as she slid the needle through the skin on my forehead. She'd numbed it so I couldn't feel much, just a gentle pulling as she tied me back together. They'd run all the tests, and nothing was wrong with me. I'd gotten knocked out when the bullet grazed my head, but other than that, I could go home.

But I wouldn't. No, I'd be taking my ass out to the waiting room.

One of the nurses told me Verona, Ru, and Hollywood had been taken to surgery as soon as they arrived. Ru had almost bled out, and the bullet that hit Hollywood passed through him and went into Verona, lodging in her rib cage right by her heart. If he hadn't been there to slow it down, she would have died immediately. Crow had popped in a few minutes ago to make sure I was okay and headed back to the waiting room shortly after. Since then, I'd been holding my breath for an update.

"You wanna tell me what happened?" Doctor Kelley maintained a steady, controlled tone while she worked, her serious gaze focused and discerning.

"Not really." Scalding, blistering rage surged through me again at the thought of those bodies on the ground, the Caputi fucks that had come after us tonight. Had Gabriella sent them? Had Leo or Nikki? I didn't know, but when I found out, nothing would stand in the way of my vengeance.

The doctor hummed to herself. "Still worried about the woman they brought in, huh?"

"My girlfriend."

She gave me a warm smile. "Well, she couldn't have hit an artery or she would have died in seconds."

That eased some of the panic in my chest, but not all of it. I stared down at her blood on my hands. I'd tried to wash it off in the bathroom, but in the time it took to get here, it had stained my skin.

So far, no one had heard from Aris, and the longer his silence went on, the more I worried, and that shit pissed me off. My mind ran through a list of horrible things that could have happened to him, especially given what had gone down with Lore. I imagined him being tortured in some basement or dragged through the woods with a rope around his neck. The Caputis would waste no time in being monstrous to one of our officers, especially the one that had "stolen and defiled" their golden child before hiding her for years under a false name.

I endured a few more minutes of the doctor's poking before she finally put the tweezers down. "All set."

"Thanks, Doc." I gave her a solemn nod.

"Let me see if I can get any scoop on your girlfriend, okay?" She winked, ripped off her gloves, and walked back into the hallway, leaving me to gather my things. My clothes had been taken as evidence since two police officers had died on the scene as well. Slip's old lady, Scribe, had run by my house to gather something for me to wear.

Then I sat there, alone and raging with my thoughts. I'd almost lost her tonight. I could still lose her, and I'd spent so much time pushing her away. God, I was an idiot. I loved her so much that I didn't know what I'd do if she didn't exist anymore. She could leave me, she could marry someone else, but if she were gone completely, my life would be over.

When the doctor came back with my discharge papers, she said, "Ru's still in surgery, but they think she's gonna be okay. You all got lucky." She nodded toward the exit. "You can go anytime you want."

Despite how much hope that gave me, I didn't buy into the lightness in my chest. Ru wasn't out of the woods yet.

I found Alba and KC sitting next to each other when I got to the waiting room, wearing twin expressions of worry. Still in her wedding dress with KC's new leather cut over her shoulders, Alba rushed to me and hugged me close. Maybe it was selfish, but I took some of the strength she freely gave.

"She's a fighter, Saint," Alba said. "She's gonna be okay."

I nodded, trying to believe her, trying to convince myself of the same. But I'd seen the damage, and I didn't know if I could. "Have you heard from your dad?"

She shook her head and sighed. "I called him a bunch."

"Yeah, me too," KC added.

She cupped my cheek and sniffed back tears. "He'll come around. He loves you both."

I nodded and glanced at everyone else in the room with us. Picasso, Slip, and Scribe sat in one corner, Coins and Thor in the other. Crow paced while Bear, Castor, and Pollux leaned up against the wall, unable to sit when the youngest Montgomery was so desperately injured.

Like all families, we had our quirks. We fought and made up and fought again, but in the end, we were there for each other. No matter what. Through thick and thin. We rose together, and we fell together, and in moments like this, I appreciated them more than any group I'd ever known. I had no idea how I'd get through tonight without their support behind me. But the person I needed the most, the only other person who loved Ru as much as I did, was nowhere to be found.

Alba sat down next to me, squeezing her fingers in between mine, and I thought that maybe, if she held on tight enough, she could carry this weight for both of us. I had been hollowed, carved clean. In the matter of a few hours, I'd alienated my only true friend and nearly lost the love of my life.

God wouldn't be so cruel, would He? The thought made me snicker to myself. What did God care for trivial human things like deserving and cruelty? He gave and He took away at His will, and this was just another way for Him to fuck with me.

When a doctor eventually came out, it was to report on Verona and Hollywood.

"Both are in recovery," the doctor said. "Things will be touch and go tonight, but if they make it, they should be okay."

"And the other woman?" I asked. "Ruth Washington?"

The doctor shrugged and said, "I'm sorry, I don't know her," before walking away.

I couldn't sit here and do nothing. Everyone stared at me with judgment, pity, or both in their eyes, and I'd had enough. I was crawling out of my skin and there wasn't enough nicotine in this Goddamn state to calm me. So, I stood, told Alba I needed to clear my head, and left them sitting in that wretched, claustrophobic waiting area.

I DIDN'T KNOW why I ended up in the chapel. Perhaps I was looking for a quiet place to pass the time while I waited for news about Ru. Or maybe I'd been pissed off at God for so long that I'd finally lost my fucking cool with the piece of shit and decided he needed a piece of my mind. I sat in a pew, my arms on the wood in front of me, my hands clasped in prayer, but nothing came out.

God and I hadn't talked in decades, and until that moment, I didn't realize how little I had to say to the bastard. What *could* I say? That I hated Him and all he'd put me through? That taking my brother and potentially Ru from me had turned me into a soulless husk of a person? Ever since I'd killed Father Darby, I figured God didn't have much place for me. To be fair, if He allowed a monster like that to be one of his chosen people, I didn't have much place for God, either. The only church I needed was the one Crow called every week. But some part of me felt responsible for the terrible things had happened to Ru. Tonight. Last August. The time in between. Was that not faith?

Why didn't you take me, you sick piece of shit? Why spare me after everything I've done?

Like all the nights before, God stayed silent, having not a word for this humble sinner full of fury and revenge.

I didn't know how long I'd been down there before footsteps sounded behind me. I assumed it was another desperate, grief-stricken person with a loved one here at the hospital, so I went on with my tirade, cursing whatever deity had allowed tonight to happen to them, too.

The footsteps grew heavier as they came closer, and I finally recognized them as boots. They stopped in the aisle next to me, and the tall fucker with gray hair put his hands on his hips while he stared up at the giant crucifix attached to the wall. Dozens of candles burned under it, flowers and decorations lining the space, all of it glowing with an ethereal incandescence that marked it as a house of worship.

"Do you think God has compassion for a man who never prayed to Him before?" Aris glanced down at me before scrutinizing the cross again. He had bags under his red-rimmed eyes and looked like shit, but I definitely looked worse.

"God doesn't give a damn about anyone, no matter if you prayed to Him or not."

Aris snorted out an indignant noise and lowered his massive body onto the bench next to me.

"Is Ru—"

"Still in surgery," he said, narrowing his eyes at the bandage on my forehead and my swollen eye. He didn't say anything, just refocused his attention up ahead. "Nobody can tell me how it's going. When they know, we'll know."

I shook my head and swallowed down the ache that caused. "My doctor told me they think she'll be okay."

"I hope so." Aris's voice was calm despite how badly he musta been wishing it was me instead of her. There was a lot of that going around. "Are you okay?"

"I've had worse."

He shook his head. "They were coming after you, ya know?"

I wished they'd taken me. I wished it was me in that operating room right now. I took a deep breath, trying to soothe the ache in my chest, but it pounded harder.

"Yeah, I know, brother." The word rolled off my tongue as easy as it ever had, but this time, Aris shifted in his seat uncomfortably.

He took a deep breath in, full of his judgment and disappointment, and let it out slow through his nose. "You were right. Tonight wasn't the right time to talk about you two."

I agreed, so I didn't say anything.

"And this doesn't mean I'm okay with it"—Aris crossed his arms over his chest and leaned back against the pew—"but in a long line of fucked-up, you and her don't rank that high."

The tension in my gut eased. "What?"

"Who Ru fucks is her own business." He pinched his nose and squinted his eyes shut. "But Christ, man, you used to scare off those little shits that came sniffing around."

"It isn't like that." I cleared my throat. "It wasn't like that for a long time. You gotta believe me."

Aris shook his head and shifted in his seat again. "Why her?"

"What do you mean?"

"You could have your pick of any of the hang-arounds. Why Ru?"

I opened my mouth, but I didn't know what else to say. I loved her. Then. Now. Since the first time I met her. "She's my girl, Aris."

He took a deep breath and ran a hand over his face. "How could you keep this from me for eighteen months?"

I cleared my throat. "Now's not the right time to talk about that, either."

"It's better than sitting around, imagining my daughter bleeding out on the OR floor."

The image made me wince, the pain a throbbing ache in my chest. "It wasn't supposed to be permanent."

Aris scoffed like he didn't like that answer.

I swallowed. "She broke it off before she went back to school, and I let her."

"Holy fuck." Realization dawned behind his eyes. All the times we'd almost been caught. All the times she'd cried over some guy she couldn't tell him about. All the times I'd spent the night and looked exhausted as hell the next day. "That was you?"

I kept my mouth shut because hurting her last year was one of my deepest shames. I was supposed to make her feel good, to protect her and love her always. Instead, I'd crushed it all in the name of doing the right thing. The road to hell wasn't paved with terrible intentions, after all.

"I knew a spineless son of a bitch shattered her heart, but I assumed it was some douchebag in Mount Vernon." He sighed. "Hell, for a while I thought it was Lore."

"I thought she was better off without me." It sounded fucked-up given all that had happened to us since then. "I told her to go have fun, go be twenty-two. I'm an idiot."

Aris whipped his eyes to mine, and I couldn't tell if he agreed or thought I was a piece of shit for thinking it. Maybe both. "I ought to rip your heart out and make you eat it for doing that to her."

I nodded and hung my head between my shoulders. "Yeah, you should."

I deserved his wrath for treating her like a dirty little secret the first time around. She was worth more than that. This moment had been etched into our future since then. It could end no other way.

A long stretch of silence spanned between us, one where we sat next to each other and stared at the light from the flames flickering across the representation of what little faith I once had. Eventually, he sighed and put his hands on the pew in front of us to tug himself upright.

"Pull yourself together." He looked down at me one more time. "If she comes out of surgery and wakes up, she'll want to see you. She's gonna look rough, and you gotta be strong."

"I'm sorry I lied to you, Aris," I said. "But I'm not sorry I fell in love with her, and I'm not sorry we're together."

He nodded and thinned his lips. "I'm sorry for bringing Noah into it. That was uncalled for." He turned to head back down the aisle, and at the edge of the pew, he stopped and looked back at me. "You treat her right from now on, or I'll slit your throat."

I sighed and nodded, knowing it wouldn't come to that. He left, and when the door closed behind him, my attention went to the crucifix hanging in front of me. I didn't know if Ru would be okay. I didn't know if I'd ever get to hear her beautiful laugh or see her smile again. God would want me to forgive, to find compassion in my heart for the ones who had wronged me, but I'd stopped believing in all that shit long ago.

In my world, it was kill or be killed.

A slight for a slight. And I'd never let a debt go unanswered.

WHEN I FINALLY MADE MY way back to the waiting room, my family had been joined by Detective Jordan and her partner, Detective Dickhead or whatever his name was. They were assigned to investigate the shoot-out last August, the one that had resulted in me getting shot in the leg and KC killing Benito's nephew.

Jordan was a short Black woman with chin-length hair and bright sunshine eyes that I was pretty sure incinerated criminals where they stood. Detective Dickhead was tall and white with an utterly punch-able face.

Tonight, they were here to pester my family about what happened. Detective Jordan stood toe-to-toe with Crow, staring up at him with her hands on her hips and her chin jutted out. He towered over her, dwarfing her with both his height and his stature.

"I've got two officers down," she said, "three Roses with gunshot wounds, and a John Doe with a bullet in his head. Someone's got to do some talking."

"I told you, I ain't saying a fucking word." Crow crossed his arms over his chest. "My daughter's in recovery, and I'm up to my ears in Caputi horseshit. You want to be useful? Go ask them why they tracked their filth into my territory the night my veep's daughter gets married, huh?"

"Who says I'm not? I wanna hear your side of the story." Jordan took a deep breath and straightened her shoulders, clearly unafraid of Crow's dominance. She might be the only person alive that could say that and mean it.

I cleared my throat, and all eyes turned to me.

"Garrett Anderson?" She crossed her arms over her chest, taking a step toward me.

I grunted at the name. I hadn't been called Garrett in a decade. "Sure. Let's go with that."

"I need to talk to you about what happened." She gestured to the hallway, taking a few steps in that direction. "If you wouldn't mind."

"Actually, he would," Crow said, moving toward me. "He minds very much."

"I'm not talking to you, Montgomery." Detective Jordan shot him a side-eye glare.

I damn near grimaced. No one spoke to Crow like that, certainly no one that hung around with him on a daily basis. With Verona still in critical condition, this detective skated on thin ice.

"If you're talking to a Rose, you're talking to me," he growled.

"It's okay," I cut in. "I don't have much to say anyway."

"Thor"—Crow nodded to me and Jordan—"take Saint back to his house. He's clearly concussed."

"No, I'm good," I continued. "I swear."

Still, Crow clearly didn't like me talking to the PD by myself, so he nudged Thor in my direction, who followed me out into the hallway with the two detectives. Jordan furrowed her eyebrows with serious concentration. Detective Dickhead remained apathetic, like he didn't give a damn what I said; he just wanted to arrest someone. "I don't have anything to tell you other than what you probably picked up on the dash cam."

Jordan nodded. "Tell me what you remember."

I gave her a brief—very brief—overview, keeping out the parts where I refused to follow the officer's orders.

"Was this the Caputis?" The look she gave me demanded an honest answer.

But I wasn't a snitch, and no matter what the pigs did, I was going after these fuckers myself. The MC wouldn't stand for an assault on four of its family members. Jordan and the entire PD would be best kept out of this. "I don't know. I don't remember."

"That's bullshit," Detective Dickhead said. "He's lying."

"No, he's not," Thor cut in. "He agreed to talk to you. He's talking. What more do you want?"

"How about the truth for once?" Dickhead rolled his eyes. "You cocksuckers are all the same."

Jordan held up a hand to silence him and nodded at me. "If I find out that you did remember, and you didn't come to me, or you take matters into your own hands, I won't be happy."

I figured as much, but if I played my cards right, there wouldn't be anything for her to find out. "You know the PD can't keep up with this game, right?" I shook my head and shoved my hands in my pockets. "You can try but this fight? It's got nothing to do with you. Your deputies would be safer if you stayed out of it."

"Hmm." Jordan narrowed her eyes, taking a step closer to me. "Those two officers that died tonight? They've got families, loved ones that didn't get to say goodbye and children that will now grow up without a father because of this stupid blood war." She adjusted the badge and gun on her belt, straightening her shoulders with a newfound sense of confidence. "And before I'm done, I'll make sure everyone responsible sees justice." She turned to her partner and nodded toward the door. "I'll be back when your girlfriend wakes up."

She left me standing there chewing on the thought of the innocent people that had suffered because of this feud with the Caputis. It wasn't just those cops tonight. Civilians had been standing near the car containing KC's parents and Crow's old lady. It was Trojan's wife, Marissa, and the children they'd never get to have.

This war might have had nothing to do with me at the start, but the minute this family took me in, it became my fight, too.

They'd gone after Ru twice now, and that was two times too many.

21

RU

Fucking. Ow.

I blinked my eyes open, and every muscle burned. It was dark, the moonlight soft in between the blinds, and the smells of hospital and disinfectant permeated the air.

Why am I in the hospital?

Before I could think too hard about that, I registered the warm hand holding mine. Saint sat in the chair next to me, his head tucked into the elbow of his other arm on the hospital bed, facing away.

"Saint," I tried to say, but my throat was scratchy and I coughed. Hell, I must have inhaled an entire ocean since I'd been here.

How long have I been out?

What day is it?

What happened?

I struggled to keep up, searching for a reasonable explanation. I'd gotten into the truck with Saint, Hollywood, and Verona. We were on our way home before we got stopped by the police. And then—

The shoot-out. Saint's head wound. Killing the Caputi that touched me. And there was something else, something important, something just out of reach...

Oh God.

Panic seized my chest, my eyes burning as realization choked my throat. I glanced at my shoulder, trying to tear away the gown and the bandages so I could see the damage. The damn things were on there too tight.

"Ru?" Saint grabbed my hand, trying to stop me, but I had to see it. I had to know. "Ru, stop."

"How bad is it?" I barely made a sound, the words coming out in wheezes and rasps.

"You're alive," he said, cupping my face, bringing our foreheads together. "You're okay. You're gonna be okay."

"They shot me." Silent sobs barreled out of my chest, the agony of their hatred too much to bear. "I killed someone, Saint. I killed him. I killed him." I kept saying it over and over again, clinging to my lover as the weight of my actions settled around me. They'd gone after Lore because of me. They'd gone after Verona because of me. I was a murderer now.

"Shh." Saint crawled into the bed next to me, holding my head to his chest, kissing my temple to soothe me. "It's okay, baby girl. You're okay."

"You're alive." I ran a finger over the bandage on his forehead, remembering the panic in my chest when I'd thought he'd died. I passed out wishing for death to take me, too. If we went down, we went down together. My heart had been broken. I didn't want to live in a world where he didn't exist.

"I'm alive." He kissed me, soft and sweet, reminding me why I belonged to him, why we belonged together.

"How is everyone? Is Hollywood—"

"Everyone's on the mend." He tilted my face up so he could kiss me again. "They came out of surgery two days ago. We've been worried about you."

Two days?

"You lost a lot of blood. It was touch and go for a while."

I didn't remember any of it. It felt like I'd passed out in the truck seconds ago and woken up here. I gasped, remembering what we'd told my dad shortly before the accident. "Where's Dad?"

"He went home to shower. He'll be back soon."

I wanted to stay there in Saint's arms forever, but the nurses came in to check on me now that I was awake. The doctor wanted to do a bunch of tests to make sure I was healing properly after the surgery. When I got the all clear, they told me I could go home in a few days if things stayed steady. I felt like I'd been run through a meat grinder and put back together poorly, but that meant I was still alive so I'd take it. After that, they gave me pain meds, and I fell asleep again.

The next time I woke up, I heard Selene's voice first.

"You know what we need to do next." She stood at the far end of the room with her arms crossed over her chest, huddled close to Thor while they talked. A stern expression glinted in her eyes, like she was serious about whatever she said.

His features softened, and he sighed. "You don't even know who did this."

"I can fucking guess." She cleared her throat and ran a finger over her eyebrow. "And it's long past time we did something about it."

"She's off the radar, Sel." Thor ran a finger over her face and brushed hair out of her eyes, pushing it back behind her ear. It was such an affectionate thing to do between two people who hadn't even kissed, but my opioid-addled mind didn't put too much thought into it.

"I can find her." She had that telltale determination in her voice, reminding me of the teenage version of herself, angry and mean and stubborn.

"Let it rest. The MC is working on it."

She squared her jaw and set her piercing glare on him, like that explanation wasn't good enough and he knew it.

"I'm serious," he said. "You running off after her ain't gonna do anyone any good."

Selene huffed out a frustrated sigh and turned to face me, her blue eyes growing bigger when she realized I was awake.

"Jesus. Look at you." She came closer while Thor opened the door to shout down the hallway that I was conscious. My best friend grabbed my hand and kissed my knuckles, tears streaming down her cheeks as she muttered something about kicking my ass for almost dying. "This is the second time now, and if you do it again, I'm going to take it personally."

I tried not to laugh too hard as the door opened and Alba rolled in Hollywood, seated in a wheelchair, my dad entering after her.

"Hey ya, Bubs!" Dad kissed my forehead and tussled my hair. "How's my little hell-raiser, huh?"

"Beat up," I teased, but smiled at the sight of my family.

"At least you still have your spirit." Alba kissed my cheek.

"There she is!" Hollywood leaned over the bed and give me a kiss on the other cheek. He had scruff around his jaw that I'd never seen before, indicating just how fucked-up he'd been as well. Bear rolled V into the room next, likewise in a hospital gown, but she had a robe over her shoulders. When she saw me, she gasped and forced her brother to bring her closer so she could give me a half hug.

"You're okay!" Her weak hold likely matched my own, but I could barely sit upright.

"I'm okay," I croaked.

They were all happy I'd survived, and while I was, too, it didn't really feel like a joyful moment. We were alive, but Lore had been badly wounded. Four of us almost died.

"Hey, look!" Hollywood pulled up his johnny, revealing the bandage over his gunshot wound in the stomach while holding his blanket strategically over his cock. "Bullet buddies!"

"Jesus Christ." Selene shook her head and pinched the bridge of her nose, appearing so much like her twin brother in that moment.

I rolled my eyes and tried to sit up farther, but the ache in my shoulder made me grimace and falter.

"Here, let me help you." Dad tried to grab the pillows and Alba adjusted my body, but it was too much too soon and I groaned, startling both of them.

"Let me see." Selene checked the dressings, but this was how I lived now. The doctors said I'd been lucky. The bullet missed my artery by a few centimeters. If it had been nicked, I would have been dead in seconds. Be that as it may, I still had a long road of physical therapy and rehabilitation ahead of me. I was young and strong and otherwise healthy. With time, I could have full range of motion again.

Visiting hours ended and everyone left except my dad, who pulled up a chair next to me and slumped into it with a sigh, his hands crossed in his lap. He had that look in his eye, the one that meant he had a thousand things to say but didn't know if this was the right time.

It wasn't, but it never would be.

"Go on. Speak your mind." I turned my head in his direction.

He shrugged. "What do you mean?"

"You have something to say. Go on."

"Nothing good." He tried to force a smile.

I cleared my throat and shifted uncomfortably. "Try me."

Dad's icy gaze shifted to me, but I already knew what he was going to say.

"I love him," I said.

"I know." He shook his head. "And he loves you, too."

I waited for him to go on.

"He lied to me for almost two years."

"So did I."

He nodded. "Yep. So did you."

"Are you angry with me?"

Dad ran a thumb over his forehead. "Furious."

I waited again because I knew my father, and there would be a lesson here for both of us.

"But," he said, "I suppose I'm as much to blame for this. I raised you around bikers. I had you breaking down tills in the Beacon once you knew how to count to a hundred."

I snorted out a sad laugh that pinched my shoulder.

"You were right." He gave me a solemn nod. "I kept things from you for a long time because I thought I was doing the right thing."

"Me too." I tried a smile, not hating how it felt on my face.

"My best friend, Ru?" He narrowed his eyes. "Really?"

"He's my best friend, too, Dad." I meant that. Saint had looked out for me, been there for me, and loved me in every way a friend could.

Before we got stuck in that blizzard a year and a half ago, Saint and I had texted every single day. We were together so much that once we did start fucking, not even my father noticed a difference in the way we acted toward each other.

"Yeah." He nodded again. "Yeah, I know that."

"Can you forgive us?"

He closed his eyes and sighed, pain and discomfort in his whole posture. "You, yes. Saint, no."

"Why?"

"Because he's the adult, Ru."

"*I'm* an adult."

"You're my child."

"I'm not a child." I kept my voice calm and level. I didn't have the strength for anything else, but I wanted to hash this out with him. "I haven't been for a long time, even since before I turned eighteen."

Dad clenched his jaw but didn't argue. I'd practically raised myself, and he knew that. It was a sore spot between us because occasionally he needed to be reminded *he* was the parent. He couldn't begrudge me the joy and happiness I'd found in someone he brought into my life. Dad didn't have any room to talk, and he knew it.

"I love you," I said. "What I have with Saint...it's real. It's pure. I wish you could understand that."

He swallowed and nodded but didn't say anything else until Saint arrived twenty minutes later. He came into the hospital room and froze, straightening when he met Dad's eyes. They didn't acknowledge each other, and when Saint looked at me, I relaxed into the mattress.

His eyes were bruised and the cut on his head looked terrible, but he'd survived. I'd lived through the fear that he hadn't, and I didn't know what I'd do without him. His presence calmed me; it always had. Saint walked to the other side of the bed and leaned down to kiss me on the lips. Right there. In front of Dad. No qualms. No hesitations.

"Hiya, baby girl." He brushed the hair out of my face and gave me another kiss on the forehead.

"Hi, Saint."

"Welp." Dad slapped his thighs and stood. "I'm gonna take off. Call me if something happens."

He kissed my cheek and headed toward the door, waving one last goodbye before turning the corner.

I met Saint's dark gaze, watching as he tried to shield the emotions behind them. Regret. Shame. Disappointment.

I grabbed his hand and squeezed. "He'll come around."

Saint relaxed his features and shook his head. "All I need is you."

Even in my heavily medicated post-op state, my heart skipped just for him.

DETECTIVE JORDAN and her sidekick came to question me, Hollywood, and Verona about what happened. That conversation had been as useful as the one she'd had with Saint. None of us would talk to the pigs. The club would handle this on their own.

The more I thought about that night, the more I felt like there was an important piece I was missing. My memory cut out right when I had looked in the rearview mirror at the assassin creeping closer to my side of the window. Something happened after that, something I needed to tell everyone. But even in my nightmares, that part remained clouded, as if my subconscious knew it would tear me in two when I learned the truth.

For the next week, Selene, Alba, and Doc took turns on Saint's couch to help "take care of" me and Hollywood while we healed. It was easier to look after two patients together, so Hollywood had moved into one of Saint's guest rooms. Saint bitched and moaned, but Hollywood's charm balanced Saint's gruff, and I suspected he secretly loved having him around.

"How long are you going to let him crash?" I asked as my naked boyfriend brushed his teeth at the sink. I soaked in the tub while the sounds of Hollywood, Bear, and KC yukking it up in the living room echoed down the hall. I didn't mind. Saint needed more friends besides my dad, and I loved those guys like brothers.

He rinsed his mouth and put his toothbrush back in the cup, giving me a sigh and a shake of his head as he prowled closer. "He was supposed to leave two days ago."

I laughed as he climbed in behind me, positioning his legs on either side of my hips, leaning me back on his chest. It reminded me of the last time we'd been in this same position, talking about how to break the news of our relationship to my dad. So much had changed since then. So much had been put into a different perspective.

I had almost died. Again. This time was much worse than before. I'd brushed fingers with Death and felt Her cold grip seize my windpipe. I wouldn't hide any part of myself again. Life was too short for that.

"I think he wants to stay permanently." I chuckled at the groan that caused behind me.

"He's delusional."

"Aww, c'mon." I rolled my ass against his cock, relishing in the rumble in his throat. "Admit it. You like having him around."

He put his hands on my hips to stop me and leaned close to my ear, whispering, "Behave or I'll have to punish you."

"What if I want to be punished?"

Saint chuckled low in his chest. "You still have stitches."

"You never let me being hurt stop you from psychological torture."

He coasted one rough hand up my back, tracing my spine to my neck and hair. He fisted a handful and yanked back, making me wince when it pulled at the stitches in my shoulder. But I didn't stop him because it was the most action I'd gotten in weeks.

"So feisty, huh?" The other hand went to my thigh, and he skated his fingers up the inside of my leg, coaxing it to the side so I opened for him. "We have a debt to settle between us."

I froze because I didn't remember any debt. What was he talking about?

"Why in the fucking world were you digging into Nikki and Gabriella Caputi?"

Every muscle in my body tightened, and I tried to squirm away from him, but he held firm.

"I was trying to help." It was the truth. I'd been kidnapped and beaten for this war. I didn't care that those alpha assholes thought I should have no part of it. I was already *in* it. Benito had seen to that when he'd taken me last August.

"This isn't your fight."

"Yeah?" My rage spilled over, tears streaming down my cheeks, my hands balling into fists in my lap. "Then why have I bled for it?" I moved away from him so I could turn around and look him in the eyes. "I know you want to protect me, and I love you for that."

"Want to?" He practically balked. "Ru, I put a ring on your finger. It may not mean marriage yet, but it means you're mine. It's my *honor* to protect you."

Heat swelled in my chest, and I twirled his ring around my finger with my thumb. I had ached to hear those words for years, and now that I finally had him right where I wanted him, I struggled to remember this was real. He grabbed my ankle and tugged me back to him, my legs going on either side of his hips as he wrapped his arms around my waist.

"Any other secrets you need to tell me?"

I shook my head. "No."

"Good." He nodded and put a finger under my chin to tilt my head up, forcing me to meet his gaze. "From here on out, you and I are a team. Don't ever hide anything from me again."

"Fine. The same goes for you."

He smirked and leaned in to kiss me, scraping his teeth across my bottom lip to tease me. Shivers raced down my spine.

"I don't have anything else to hide." He smiled and leaned back against the edge of the tub. I licked my lips, staring at the muscles in his tattooed throat. What he would do if I bit them? I wrapped my good arm around his neck and pressed my forehead against his.

"What is the club going to do now?"

He gave a reluctant growl and kissed me again. "Crow is still deciding, but I'm gonna hunt them down, every last one of them."

I nodded, anxiety churning in my stomach. I didn't want him to get hurt again. Last August, it was a bullet in the leg. Last week, it was almost one to the head. What would happen next? What else would they take from my family before this was through?

Rage burned in my chest, and a desperate part of me wanted to join him, maybe hunt every single Caputi down *Terminator* style. But what good would that do? Someone else would rise up in their place. This war would never end, not until every last one of us was dead. The thought broke my heart.

We'd never know peace, not really.

Neither would our children.

"Hey." He rubbed his thumb over my bottom lip, drawing my attention back up to him. "No one's gonna touch you again, Ru. I swear it."

I swallowed down my anxiety and tried to believe him, but he couldn't promise that. I'd never be safe again. For right now, I had him under me, his arms around me, his soul wrapped intimately with mine. Nothing could sever us again. "All you need to worry about right now is how you're going to make this up to me."

I balked and pretended to be surprised. "Make it up to you?"

"The spying. Almost getting yourself in trouble." He raised an eyebrow. "You're my old lady now, so I have to keep you in line."

"Oh, am I?" The title made me smile, and I kissed him again. He clenched my ass to pull me closer. My cunt bumped up against his cock, already hard and ready to go. One tilt of my hips would line him up and then...

He pushed me farther down his thighs, separating the contact so suddenly I gasped.

"Yeah." His evil grin stood out against his dark beard, and I tried to hide the tremble that shot through my body. "Now I have to put you in your place, both as your old man and your sir."

I snorted out a laugh and tried to get closer to him, but given the fact he was so much bigger than me and I'd been shot two weeks ago, he easily held me back.

"Hmm." My noise told him to give it his best shot. I matched his biker dominance with my MC princess brat energy, and he knew it.

"Don't tempt me, little sinner," he said, a predatory stare in his eyes. I had to tread carefully if I didn't want him adding a million spankings to my sentence once I was better. "You put the club in danger, and most importantly, yourself."

The confidence I'd felt a second ago dissipated in my chest, leaving an ache that would take me a while to soothe. Maybe Saint thought he was going too hard on me because he put his hand under my chin and lifted my face to his again.

"You're my most favorite person, Ru. And you scared the shit out of a lot of people. It's not your fault this war started." He brushed his lips over mine gently, reminding me he adored me and cherished me in equal parts. "But you die on me, and I'll never forgive you."

"Same goes for you." I grabbed his face the way he held mine. "Promise me, Saint."

"I promise." He gave me another kiss. "I promise."

We held each other for a while, letting the water get cold while our fingers pruned. And when we eventually did venture back to Saint's room, the guys were still in the living room watching a football game. If I didn't know any better, I would swear we were a normal family that did normal family things. In some ways, we were. But that had never been my life, and as much as Saint wanted to keep me out of this, I'd been born into it.

I'd never be free of it, not unless I abandoned everyone I'd ever loved.

And that wasn't my style.

22

SAINT

Sometimes, it took a fucked-up thing like getting shot in the head to put shit in perspective. Like all the time I'd wasted being worried about Aris's opinion instead of loving the one woman that made my life worth living. I shoulda gone to college with her. I shoulda been up front with her father from the beginning. But regretting what I'd done didn't undo it, so I showed up at the clubhouse with my head held high.

"Aris will get over it," Hollywood assured me, clapping me on the shoulder before walking ahead to find his buddies. That mother-fucker was still crashing in my guest room a whole month after he'd been released from the hospital. But I had to admit, having him around made things a little less somber, so I hadn't tossed his ass to the curb...*yet.*

I scanned the living room and bar area for a set of piercing, ice-cold eyes. KC, Bear, and Hollywood crowded around the pool table while Switch, Slip, and Thor sat on the couches. Crow and Doc stood in the back, their arms crossed over their chests while they talked quietly together. Lore was still on the mend and hadn't officially returned to MC duties, but I suspected that was more outta pride than needing more time to heal. A few hang-arounds laughed and carried on while Verona and Selene chatted at the bar. Aris was nowhere to be seen.

"He's in the back," Alba said, walking up to my right. She gave me a sympathetic smile and squinted her eyes, clearly uncomfortable with whatever she wanted to say next. "He's, uh...sublimating."

I cleared my throat and straightened my shoulders, pretending like the stab between my deltoids had nothing to do with him. I was a grown man. So was he. Now that the truth was out there, we both had choices to make.

I still loved the son of a bitch, even if he couldn't stand the sight of me anymore.

"I got nothing to say to him."

She laughed a sad noise and rolled her eyes, pushing up on her toes to give me a friendly kiss on the cheek. "I doubt that very much."

"All right, you fuckers. Round it up!" Slip stood and waved his finger in the air, calling the rest of us to church in the big room behind the bar. I found KC and fell in beside him, taking my normal position in the back corner.

Crow went to the head of the table, and Slip sat down on his left, leaving the seat on his right open. Doc, Thor, and Coins took their positions, and once the room filled with the rest of the brothers, one of the prospects closed the doors to the main area.

I raised an eyebrow at Aris's absence, but didn't mention it. Just as Slip stood to call everything to order, the door to the back rooms opened and Aris stepped in, yanking his shirt over his head before pulling on his cut. One of the hang-arounds giggled in the background, racing through the hallway to the living area. I cleared my throat and shifted my weight to the other leg, furrowing my brows. Eight years I'd known this bastard, and not once had he fucked a hang-around.

As soon as I'd found out about Penny, I understood why. But hell, Penny had only been in the ground eleven months. I ran a hand through my hair and met his gaze as he passed me, but he gave me nothing, just walked to his seat and banged his rings on the table.

"Everyone, shut the fuck up," Aris bellowed. "Church is in session."

Crow rose and put his hands out on the table in front of him, his eyes focused on the MC's emblem burned into the middle: a rose with a blade going through the center of it.

"Brothers," Crow started, "I once again must ask too much of you. This war comes at a cost, one we signed up to pay when we took our oaths and patched in. We all knew that. And yet, sometimes the price is too high." He paused and looked around the room, his attention landing on Lore's father, Titan. "They mutilated one of us. They nearly took my daughter from me, and if Saint had been leaning two inches to the right, we'd be drinking in his honor." All eyes shot to me, all except a set that looked to the ground at the mention of my name. I shifted uncomfortably, my burning skin prickling at being the center of attention.

Crow gazed at Hollywood, the expression in his eyes turning soft and tender, almost like a proud father looking on a triumphant son. "If it wasn't for Hollywood, we'd be praying for Verona. I thank you, brother."

"We thank you, brother!" The entire MC echoed Crow's sentiment, knowing that when the president personally offered gratitude, it meant it was in the best interests of the entire MC. We were one because of our tie to him. A favor to Crow was a favor to us all.

"It's an honor to protect the Roses," Hollywood said, looking and sounding surprisingly sheepish.

Crow returned his attention to the MC. "We can't let this stand. But we also can't charge in guns blazing."

"That's worked out for us before," someone said, making Thor crack an indignant smile.

"That was different," Thor added. "We knew where they were. We knew what they were packing. Now?" He shook his head.

"Gabriella is unpredictable," Bear said. "She laid dormant for ten months, then attacked us in the middle of a public street." He widened his eyes, looking from his father to me and KC and back again. "Doesn't make any sense. Why the big show? Why the drama?"

"They were looking for Saint," Aris said.

Again, all eyes glanced in my direction.

"They thought Lore and Saint were the same person," he continued, finally setting his gaze in my direction. "Because of their connection to my daughter."

I hated that Lore had gotten hurt, but I wasn't going to be shamed by Aris's stare. I loved Ru. Lore had protected her. I couldn't help it if the Caputis were idiots that didn't know their ass from a hole in the head.

"He doesn't remember much from his time with the Caputis," Doc finally said, drawing attention back to the real issue. "But he's sure about that."

"What else does he remember?" Bear asked.

"Bits and pieces. Small parts of conversation." Doc glanced at Titan before returning his focus to Crow. "They're trying to undermine us, which we already knew. But they're also getting more violent. Taking out Julian and Benito set Gabriella on a warpath."

I wasn't so sure about that. Gabriella had been precise and calculated up until now. Being raised the mafia princess of another crime boss meant she rarely got her hands dirty. Going to McMurphy behind our backs, buying out the Canadians, that had her stink all over it. Striking out after KC's wedding didn't seem like her style. It felt more like Leo—ostentatious and impulsive.

"Lore says he heard seagulls in the morning," Titan said, clearly struggling to keep a lid on his fury. I didn't blame him for it. They'd carved his son's eye out of his head. Lore couldn't ride a bike anymore. Hell, he'd have to relearn how to drive.

"That means they were keeping him on the docks," Pollux added.

"Well, it's a good thing Maryland and Virginia aren't covered in coastline." Thor groaned, rubbing at his forehead.

"Caputi businesses own a few waterfront condos and countless storage units across the state." Castor typed on his laptop, clicking tabs open on his screen faster than I could keep up.

"They don't shit where they eat," Slip said, shaking his head.

"I'm still waiting on a lead from the IRS," Switch said, adding to Castor's symphony of keystrokes. "I'll reach out to them again."

"Didn't you mention a vacation home on the Eastern Shore in your report?" Bear looked at me before walking to the table to flip through the folder I'd put together, tossing pages to the side until he found the one he wanted.

"Yeah," I said. "Leo Caputi brings his female entertainment to a two-story mansion near Benoni."

"That's on the other side of the fucking Chesapeake," Thor said.

"Lots of privacy." Doc ran a hand back through his dark hair.

"And seagulls," KC agreed.

Crow nodded, giving the report another look. "Leo Caputi. I thought he and his aunt didn't get along."

"They don't," I said. "He's an idiot, and she's trying to run an empire." I crossed my arms over my chest. "I've been investigating these assholes for the better part of a year. The whole thing reeks of Leo, not Gabriella."

"Didn't she promise you vengeance and blood?" Bear shook his head, raising an eyebrow.

"She's the type to choke us out, not kill everyone in one blow." I looked at Aris, who still didn't glance in my direction, before shifting my gaze to Crow. "I say we hit Leo first."

"All right, listen." Crow tossed the folder to the table and leaned forward, putting his hands out in front of him. "Thor, take Aris, Saint, Bear, and KC out to Benoni. See what you can find."

Hearing Aris's name before mine snapped my spine straight.

"Meet me here tomorrow afternoon," Slip said. "We'll check the place out at night."

"I'll split the condos and storage units between the rest of us. Let's run a sweep, top to bottom." Crow stood up straight and glanced at the crowd. "Even if we find nothing, it'll let them know we're coming. The Roses never let a debt go unpaid."

Under any other circumstances, we would have talked about the charity ride next week and confirmed that everyone still planned to attend. Now, our hearts were too heavy for that. With one more glance at Titan, Crow nodded and held a hand over his heart. "I promise you, brother. We'll find the fuckers that did this."

"I'm with you," Titan said, honoring the vow of the Roses.

After Crow closed the session, everyone stood, and the prospects opened the doors to the front room again. Most of my brothers filed out, but I waited to see if Aris wanted to clear the air before we were supposed to have each other's backs tomorrow. He didn't even look at me before he turned on his heel and walked to the bar, wrapping an arm around the hang-around from the hallway.

I WENT HOME and fucked my girl, holding her down while I buried myself deep inside her, swallowed her moans and brought her to release over and over again. After I came, I cleaned her up and wrapped her in my arms until she fell asleep.

Then I sat there like a creep and watched her well into the morning. I'd be tired as shit for the ride, but I didn't care. Once upon a time, something like this woulda excited me. This could be an ambush. This could be a trap. We could get our shit blown up. The anticipation in my gut woulda had me wired for days, especially if I got to kill some Caputi cocksuckers along the way.

But there was a possibility I might not come back. That wouldn't have been a problem if not for the brilliant brunette snoring next to me. What if we did meet some Caputis and they finished what they started when they abducted Lore? Me, Thor, Bear, KC, and Aris all in the same spot at the same time was a treasure trove of Roses to pluck.

I rubbed my fingers over my eyes again and sighed.

"You know," Ru murmured, "for someone who doesn't talk much, you think really loud."

I laughed and scooped an arm under her to tug her closer, giving the top of her head a kiss. "Did I wake you up?"

She shook her head and stretched, letting out a big yawn. "No. I had to pee." Giving me a smile, Ru sat up and swung her legs over the side of the bed so she could stand. I tracked her as she walked across the room and headed to the bathroom, resisting the urge to get up and follow her to make sure she was still okay. When she came back, she curled in next to me and rested her head on my chest, under my chin.

"Why are you still awake?"

"Just thinking about the run."

"Hmm." She sighed and held me closer. "Is it a tough one?"

I debated telling her the truth. Some of the guys were more open with their old ladies than others, and Ru had more than bled for the club. Keeping her in the dark might be safer for her.

No. All Aris ever did was keep her in the dark, and it had almost gotten her killed twice. "We think we know where they tortured Lore. It's one of Leo's fuck pads."

She widened her eyes and looked up at me. "You're going?"

I nodded, watching the urge to ask why I had to be the one form behind her expression, but she never said it. Instead, she nodded and leaned in to kiss me, her warm scent ambushing my senses. I pulled her on top of me, her legs going to either side of my hips, and wrapped my arms around her waist, leaning my forehead against hers.

"I'm going to kill him, Ru. Whoever did this to you." I brushed my fingers over the fading remains of the bruises on her face, running them down to the wound on her shoulder. "Whoever ordered it. All of them. I'm going to make sure they never do it to anyone else ever again."

"Saint," she murmured, kissing me. "Please be careful. I can't..." She cleared her throat and rocked against me, rubbing her warm cunt up against my cock, which responded to her greedy motions. "I can't lose you."

"You won't, baby girl," I said, shifting my pelvis so I easily slipped inside her again. *Fuck,* she was amazing, so warm and tight. I relaxed against the pillows and watched her ride me, pressing her hands into my chest for leverage, her face relaxed as she used me for her own pleasure. God, she mesmerized me, and I'd never understand how I got to be the lucky bastard she chose to keep her safe. She had become the one good thing in my lifetime of darkness, and I'd been such a Goddamned idiot for not owning up to it sooner.

I missed Aris, and if he never talked to me again, I always would, but I shoulda made this decision earlier. I'd lost so much time with her, and because of it, she'd gone through a rough part of her life by herself. I shoulda been there. From that point on, I swore to be a better man, more deserving of her, of this.

I rolled us so I was on top, and I held her body under me while I slowly rocked into her. She moaned and kissed me, wrapping her legs around my back so her ankles hooked across my lower spine.

"Talk filthy to me," she whispered, her wicked grin making me surge into her harder.

"Oh, does my sinner want dirty words?"

She bit her bottom lip and nodded.

I leaned down so my mouth was right by her ear, keeping my voice low so I didn't wake Hollywood in the next room. (Not that I gave a shit if I did. If he didn't like it, he could get the fuck out.) "You're my dirty slut, aren't you? Fucking me so good before the run. Draining me. Marking me with your scent."

She laughed and rocked into me harder.

"You want everyone to know you were in my bed this morning, don't you?" I whispered the most depraved shit I could think of, anything to turn her cheeks red with shame. But Ru had long ago lost her inhibitions around me. When I rolled around in the filth, she rolled with me. After we found our release in each other, we collapsed in a heap of sweat and hormones, silent but content.

"Please be safe," she said, sitting up to press a small kiss to my chin. "Promise me."

"I promise," I told her. But even then, I worried if I could keep it.

Eventually, I extracted myself from our lazy lovemaking to shower and dress. When I came out, Hollywood and Ru sat around the breakfast table, laughing and ribbing each other.

"Are you sure that bullet didn't hit your brain?" Ru said, shoving his shoulder while he swallowed a spoonful of cereal.

"I'm serious," he said, taking a gulp of water. "No more random hookups. It's just me and my right hand, like you said."

She raised an eyebrow as I approached. "You hear this?"

"Hmm." I made a noise that said I didn't care where Hollywood stuck his dick so long as Ru wasn't involved, and I poured myself some coffee. I furrowed my brows and studied him, the lines on his face more pronounced. It had been a rough year for him, and getting shot hadn't made that any better.

"Wait, do you guys feel that?" Ru sipped at her coffee and set it down before grabbing his shoulder and widening her eyes playfully. "It's like a million hearts just shattered all at once."

"Aww. Don't be a tease. Not in front of your boyfriend." Hollywood pretended to whisper like I wouldn't hear.

Even if he'd done it just to fuck with me, I ignored him because Ru had never shown any interest in the playboy. Now that I'd put that ring on her finger, everyone knew I'd come for them if they so much as touched her. Besides, since Hollywood and I had been living together, something had changed in our relationship, too. Even if I didn't want to admit it.

23

RU

I n the weeks since I'd been out of the hospital, I'd seen almost everyone in my life. Although things were weird between us, I'd even managed to see my dad. There was one person, however, I'd been avoiding, one person that needed more than a casual catch-up.

I stood outside his apartment door and took a deep breath, steadying myself for the rejection I was sure I'd face. Just as I raised my hand to knock, the entry opened.

Selene narrowed her eyes at me. "What are you doing, standing out here?" She raised an eyebrow, tugging her coat tighter around her body.

I held up the lasagna I'd baked as a show of solidarity. "I was hoping he'd see me."

"Sure." She sighed and stepped outside, leaving the door open so I could go in. "I came by to check on his progress, but I'm leaving." Selene took a step down the hall but paused to turn back around. "Hey, stop by the shop after this. Your truck's done."

"Really?"

She nodded. "Yeah, Bear worked overtime yesterday to finish it for you."

"I guess I owe him a lasagna, too, huh?"

She smiled, waved goodbye, and left me to my business with Lore.

I entered and froze, immediately meeting his gaze at the small dining room table. He looked rough, his cheeks sunken and his skin pale. A dark eyepatch hid his injury, but other than that, he still looked like the guy who'd gotten me through my heartache last year. My pulse raced and my hands shook. I'd been a terrible friend, hadn't I? I should have come by earlier. I should—

"Stop that," he said, pushing to his feet. Lore held his arms out, welcoming me into them. "C'mere."

I set the meal down on his table and pressed myself into his embrace, circling my arms around his waist and tucking my head under his chin. We weren't meant to be romantic, but that didn't mean I stopped loving him. He was still my friend.

"I'm sorry," I told him. "I'm sorry this happened to you. I'm sorry I took you to Mount Vernon with me in the first place. They thought you were Saint because of me."

"Hey." He put a hand under my chin and tilted my face up so I had to look at him. "I wouldn't have done it if I didn't want to. And this ain't no one's fault but the Caputis. Understand?"

I nodded and swallowed down my shame, remembering this visit wasn't about me. I put the lasagna in his refrigerator, noting that it was mostly empty except for beer and a few boxes of leftovers. I thought the prospects were supposed to be bringing him food. Perhaps I'd been mistaken, so I kept it to myself and walked to the spot next to him, taking a seat while he poured me a cup of coffee. "How are you? You feeling any better? I can bring over more dinners."

"That would be great, but only because I like your cooking." Lore smiled and reached out to grab my hand. "How are you? I heard we both almost died that night."

I sighed and ran a hand over my face, the wound in my shoulder pinching despite the weeks since the injury. "Yeah. Zero out of ten stars, worst experience ever."

He laughed, and the sound lifted my spirits. Despite being

maimed, he hadn't lost that spark of joy that made him who he was. "You finally told Aris about Saint."

I nodded. "I wouldn't recommend that, either."

"Eh, fuck it. He'll get over it."

"It doesn't matter anymore. I'm not going to live without Saint in my life, and if my dad can't accept that, it's his problem."

"Hell yeah." He lifted my hand to his mouth so he could kiss my knuckles in approval. "That's what I told my old man."

That surprised me.

"He wanted me to pack up my shit and go stay with my mom, but I'm not some coward motherfucker that runs at the first sign of a fight." Lore shifted in his seat, righting his shoulders as he went on. "Those Caputi bastards took something from me, and until they pay up, I ain't going anywhere."

His fighting spirit had always been one of the things I admired the most about him. "Do you remember who was there? Did you hear any names or recognize any voices?"

He shook his head. "I don't remember much. They kept me unconscious for a lot of it. I thought they'd torture me. I don't know, tear out my fingernails or some shit. They kept me tied to a table until..." He cleared his throat and looked down to his lap. "I remember seagulls. I remember hearing water outside. I remember... Leo and Nikki coming to see me, and she spit in my face."

"Nikki?" That piqued my interest. After she'd betrayed us last year, she'd run off with the enemy, taking her newborn baby with her. It was because of her that Alba and I had been taken last August. Something about Nikki stuck out, something monumental, like I was standing at the cliff of understanding and I just needed to toss myself over the edge already. Whatever it was didn't come to me while I was at Lore's table, so I ignored the feeling and refocused on him.

"Nikki's scared." He sighed and shook his head. "She's afraid of them, and she's afraid of the Roses."

"She's got good reason for that."

Lore pulled one side of his mouth into a smile. "I missed you, you big stupid idiot. Don't stay away from me again."

I leaned in to give him a hug, and he hugged me back, kissing me on the temple when I finally pulled away. I hung out for a few more hours, catching up with him and telling him how Dad had finally found out. He laughed and commiserated, promising to meet me for lunch later in the week. Eventually, I said my goodbyes and headed to pick up my truck.

My Tacoma sat in front of Rose Garage, gleaming in the sunlight. They'd even had a prospect detail it for me, which was an unexpected surprise. I ran my fingers down the front fender as I passed, heading into the office to find out how much I owed them. Praying it wasn't too expensive, I went inside to find Verona sitting across from Selene, both of them huddled close to each other while they talked.

I'd seen Verona a few times since the accident, but always around other people. Today, her smile brightened when I entered, and she struggled to push herself upright to give me a hug.

"What are you doing here?" I furrowed my brows and looked at Selene, who shrugged and went to the plastic bin to find my keys.

"My car died." She ran a hand over her forehead. "It's a good thing I got that job at the Beacon when I did. I need the extra cash." Verona pointed to the spot on her chest where she'd gotten shot. "Only a few more days before I'm cleared to work again."

"Uh," Selene cut in, "better make that a week, at least."

Verona gave her a salute and nodded. "Sure thing, Doctor Montgomery."

The moniker made me laugh. Technically, Selene was a doctor. She'd gone to medical school, graduated, and almost completed her residency. But life at the MC pulled her back in and doing both wore her out. So, she stayed here with her family. I wondered if she ever resented us for that and if the toxicity of letting it fester would come back around to bite her one of these days.

To me, she was always Sel: my best friend, my older sister, my fellow MC princess. We weren't *in* the club, but we'd sacrificed just as much for this family as the brothers, some of us even more so. We were the heart that kept the Roses human, the soul that grounded them to this reality. Without us, their rough edges would cut anyone who dared get close.

The door to the auto shop swung open and Thor walked in, his grey gaze looking between the three of us before landing on Selene. "You get that Honda written up?"

She nodded to the bin containing the work orders before returning her attention to the computer in front of her. The tension between them amplified with Thor's rigid posture as he reached inside and yanked out the one he wanted. He walked back into the shop, letting the door slam closed behind him.

Verona raised her eyebrows at Selene. "That was frosty."

She cleared her throat and shook her head. "I went on a date the other night."

I blinked and straightened, shocked to hear this. "A date? What date?"

Sel gave an awkward laugh and ran a finger over her eyebrow, her cheeks turning a bright shade of pink. "A guy I knew from high school."

"Who?" Verona and I said at the same time like a set of owls. We looked at each other and laughed.

"Blair Edwards." She rolled her eyes and blew out a breath. "It wasn't anything serious. Just a catch-up. He's back in town for some marketing expo in DC, thought he'd swing by to see his family."

"And get a little nostalgic booty call?" Verona nudged Selene with her shoulder, but I understood what Sel wasn't telling us. Thor had found out about the date and whatever happened after that had caused the awkwardness between the two of them now.

"I've gotta get my own place," Selene murmured under her breath, typing on the keyboard with harder, more pronounced strokes.

"Me too." Verona raised an eyebrow. "Wanna be roommates?"

Selene paused and looked at her. "Are you serious?"

Verona nodded. "Yeah, anything to get out of my brothers' house. I'm going to choke them all out one of these days."

"If you're serious, I'm serious." Selene leaned in closer to her. "There's a two bedroom—"

"Goddamn it, Selene!" Thor's voice roared from the garage, making me jump. "Selene! Come here!"

"What?" she roared back, stomping over to the door and shoving it open so she could peer behind it.

"Hey, I've been meaning to talk to you about something." Verona narrowed her gaze on me. "You wanna get some coffee?"

"Yeah. Everything okay?"

"Of course." She smiled. "This is a good thing."

Before I could ask anything else, Selene came back with my keys and tossed them across the counter to me. "It's on the house."

"What?"

She nodded. "Crow took care of it. The MC owes you." Selene didn't explain, but she didn't need to. In return for my injury, Crow had paid for the repairs. There would likely be other things like this too, bills miraculously cleared, debts unceremoniously settled.

"Thank you," I said.

"Thank Crow." She nodded toward the door. "Go on, get outta here. I've got smut to read and a pissed-off biker to ignore."

"All right." I nodded at Verona and tossed Saint's truck key at her. "Drive Saint's truck back to the clubhouse, and I'll make us lunch when we get there. Deal?"

She caught it and smiled. "Deal."

MOST OF THE brothers were out, leaving the old ladies and hang-arounds to nose about the clubhouse. Slip's wife, Scribe, sat in one corner with her laptop open in front of her, no doubt typing up the next mystery bestseller. Sheridan, Hollister's wife, sat in the back, talking to Picasso. When Verona and I walked in, everyone looked up to say hi.

We walked to the kitchen, and she sat at the island in the middle while I found stuff to make turkey sandwiches.

"So, here's the thing." She ran a hand over the back of her neck and cleared her throat, seemingly uncomfortable.

I narrowed my eyes but kept working, hoping she'd think I was open for anything and it would put her at ease. "Shoot."

"Were you serious about trying to turn the Beacon into a sex club?"

I froze, shifting my attention to her. It was a sincere question, so I nodded. "Yeah. We start renovations in two weeks."

"Do you know anything about running one?"

I shrugged. "I know about running a strip club and a porn website. How hard could it be?"

She licked her lips and ran a hand over her face. "Okay, listen. I'm about to tell you something, but you have to promise me you won't tell anyone. At least, not yet."

"Okay." My heart kicked behind my ribs, anticipation circling in my veins. What the hell could Verona have to tell me that—

"I used to work at a dungeon on the Upper East Side."

"What?"

"I was a dominatrix. A good one. Until one of my clients..." She took a deep breath, unclenching her hands. "It doesn't matter. I can help you."

I blinked, struggling to keep up with the fact the angry goth girl I'd known from childhood had turned into a full-fledged dominatrix. Actually...now that I considered it, the idea made a lot of sense. Curiosity took over, and I needed to know everything, the whole story. "Jesus Christ, Verona Leigh Montgomery. You've been sitting on this the whole time? Why didn't you say anything?"

She put a hand over my mouth. "Shut up, Ru. Someone's gonna hear you."

"Tell me everything," I mumbled behind her palm.

Verona pursed her lips, but let me go so I could finish making our lunch.

"After I moved to Manhattan, I lied to Dad about how expensive it was. I didn't want him knowing I'd made a wrong decision, that I hated living there almost as much as he hated me being away from the family." V went to the fridge, retrieving two waters for us and cracking them open. She took a long swig before sighing and sitting to continue. "That's when I met Greg. He was some rich venture capitalist that liked women to degrade him. One thing led to another…"

"Wait… No… Back up. How does that come up in conversation?" I finished her sandwich, put some chips on her plate, and slid it across the counter to her. Then I sat next to her to enjoy my own. "Were you just like… Hey, want me to treat you like shit?"

She laughed. "We were drunk. It just came out. I don't know. I told him I'd do it for two hundred dollars, and he said okay. I didn't think he was serious." She shrugged. "It was fun. Afterward, he told me I was a natural and I should check out Vertigo, this social club a few blocks away." Verona shook her head. "Again, I didn't think he was serious, but I went. I auditioned and got taken in by a mentor named Mistress Devi."

I was captivated by her story. I couldn't believe she'd turned into this powerful, confident goddess. Now I knew how that happened. Spending your days being literally worshipped would change a person. "And then?"

"I learned about findom and femdom and all the ways to make other people pay me to do what I always did to men…except now they consented to it beforehand."

"Wow." I took a drink of water and swallowed down my surprise. "Look at you. All grown up."

"I could say the same of you. The Ru I left behind had just figured out how to wear a miniskirt. Now, you're running a woman-empowered business and you're about to open up Madison's first sex club." She paused before furrowing her brows and leaning in to whisper, "Who *are* you?"

We shared a laugh before she continued. "Things with Greg ended badly, so I came home. I don't regret the people I left behind, but I don't know how to do anything else. I liked what I did, and I worked there for a few years so I know how to run the space. I mean it, Ru. I can help you."

"Done." I held out a hand for her to take. "I can use all the help I can get. What do you want? Co-general manager? It's yours."

"That's a start," she said. "I want to train the employees. I saw both sides of this world while I was there, and I know how to do it ethically."

"You got it." I told her all my ideas, how I wanted to change what we had into something more modern and clean. She agreed with me and threw out a couple of ideas she'd been sitting on. While we talked, I remembered how much I liked Verona and how disappointed I'd been when we drifted apart. I always wished we'd been closer, and now that we'd found our way back to each other, I thanked the fates for the reunion. Between me, her, and Alba, we could create a gigantic sex-positive slice of Madison County.

I couldn't wait.

24

SAINT

The ride to Benoni tasted like vengeance from the start. Thor went through the plan four times, just to make sure we knew what we were doing. Switch had hacked the security earlier in the day. Leo Caputi was holed up in the mansion with his small army of guards keeping him safe. As of twenty minutes ago, there were ten of them to the six of us, and they were much more heavily armed.

But Thor's style of get in quick and quiet had proved efficient last August, so I trusted him again this time. We'd stick together, let him take the lead, and shoot any Caputi fuckers that got in our way.

The house sat back in the woods, nearly two miles from the main highway, with floor to ceiling windows showcasing everything going on inside. Except we hadn't come from the front. Oh no. We wanted blood, and our plan made for an easier escape.

"What do you see?" Slip said from behind the boat's wheel, keeping us far enough out in the water as to not be suspicious but close enough that we could see inside with binoculars.

Men with assault rifles stood on either side of the back porch, and more guys with guns were strategically placed through the rest of the house. Leo talked on his phone, pacing through the living room as he rubbed a hand over his face and expressively yelled at whoever was on the other end. A few women in heels snorted white powder off the kitchen island, laughing to each other in a hazy, drugged-out way. The upstairs was empty and dark, but I assumed more guards waited sentry.

"It's just Leo. He's having a normal night in," Aris said.

"How fucking cozy," KC added.

I only hummed a response, debating whether I wanted to stab the fucker in the eye with my knife or shoot his brains out. Neither would fully satisfy me. He was just another Caputi prince in a long line of them. Those assholes bred like rabbits, convinced the only true family member was blood. While both families valued loyalty and respect as principles, the Roses had proved their worthiness through actions rather than being born into it.

Which explained the piece of shit in that house. He had money and privilege but chose to snort it up his nose and fuck it into bankruptcy. While he basked in his life of luxury, unaware of the consequences of his family's actions, we rowed, rowed, rowed our boat right up to his shore.

They'd come after me and Ru. They'd come after V and Hollywood. They'd come after Lore. And tonight, we planned to end the last of the male Caputi heirs. I personally didn't subscribe to the idea women were lesser or some shit, but those Caputi cocksuckers did. They valued their male children higher, and Leo was the last male cousin in his generation. After him, there would only be his brother Julian's five-year-old son. Knowing that, Leo's life seemed a fair trade for what they'd done to us.

I shoulda been okay with this reasoning, especially given I'd almost died myself. But the closer we got to the pier, the more my stomach churned. My pulse raced, and my hands shook, something in the back of my mind warning me to be cautious.

Move with patience tonight, it said. I swallowed that down and refocused on the present.

"We play this like last time," Thor said, rechecking that his gun was loaded. "Be quiet. Be quick. Don't think twice."

KC and Aris nodded, the latter's eyes shifting to me for a moment before glancing back to the house. I agreed and turned to Bear, giving him a clap on the shoulder before he switched off the safety on his rifle. We'd brought out the big toys tonight, and we weren't taking any chances.

"You're a go," Slip said, holding his earpiece tighter to his head. "We've hacked the security."

Fuck yeah.

When we got to the pier hidden behind the trees, the five of us hopped off as silently as we could. They likely had cameras here, but we were counting on Switch to keep us hidden. I followed Thor, the feel of my gun in my hand calming me and urging me on at the same time. Memories of sneaking into the Caputi compound to save Ru and Alba floated through my mind, this same group of rough motherfuckers coming together then to get the job done. There was a reason we worked, a reason we called each other family. We had an unshakable bond that could only be forged through blood and sweat.

Well, most of us anyway, I thought as Aris passed me to move next to Thor. We stalked through the undergrowth on the pads of our feet, making as little noise as possible. When we got to the tree line in the backyard, Thor held up a fist to pause us, squatting down to hide in the brush. I followed, holding my nine up higher, waiting until he gave us the signal to move forward.

Thor perched his rifle on his shoulder, leaned down to look through the scope, and fired off two rounds. The men by the doors fell to the ground, landing in loud thumps that surely shook the whole house. If they didn't know we were there before, they certainly did now.

We raced across the yard, our boots hitting the grass with soft thuds until we got to the porch and climbed the steps to the sliding glass door. Thor tried to yank it open, but it was locked, and when the women inside saw us, they screamed and ran farther into the house. He shot the lock with his handgun, exploding the glass window in the process. KC stepped inside just as two guards barreled down the stairs, headed straight for us with their weapons raised.

I got both of them between the eyes, dropping them on the spot and saving KC's life.

A bullet whizzed by me, millimeters from my face, and I jumped back, turning in that direction to squeeze the trigger before I thought about it, nailing one of the girls in the shoulder and making her drop the gun. She screamed like a banshee, her wail nearly splintering my ears, and grabbed a knife from the rack on the counter, throwing it at me blade first. I dodged out of the way in time to miss it and shoot at her again, this time skimming the side of her leg, taking her down to the ground before I kicked her gun farther away.

"Jesus Christ, lady. I'm not here for you."

She said something in a language I didn't understand, but judging by the tone and emphasis, it was better I didn't know. While she writhed in pain, I went searching for the target. We'd come here with a purpose, and once we'd taken out all of Leo's guards, he wouldn't have anyone else to protect him.

Aris and Thor split off to the left, combing through the living room to the front end of the house. Bear, KC, and I went right, continuing through the kitchen to the dining room and hallway leading to the staircase. When we met our brothers in front, Thor pointed to the two of us and gestured up. He nodded to Aris, indicating they'd sweep the rest of the first floor.

As we climbed the carpeted staircase, I marveled at how the other half lived. If I wasn't here to take retaliation for what these assholes had tried to do to me, I mighta appreciated the moonlit view over the Chesapeake Bay or the glittering chandelier hanging from the ceiling. What a far cry from my humble rancher. But this opulence was what you got when you played the dirty game, and the Caputis had been playing a lot longer than the MC.

The first room we checked turned up empty, as did the second. But when we got to the third, one of the girls launched herself out from behind the bed and held her hands up.

"Please," she blubbered. "I'm just an escort. I didn't know who he was. Please."

KC looked at me and then to Bear, trying to get our opinions, but I didn't see any reason to kill her. She coulda fought back like the woman downstairs; she gave herself up instead.

"Where is he?" Bear whispered.

She gulped, shifting her gaze to the room across the hall long enough to give us the answer.

"I'll keep an eye on her," KC said, gesturing to me and Bear. "You two, keep going."

Bear nodded and turned, heading back toward the hallway. I followed, aiming just over his shoulder at whatever came out of the room when he opened the door. He reached for the knob with his tattooed hand, waiting half a heartbeat before turning it and shoving the door open.

Gunshots exploded from inside, and I jumped to the right to avoid them. The escort wailed and leaped behind the bed while KC darted forward. Bear rolled to the left, pressing his back up against the wall, and KC came to stand next to him. I squatted to the ground and peered around the corner, aiming the barrel of my pistol at the Caputi inside. Leo stood in front of a big ornate chair, his assault rifle firing off rounds that hit the plaster above our heads rather than anywhere close to our bodies.

He shouted in Italian, every other word laced with an added "fuck" or "piece of shit Rose motherfuckers." Maybe he was too high to see me; I didn't know. I aimed at his kneecap and fired, taking the asshole down to the seat behind him. He dropped the rifle, and it skidded across the floor while he writhed, grabbing at his ruined trousers and the bloody mess behind it.

"You bastards," he spat and tried to stand again, only to buckle under his own weight. "You come to my fucking house to do this? My house?" Forehead sweaty and pupils dilated, Leo stared at us with insult in his dark expression. Sweat matted his black hair to his forehead, but the fact he was insulted by us ruining his house rather than shooting him amused me.

"Shut up." KC hit him across the face with his nine, making Leo slump to the side and grab his cheek.

When he looked up again, I pointed my gun at his forehead,

placing the barrel between his eyes. Leo stared at me, misery and hatred radiating from his brown gaze, his lips twisted in agony, his nose bleeding and busted. The time had come to even the playing field, to remind Gabriella what loyalty meant to the Roses. The Caputis had come for us, and we'd never forgive something like that.

But now that I was here, my trigger finger wrapped around its namesake, revenge coating my willpower, I hesitated. The last time I'd been in this position, Father Darby had begged and pleaded for his life. He'd reminded me of my own salvation, that killing him would only leave a stain on my soul.

Maybe he was right. Maybe that was why he still haunted my nightmares.

God fucking knew the world wouldn't miss men like Father Darby or Leo Caputi or Saint Anderson. But taking Leo's life today wouldn't fix the war between our families, either.

"Well," Leo started, "go on then, you piece of shit. Pull the trigger. You've got me, huh? You've got the bastard that tried to kill your precious little bitches."

Hearing it confirmed my suspicions. It *had* been him that sent those assholes after us on KC's wedding night. Gabriella mighta known about it, but that wasn't her style. It was his. It shoulda enraged me further, especially when Leo pulled his lips into a toothy, bloody smile, staring at the gun like it might bring him peace. He didn't deserve that. He didn't deserve a quick death. None of them did. Not even Julian and Benito.

"Saint?" KC took a step toward me and put a hand on my shoulder, bringing me back to reality. Bear furrowed his eyebrows, giving me a look that questioned if I'd lost my mind. Maybe I had.

The door opened wider, and the others stepped through, Aris going to stand next to KC and Thor coming to the other side of me.

"The rest of the house is clear. I let the girls go so they could tell the rest of those cocksuckers who did this." Thor looked from me to Leo and back again. "We good here?"

Leo laughed and spat blood at our feet, muttering in Italian.

"Yeah?" Bear said, grabbing a handful of Leo's hair to yank his head back. "Bring your piece of shit family here. I don't give a fuck. I'll kill them in front of you and not even blink."

It didn't surprise me that Bear knew another language. The kid was smart as hell.

"Bear," Thor said. "Stand back. Let Saint finish the job."

Fuck.

I thought about Ru in that hospital bed, the absolute panic I'd felt when I almost lost her. I shoulda done it already. I knew that. I had to do it. But…

"We could take him back to Crow." I regretted it the minute it came out of my mouth.

"What?" Bear and Leo both said at the same time.

"Sober him up. Interrogate him. He might be worth more to us alive." I couldn't believe I was suggesting it, but that feeling rose in my chest again, the one that told me to hold off.

Move with patience, the voice whispered, and if I focused on it hard enough, I might have even said it was Noah, reaching out from whatever great beyond there was.

"What are you talking about?" KC squinted at me, clearly confused by my suggestion.

"Fuck this," Bear said, pointing his own weapon at Leo's temple. "I'll do it myself."

"Wait," Aris cut in, shifting his gaze to me. It was the first time in weeks he even acknowledged I was in the same room. "What are you saying?"

All the shit I knew about their family surfaced, all the fucked-up connections. Leo had been the one to arrange our deaths, and he deserved agony for that. Death would be too easy. "Think about it. Leo's the fuckup, the younger brother of the man that should have been heir."

"Hey, fuck you," Leo said, spitting at me again.

"Do that one more time," Bear said, "and I'll end this conversation right now."

"Go on," Leo muttered. "I'm ready for it to be over."

I nodded to the side, gesturing Aris and Thor to come with me out of Leo's earshot. "Look, it might be a dead end, but I say we take him. He might know something valuable about the Caputis."

"Yeah, I'd say there's a lot he knows," Thor argued. "But he's not going to share it with us."

"Not now. But..." I ran the length of him again, seeing nothing but a scared little boy in a grown man's body. He'd lived in his big brother's shadow his whole life. He'd only gotten thrust into power at the expense of his family's lives, and now he had to fight with his aunt for the title. "Everything I know about them says he and Gabriella don't get along."

"So?" Thor crossed his arms over his chest.

"What if we could use that to our advantage?"

"Take him hostage?" Aris raised his eyebrows.

"Rehab him," I said. "Get him cleaned up. See what he knows."

Thor pinched the bridge of his nose and shook his head. "I don't like it."

"Yeah, I second that," Bear cut in.

Aris studied me, remaining silent while he considered my plan.

"If it doesn't work, we'll shoot him then."

"Why him?" Aris put his hands on his hips and narrowed his icy eyes, giving me the judgmental stare his daughter had inherited.

I shrugged. "He deserves to die. God knows he does." I took a deep breath, praying I didn't get my ass handed to me when I said the next piece. "I don't know, Aris. This could be our chance to do things differently, to stop the bloodshed for once. Putting him out of his misery is too quick. Showing mercy is more vicious." I cleared my throat and straightened my shoulders, growing more confident as I talked. "In this case."

Aris considered me while Thor looked back and forth between us.

"Really?" Thor asked. "You're going against Crow's orders?"

Aris shoulda told me to go fuck myself and pulled his own gun to end the discussion. But whatever respect he still had for me shined through his eyes as his features softened. Finally, he nodded and gestured to Thor. "Knock him out. Load him up."

"What?" Bear said.

"We're taking him?" KC looked appalled.

"No, no, no," Leo sputtered, glancing wildly between us. "Shoot me. Just fucking shoot me."

"Saint thinks we can turn him." Aris nodded. "I think we can, too."

"What?" Leo dropped his jaw and glanced at me. "No. Never. I would rather cut off my own cock with my teeth—"

Thor hit him across the face so hard that he slumped to the side, and that was the end of Leo's protests.

"THIS IS the stupidest idea you've ever had," Aris said, standing at the bow of the boat while we watched the mansion burn in the distance. Leo Caputi was still passed out on one of the beds in the hull while Bear whispered to Slip behind us, filling him in on why we'd came back with extra baggage.

"Yeah." I ran my thumb over my eyebrow. "Yeah, probably."

"Besides fucking my daughter, of course." He meant every syllable, and when he looked at me, the weight of his righteousness echoed in his stare. I cleared my throat and swallowed the fire twisting up my throat.

Enough of this. Enough now.

"Aris, I love her. One day, I'm gonna marry her. I hope you can accept that." I nodded before returning my attention to the house. "But if you can't, that's not my problem. If I have to take a hit to prove that, you better swing."

He snorted out a sad laugh and hung his head between his shoulders, silent for a few moments before saying, "These past few weeks, I've been trying to figure out how I fucking missed it, how could it have been under my nose this whole time." He ran a hand over the back of his head and sighed. "It's none of my business, and I shoulda left the two of you alone, but Christ. I guess I thought I'd never have to worry about you hurting her." He pierced me with an angry glare. "Again."

"You don't." I shook my head. "The only thing that's gonna separate me from her again is death." I didn't say it for his benefit; I said it because I meant it. I'd go to my grave loving my girl. End of story.

Aris kept his gaze trained on me, his expression turning more empathetic. I didn't know if he liked what he heard or it pissed him off, but in the end, he clapped me on the shoulder. "It's never gonna be the way it was, brother. But between you and me, I rest easier knowing you're sleeping next to her every night."

I gave him a nod and a hesitant smile. "Thank you for backing me up." I paused, waiting for him to meet my gaze again. "With Leo."

"I hope you know what you're doing, brother."

"Yeah. Me too."

"Don't sound too cocky, now." Aris chuckled and turned to head back toward everyone else, leaving me to watch the ruins collapse around the flames alone.

No, it never would be the same between us, but I didn't want that anymore. What we'd had before didn't allow for me to be honest, and whether that was because of him or me, I'd never know. What we needed now was different. So I hung my hat on that one word.

Brother.

We were family, no matter what. I planned to marry his daughter. I was going to be in his life for the rest of it, like it or not. We may never get back what we'd had before, but we could have something different. Better even, and the hope of that was okay with me.

When we got back to the Virginia shoreline, we loaded Leo into the trunk of Thor's '68 Impala. Christ, the thing was the size of a house, ensuring Leo had a comfy ride despite tied wrists and ankles. The rest of us found our bikes and loaded up, preparing for the long ride back to the clubhouse. Aris had gotten an earful from Crow when he called to let him know what we'd done, but after he explained, he told him to bring the Caputi fucker back with us.

"He's not happy," Aris said, "but he'll hear you out."

Once we arrived at the clubhouse, most of the other brothers were back from their respective runs. We'd raided four storage units, two condos, and the house in Benoni. We were supposed to kill on sight, to take out as many of their ranks as we could. Hit them hard and fast. One quick blow.

I'd gone off script in a big way, and I was probably about to get my ass handed to me.

"Whose idea was it to leave him alive?" Crow bellowed, storming out of the metal door with murder in his eyes. He set his sights on Bear and KC, but ultimately landed on Aris, expecting an answer from his veep.

"Mine," I said, unsnapping my helmet so I could take it off. "We can use him."

Crow put his hands on his hips and raised his eyebrows. "What the fuck does that mean?"

I swallowed, knowing he could command these other fuckers to beat the shit out of me for disobeying him and most of them would, including Aris. However, I'd always known him to be a reasonable man, and the fact he hadn't already done it meant I might still have some sway.

"Look, I know what it's like to grow up thinking you're a piece of shit. When the world tells you what you are, you start to believe it." I explained my theory about Gabriella and Leo, watching as Crow took a deep breath and put the pieces together in his own mind. With him out of the way, he was less of a wild card. Gabriella would have complete control, and we already knew what her plans were. Leo *wanted* to die. "Sobering him up, making him deal with himself, it's worse than death for him. We can use that to our advantage."

"I didn't see any harm in considering it." Aris shrugged, moving to stand next to Crow so they could appear as a united front despite him taking my side. "If you don't agree, we can shoot him now and get it over with."

Crow looked back and forth between us, his steady gaze assessing the situation before he spoke. "Are you two back together or some shit?"

Aris shook his head. "It's a good idea either way."

Crow took a deep breath and let it out on a deep, agitated sigh. "All right. Fuck." The prez ran a hand back through his long dark hair and nodded toward the car. "Take him to the farmhouse. Lock him up." Then, he turned and headed back inside, muttering to himself about his own brothers being the death of him. "I'll send Doc in a bit."

The weight of the last few hours lifted off my chest as I exhaled. Aris patted my shoulder and smiled, turning to follow Crow inside the clubhouse. Bear and KC, on the other hand, both eyed me with skepticism as they followed.

I understood why. Ru and Verona were their sisters, their girls. They deserved their vengeance on Leo, and I'd robbed them of that. But if we could end the war by showing the least bit of restraint, I'd do it. If we could stop losing brothers, if we could find some kind of peace in the chaos, I'd rein in my most savage impulses.

Just this once.

25

RU

When Saint told me what he'd done, I struggled with my reaction. On one hand, his infinite patience made me love him even more. On the other, I had to physically restrain myself from going to the barn and shooting the mother-fucker myself. I understood what he was trying to do, but it didn't mean I had to like it.

Instead, I focused my attention on renovating the Beacon. After everything that had happened, I needed somewhere constructive to put my energy, and I'd been itching to do this for a long time.

"I like the black granite better than the white," I said to the contractor, who nodded and stuck a pencil behind her ear.

"I agree," she said. "Especially given the vibe you're going for."

The Beacon had officially shut down for two months while we completed the upgrades, but the staff hung around to help wherever they could. Candy had done drywall in a previous life, so she rocked out with her putty can in one hand, the knife in the other, earbuds in and music cranked. Hollywood and Verona bickered by the reno-vated stage about whether pineapple was an acceptable topping for pizza while Lore shook his head and laughed, sweeping sawdust into a tray.

"Everyone knows you don't put fruit on pizza," Hollywood said, narrowing his eyes on Verona.

"Tomatoes are fruit." Verona ran her hand over her face like he was the most frustrating individual alive.

"Barely." Hollywood rolled his eyes.

"Why do you have such strong opinions about pizza, anyway? Aren't you pansexual?"

Hollywood balked, looking outraged when he gasped and responded with, "How dare you compare the sanctity of pizza toppings to a silly thing like sexual orientation?"

"I'm surprised you know what the word sanctity means." Verona rolled her big eyes and tilted her head at him.

"I'm the smartest person you know." Hollywood flashed her his charming smile.

"I'm sure you think so." That was one of the things I loved the most about Verona. She didn't put up with anyone's bullshit, especially not his.

The contractor asked me a few more questions about what to do with the plumbing issues they'd found in the back, and after she left to finalize the rest of the rebuild, I returned to the Excel spreadsheet on my laptop. I needed to complete the quarter-end reports for Crimson and balance the accounts for all of our performers. Membership was up over two hundred percent, and we'd brought on more associates than in the last six months combined.

"Hey, baby girl," Saint cooed, wrapping his arms around me from behind. "You about ready to head out?"

I bit my bottom lip between my teeth, remembering the reason we were leaving early today. He had big plans of tying my ass to his bed and torturing me for the next three hours. If he played his cards right, I might even get him to put it in my ass.

"Yes, sir," I whispered, leaning in to kiss him.

He smiled. "I like the sound of that."

Just as he stepped away, the front door opened, and I swung my attention around to see who it was. My heart nearly stopped when my father walked in, taking off his aviators with a loud whistle. I'd seen him a few times since the wedding, but always on my own. The only time he'd been in the same place as the two of us had been those few brief moments at the hospital. Whatever prompted his visit must have been important.

"Dad?" I hopped off the barstool and walked closer, holding out my arms to give him a hug.

He tugged me in close, kissing the top of my head like he always did. "Hey ya, bubs."

"What are you doing here?"

He shrugged. "I was in the neighborhood. I thought I'd pop in to see the mess you've made."

I rolled my eyes and shoved his shoulder. "Shut up."

He laughed, rubbed a hand over my curls, and nodded at Saint. "Hey, brother."

"Hey." Saint gave him a similar nod in return, and I pursed my lips, ignoring the awkwardness between us.

"Wanna see what we've done so far?" I cut through the tension and gestured toward the showroom. We'd already increased the size of the stage and added another two catwalks, but that didn't compare to the space we'd added to the back. He walked around with his jaw open, eyes roaming the space while I talked. "I'm talking new locker rooms, new bathrooms, new showers, the whole thing."

"She even added a second floor," Saint said, stuffing his hands in his pockets while he trailed a few feet behind my dad.

Dad beamed when he smiled down at me. "Show me."

I took him upstairs, explaining my vision for the place once it was complete. "Right now, it's not much more than two by fours and studs. But once we get the drywall done, it'll be rooms for people to rent, adding to our revenue stream." I practically shook with excitement. "We'll have to pay staff to clean them, of course. But if we charge by the hour, we could increase our profit margin."

"Jesus, Ruthie." Dad shook his head and leaned against a beam, the other hand on his hip while he looked around. "You pulled this all together?"

"Yeah." Was there something in this about sublimating instead of facing my problems? Absolutely. I'd taken Alba's approach to healing, reaching out to one of her therapist's colleagues for support. Once I explained my backstory, they'd wished I'd come to them sooner. Everyone carried trauma, some of us more than most, and I'd lived a hell of a life up to this point. I was a fighter and a survivor, so I carried it well. But even I had scars to heal.

"Good job, bubba." Dad pulled me into another hug, kissing the top of my head again. "Good job to both of you." When he stepped back, he held his hand out to Saint, who grinned and shook it, alleviating whatever weirdness had been lingering since my dad showed up. "I'm impressed, truly."

"Well, wait until the grand opening before you say that." I grimaced and shook my head. "It could go sideways. We could have an empty house."

"Doubtful," Saint said. "You'll have this place packed, I guarantee it."

I smiled. "And once we announce it on Crimson, I bet we'll have people flying in to visit their favorite stars."

That made Dad's grin widen, and he tugged me in for another tight hug. "My little entrepreneur. Jesus Christ, you're so smart."

Saint laughed while I struggled, and when I freed myself, Dad clapped and turned to head downstairs. We followed, and when we got to the open space next to what remained of the bar, Dad faced me and put his hands on his hips.

"Well, I'm gonna head to the clubhouse. Crow's called church later this evening."

"Yeah, I know." Saint ran a hand over the back of his head, coming to stand next to Dad. "Leo's still all fucked-up, huh?"

He nodded. "He's been on a bunch of shit for a while. Three weeks is enough to wring him out, but now he's just pissed off. He's refusing to eat or drink."

Saint sighed. "Maybe this was a bad idea."

Dad shook his head. "No, I stand by my decision. You were right. We'll get through to him, sooner or later."

Saint nodded. "Thanks."

"Sure." Dad looked around again and gave us one last nod. "I'll see you both later. Love you, bubs."

"Love you," I told him.

He turned and walked away, the sound of the hammering going on in the background drowning out his boots. I thought back to a few weeks ago, when the three of us had sat out on the porch in the summer night air before Alba's wedding, drinking and laughing together. Dad and Saint had been as close as brothers, and even though they still called each other by that name, I sensed the shift in their relationship and hated that I was the cause of it.

"That's distorted thinking," my therapist's voice said in my head. *"Your father's reactions are his own."*

If he wanted to drink himself into a stupor and fuck random hang-arounds at the club, I couldn't stop him. If he wanted to resent his best friend for loving his daughter, I couldn't change that. I owned my actions, nothing more, and I loved Saint deeply. That would never change.

Saint wrapped his arms around me, pressing his chest against my back and bringing his lips to my ear. His beard brushed against my skin, scratchy and soft at the same time.

"Don't forget what I had planned for your tight little ass," he murmured, biting my earlobe and sending a jolt of steaming lust down the center of my body. I prayed I never stopped wanting him, and I prayed he never stopped wanting me. When I turned in his hold so he could press a deep, sensual kiss to my lips, I knew my prayers would be answered.

If I had to bet, I'd say Saint had pined for me as long as I had for him, and in that desperation, we'd grown an itch impossible to scratch. It would take the rest of our lives to try, and I was prepared to do it.

I COULDN'T REMEMBER what happened after I'd shot the guy in Saint's truck. I vaguely recalled two people walking up behind us, a familiar female voice calling out into the night. But when I focused on figuring out who she was, I came up empty every time. Eventually, I stopped trying, my therapist advising that it would come when it was supposed to, if it ever came back at all. There was something I was missing, some bigger part of this whole thing that needed to be resolved, and I was the only one who could do it.

Life went on. I officially moved in with Saint, as did Hollywood, much to our chagrin.

"Having his help with the mortgage has been useful," Saint told me one night while we cuddled in bed. "We can save for a bigger place."

I smiled, curling into him so I could look up at his soft brown eyes. "A bigger place?"

"Yeah." He brushed his nose against mine. "For all those babies I'm gonna put inside you."

"I figured you'd want to adopt." Saint had been an orphan himself when he was a child and spent time around the holidays visiting local children's homes in the area.

"Oh, we will," he said. "We're gonna have a whole pack of little Roses running around."

The thought made me so happy, I could burst. I pictured miniature versions of us, both biological and found, and wanted it with such a painful yearning that I didn't know what I'd do to get it.

A few days later, Selene had a sleepover at her house for her birthday. She didn't want anything huge, especially after all the shit that had happened recently. The women of the Roses needed a break, so we gathered around the enormous sofa in her living room, snuggies on and popcorn popped, gearing up for a *Vampire Diaries* marathon of epic proportions.

Verona stretched out to my right while Alba painted my toenails on my left, my foot up on her knee.

"I can see why you're into Uncle Mason," Verona said with a

wistful sigh. "All those muscles. I bet I could make him squeal like a stuck pig."

I laughed, and Selene gasped, glancing up at Verona with wide eyes.

"Don't look at me like that." She threw a piece of popcorn at Selene, who caught it with her mouth and gave it a loud chomp. "I told you I wasn't the same girl you knew."

"No kidding." Alba shook her head and laughed, dragging the brush across my big toenail. "You're gonna make so much money on Crimson, it's ridiculous."

"I'm already doing pretty well." Once the wound in her chest had healed enough to do solo work, she set up her site and switched her fanbase to our app instead. No one in her family knew, and the girls planned to keep it that way. For now, it was our secret, but I didn't know how much longer that could go on. "I can't wait until the club opens."

"Same," Alba and I said together before looking at each other and laughing. The more I got to know her, the more I realized how much the whole nature versus nurture debate had merit on both sides. Despite spending our whole lives apart, we were similar in a thousand different ways.

"Sunshine," called a deep voice from the back door. KC walked in carrying a paper bag full of groceries. Selene and Alba had sent him on a munchies run, and now that he was back, my stomach grumbled in anticipation.

"Hey, thank you so much!" Selene stood to take the bag, her dark hair in a plait down the side of her body. But when she rose, her phone fell off her lap and knocked into the table on its way down, landing in a sickening crunch on the hardwood floor. "Fuck!"

"Oh no!" Alba said.

"That sounded expensive," Verona added.

Wincing, Selene bent over to pick it up, groaning at the cracked screen. "Damn it!" She pressed her fingers against it, but from the expression on her face, it wasn't working the way it should. She hit something else, and a voice came over the speakerphone.

"Hey, Sel. It's Nik. We're running late."

"Jesus Christ, how old is that voice mail?" KC raised an eyebrow and sat down next to Alba, rubbing a hand over her back. She preened into the touch but continued painting.

"Jer got off work late. Again. I'm sorry."

"Ah, fuck." Selene frantically pushed at random parts of the phone, trying to get the voice to stop talking, but it wouldn't work. "I'm gonna turn it off."

"Do you have to get a new one?" KC took the phone from his sister and looked it over.

The hair stood up on the back of my neck, a shiver snaking down my spine.

I'm sorry.

I'm sorry.

I'm sorry.

The tone and cadence shook through me, taking me back to a dark, hazy night. I knew that voice.

Verona clenched my wrist, digging her nails into my skin. I focused on her wide eyes and panicked expression, her deep inhales making me even more concerned.

All of that faded to the background. Something about the combination of the two of them, Verona and the voice, unlocked a missing puzzle piece in my mind. I went back to the night in Saint's truck when I was bleeding out in the passenger seat, having just killed the man sent to murder me.

"I'm sorry," the other assassin had said before she'd taken off in a puff of blond hair.

Nikki.

The memory cleared in my head. She'd been in one of the Caputi's cars that night. She'd been the one standing outside Saint's window.

"It'll give you a chance to prove your loyalty." The guy I'd shot had muttered that to her on their way down to the wrecked truck. It didn't make sense at the time, but it did now. The Caputis didn't take in random people, no matter what deals Benito or Julian might have

made. If Nikki wanted to stay, she would have to do more than fuck one of their princes.

Rage burned through every molecule in my body. I understood why Pie betrayed us. Money could make people do despicable things. But Nikki's treachery hurt particularly deep because I thought we were friends. While I didn't like her with KC and I thought they were toxic for each other, I had wanted the best for her after it was over. She was one of us, and she'd used that against us.

We, the women of the Steel Roses, owed her for that, and by God, it was time we paid up. Now, the question came...did I tell the rest of them?

"She was there," Verona said, answering for me.

Selene's raised her eyebrows. "Who?"

"Nikki." Verona sat up and pushed to the edge of the sofa, her elbows on her knees. "Ru, tell them. You know it, too. I saw the look in your eyes just now."

I swallowed and nodded. "At the time, I thought the voice was familiar, but she was scared." My heart raced as I looked at Selene, KC, and Alba. For as long as KC had dated the bitch, Selene had to put up with her screwing around with her twin brother and fucking with his heart. She had *hated* her, and after they broke up, she took every opportunity to put Nikki in her place.

"What are you saying?" KC's focus shifted between me and Verona. "That Nikki was there the night you got shot?"

Verona nodded, her eyes getting wider. "Tell them, Ru."

I explained what the other guy had said about proving her loyalty, but she must have gotten cold feet because she obviously didn't finish the job.

"That bitch!" KC's temper hit a boiling point, and he lit a cigarette, pushing to his feet while he grabbed his phone. "I've gotta tell Crow. I knew that cunt was up to something. I fucking knew it." He rattled on, roasting her ten ways to Sunday while Alba tried to calm him down.

"We'll get her," she said. "The Roses will go after her and bring her in. If Doc's too sexist to do it, I'll kill her myself."

"That's not his hang-up. It's the baby. It always has been."

"So, because she got knocked up, she gets away with whatever she wants?" Verona chimed in, rising so she could talk to whomever answered on the other end of KC's phone. But I stared at Selene while she processed. She wrapped her lips around a blunt and pulled, going eerily still and calm, which wasn't a good sign. It meant her brain was going at the speed of light, and there was no stopping her now. It had made her a brilliant surgeon and an even better hunter.

Growing up, Selene had been my best friend, my confidant, and the older sister I thought destiny had forgotten to give me. I knew her better than almost anyone in the world. I'd seen her patch up wounds I thought would kill the recipient, and I'd seen her hit rock bottom only to rise up again from the ashes. Like everyone, she had her flaws. She and KC were truly twins in a lot of ways. They looked alike, sure, but they both had a fiery white temper. Where KC raged and burned bright hot, Selene turned cold and frozen with her fury. Underneath this relaxed, unbothered facade, she was ruminating, and when she got to ruminating...

"How sure are you?" she whispered, tapping ash into the bowl on the coffee table.

"Maybe ninety-five percent," I murmured low enough just for us to hear. "I recognized her voice that night, but I was losing a lot of blood."

"I'll take those odds." She nodded, stabbing the blunt out.

My stomach churned. "What do you mean?"

She didn't answer, just refocused on the three people arguing on the phone with Crow.

"It's her, Dad. I know it." Verona ran her hands over her face.

"I told you," KC said, holding the phone up so Crow was on speaker. "We shoulda dealt with her when we had the chance. She's not gonna stop."

"All right, let me take it to the club." Crow let out a deep sigh, uneasy lies the head and all that. "Be safe tonight, and for the love of God, don't go running off like a jackass to handle it yourself, okay?"

KC stayed silent, squaring his jaw and murmuring a quiet, "I shoulda called Saint."

"What?" Crow bellowed. "That better a been a 'Yes, Prez. Whatever you say, Prez. I'll keep my fucking mouth shut, Prez.'"

I looked at Selene, who raised an eyebrow and pursed her lips.

"Yes, Prez." KC said the words like they tasted like hot garbage.

"Thank you, KC. Have a good night." And he hung up.

"C'mon. I'll go calm you down." Alba grabbed KC's hand and dragged him outside, closing the door with a mouthed, "I'm sorry."

Verona sighed and turned back toward Selene and me, slumping down on the couch where Alba had once been. "What do we do now?"

Selene grabbed the remote and clicked unpause on the *Vampire Diaries*. "Now, we watch Elena get turned into a vampire."

Verona gasped and threw a pillow at her. "Spoiler alert!"

EPILOGUE

Ru

Two years later

"Is V ready?" I looked around the backstage area of the Beacon, searching for my star dominatrix. People drove from all parts of the country to see her perform, especially with her infamous, beautiful submissive.

"Yeah, she's oiling him up." Alba appeared around the corner and smiled, clapping. "Are you excited?"

I rolled my eyes and nodded. "It's not that big of a deal."

"Saint is taking you on a surprise all-expenses-paid vacation. You're definitely coming back married." My sister seemed more excited by the prospect than I was, but I just shook my head and nodded toward the green room.

"Can you tell them they have five minutes?"

"Sure!" Alba turned and headed back the way she came, but big, strong arms wrapped around me before I could follow her.

"It's time to go, sinner."

"I've got three more emails to send." I tried to pull up something on my iPad, but he yanked it out of my hands and gave it to Candy, who immediately took over whatever I'd been trying to do.

"Hey!" I turned in his arms and set my glare on his gorgeous face.

"Our plane leaves in a few hours. We need to go." He whispered the words in his dominant voice, ricocheting a shiver down my spine. I loved him more every day, especially because of how he could make me tremble.

I narrowed my eyes. "Alba thinks you're taking me away to marry me."

He pursed his lips. "I already put a ring on your finger. I could marry you anytime I wanted."

It had been two years since the night he gave me a symbol of his devotion, but getting married had never been a priority for either of us. I had *Saint* tattooed on my wrist, and he had *Ru* tattooed over his heart. No one and nothing could ever come between us again. Despite what the Commonwealth of Virginia had to say, we were committed in all the ways that mattered. Yet, something seemed off about him. He'd refused to mention *exactly* where we were going, only saying that the *sinner* in me would love it.

"Are you sure I don't need to pack anything?"

He rubbed his nose against mine. "Trust me."

"I do."

He grinned, kissed me, and grabbed my hand to lead me out of the side exit, where his truck was parked in the alley. The closer we got to the airport, the more suspicious I became. Once we were seated on a flight to Vegas, the excitement inside my stomach had reached epic proportions. I couldn't contain myself anymore.

"Are you taking me to the City of Sin?"

He licked his lips and grinned, his smile spurring my giddiness. When he said nothing, I interlinked my fingers with his and ran through a list of things it could be, each one getting more and more ridiculous.

"The world's largest cheese display." I waited for a reaction and got nothing. "The Adult Video Awards."

"You would be so lucky." He chuckled low in his chest and sipped his whiskey, relaxing his head back against the headrest. "But you're getting warmer."

My heart pounded against my ribs. "A sex club?"

He adjusted his hips. "You've been to dozens of those. What's another dungeon?"

He shifted around, an obvious tell, so wherever we were going, it must have been something to do with that. Deciding I'd rather be surprised, I leaned my head against his shoulder and sighed, contentment filling my heart and spilling over to the rest of my body.

Saint and I'd had a rough road to get here, but I would walk it all over again if it meant I got this far every time.

Saint
The middle of nowhere - NV

"Are you sure?" I cracked the flogger in front of me, stalking around Ru with a huge grin on my face as she jumped. I'd tied her arms above her head, attaching her wrists to a hook in the ceiling with a thick piece of rope. She'd been blindfolded for about an hour, her sense of touch so attuned to me by now that she musta been able to track me by heat signature.

"Yes, sir," she whined.

"Excuse me?" I couldn't possibly have heard her right.

"Yes, husband," she corrected.

It was too late. She'd made the mistake, and I had to punish her for it. I slapped the leather tails against her ass, pleased when she moaned and sagged into the pain.

Yeah, I'd whisked her off to marry her at a Vegas kink camp

before bringing her to my cabin on the outskirts of the desert. No one knew about this place, not even Aris. I'd spent every cent the church ever gave me on it, and once upon a time, I'd delighted in bringing women back here to do unholy things to them.

Now, I just brought Ru. It was our playhouse away from reality. Since I'd made things all official and shit, her ass was mine for the next week. Was it ethically ambiguous to make my new honorific *husband*? Possibly. But I liked the way her cheeks turned bright fucking pink every time she said it, and when I called her *wife* in public, she had to grab on to me to keep from dropping to her knees and opening her mouth.

That shit turned me on.

"I don't think you've been good enough for this." I lifted one of her legs and put it around my hip, leaving her to balance all of her weight on the ball of her other foot.

"Please, husband. Please." She milked the role-play for all it was worth. Ru loved to play the brat; she loved to resist and put up the fight if only to make me break her down. But this week, she'd been exceptionally submissive, as if I'd given her everything she'd ever wanted by whisking her off for this little adventure. Maybe I'd waited too long to do it, but fuck it.

I held on to her hip and pushed my cock inside her, sighing at how warm and tight she always felt. She groaned, and her head fell forward onto my shoulder like she simply couldn't hold it up anymore.

Which was fucking okay with me because I couldn't wait much longer myself. While I'd been edging her, I'd been doing it to myself, too. Normally, I had infinite patience when it came to Ru, always had. But now that she was mine, I wanted her more than I ever had before.

Maybe I'd put a baby in her one day. Maybe I'd give Aris the grandkids he kept bugging us for. But until then, I'd be happy to call myself hers. I'd taken on the honor of protecting her with every breath I had, and heaven help anyone that came for her again.

WANNA JOIN THE ROSES?

Thank you for reading! If you enjoyed this book, please consider leaving a review.

Want more? Read about Ru and Saint's night stuck in the snow, check out the prequel novella, **THEY CALLED HIM SAINT,** for *FREE* when you sign up for my newsletter.

http://join.jenadoyle.com/roses

(No spam, only smut. I promise.)

But wait! There's more! The next book in the Steel Roses is out now. Check out **SELENE and THOR's** story, **OLEANDER OATHS.** Keep reading for a sneak peek!

She's a monster.
He's the man who made her.
When she runs, he chases,
even into hell.

STEEL ROSES
MOTORCYCLE CLUB

OLEANDER
OATHS

JENA DOYLE

OLEANDER OATHS

Thor and Selene get their chance at primal forbidden love in this raw and fiery addition to the Steel Roses Motorcycle Club. She's a monster. He's the man who made her. When she runs, he chases, even to hell.

<u>Selene</u>

I've always known what I am: a monster wrapped in pretty skin. When a traitor targets my club, I don't think. I hunt. I bleed. I make them pay.

But Thor won't let me do this alone. He's my dead aunt's husband. My mentor. My obsession. And he's spent years chasing me, training me, breaking me down until every breath I take tastes like him.

When he finally catches me, I know exactly how this ends: against a wall, under his control, with no way back.

<u>Thor</u>

She runs. I chase. It's the only game we've ever played, and I've never lost. But the woman she's become isn't the girl I used to protect. She's wild, vengeful - decadent sin wrapped in leather and blood.

I shouldn't want her. I sure as hell shouldn't touch her. But the moment she kisses me before she disappears, every line I've drawn burns away.

When I find her, I'll remind her exactly who taught her how to fight... and how it feels to surrender.

OLEANDER OATHS

SELENE
Thanksgiving

I ducked out of the way before Thor's massive fist connected with my cheekbone, but I missed the cues indicating he'd swiped his foot out. When his leg connected with the back of my knees, I melted like ice cream on a hot summer day, landing on my back with a loud *oof*.

Fuck.

The air rushed out of my lungs, and I blinked up at the shadow of my mentor, holding out his hand for me so he could yank me to my feet. Grimacing, I shoved it away. I didn't need his help, not anymore.

"You're distracted," Thor said, his steel eyes twinkling in the sunlight.

I ignored his comment and peeled back the tape around my wrist to make it tighter before slapping it down again.

"Let's go." I held up my hands, ready for another round, but Thor only raised an eyebrow and smirked before picking up his water bottle. He tilted his head back to squirt some into his mouth while I stared at the drop that trickled down the side of his jaw and onto his neck. The muscles worked under his skin as he swallowed, and for the millionth time, I wondered what it might be like to lick that throat as he slid inside me.

Get your shit together, Montgomery. I shook my head to bring my attention back to reality. Not that there was ever a good time to lust after the man who'd married my aunt before her untimely death, but it was definitely the *wrong* time when my focus was supposed to be on hitting him in the face as hard as I could.

"Why don't you tell me what's on your mind?" Thor sat on a fallen log to take another long drink, tossing his bottle to the side so he could adjust his own wrappings.

Of all the people on this great earth, he would be the last person I spoke to about my dark, twisted secret. He would do everything in his power to talk me down, to remind me it was Rose business, not mine. I didn't care.

The Steel Roses Motorcycle Club had been dragging their fucking feet for three months since my best friend, Ru, and her boyfriend, Saint, had gotten shot. As soon as the time was right, I would take action.

"I'm just tired."

He narrowed his gaze, tilting his head to the side while he waited for me to continue. It was always this battle of wills between us, who had the most patience, who had the courage to hold their tongue the longest. He read me like a book most of the time, and even when I tried to keep my walls up, he found a way to bring them crumbling to the ground.

"Are you having trouble sleeping?"

I chuckled softly, forcing a tight smile I knew looked fake. No, I wasn't sleeping. I hadn't slept in over a year, and he knew why. Nikki McNally, a woman I'd known since childhood, a woman that had dated my twin brother, Jericho, for over a decade, had defected to our enemies last July. Since then, the information she'd given to the Caputi crime family had led to the abduction and brutalization of multiple Roses, the shootout this August only being the latest. Ru had barely made it out alive, and as I stood over her hospital bed, debating with myself about the odds of her survival, I made myself a promise.

I wouldn't stand for this any longer.

The only problem was Nikki had *also* gone after the Roses by attacking Saint and the other brother in the vehicle, Hollywood. They claimed it was club business, that I wasn't a member of the MC so I had no reason to get involved.

What these fuckers failed to understand was the women of the club, people like me, Ru, and the hang-arounds, existed in a liminal space—not quite in, not quite out. Nikki had lived in that gray area *with me.* In here, the women of the SRMC took care of each other. We were the heartbeat of this family.

"I can't help you if—"

"I don't want your help," I snapped, shooting him a sharp look.

He sat up straighter and smiled, knowing he'd hit a nerve. There was only one person in the world I trusted beyond reason and logic, and he couldn't resist needling my temper.

"I know what you're thinking," he said.

Again, I glared at him, waiting for him to show his cards.

"If you go after her, Selene, so help me fucking God..." It came out more as a growl than a calm, controlled statement.

Yes, yes, I knew what he planned to do. He'd come for me, just as he came for me all the times before. But I'd done my research and I was good. I could get in and out without anyone knowing, and once Nikki was gone, the leak would be patched and she wouldn't be a threat any longer.

"Tell me that's not what you're planning, and I'll leave it alone." He stood and took a step toward me, raising his eyebrows in expectation of a response. "Be honest."

I cleared my throat and focused on the ground between us, unable to look him in the eyes because he'd see right through me. He always did.

"That's not what I'm planning," I lied, although technically, I wasn't planning to go after her *yet.* I wanted to be sure. I needed a solid plan, and until I had that, I had to keep up the great facade.

"Hmm." Thor didn't believe me. Why should he?

I'd spent the last three months trying to find her, calling in every favor I had. The information ultimately came from the most unlikely of places—an old friend of mine, Marissa. She'd been an old lady in the club for years until her husband, Trojan, died protecting Ru and Alba the first time the Caputis attacked. After that, Marissa had taken off to start a new life... until a few weeks ago, when she'd reached out from Buffalo, New York with pictures of my most favorite hang-around slung all over a biker from their local club, the Kings of Carnage. Marissa said she saw her in the bar with the same group of bikers almost every night, and up until now, Nikki hadn't recognized the former SRMC old lady. Or if she had, she hadn't been provoked by Marissa's appearance nor asked for a reunion. In the absence of a safety net, Nikki had done what she always had... infiltrated a group of men and found one to fall in love with her and protect her, the idiotic sap.

Once upon a time, Nikki and I had been kids together—running in between the sheds out behind the clubhouse, making mud pies until our clothes were filthy, playing hide-and-seek under the summer moonlight. Nikki's mother had been a hang-around that had taken up space at the clubhouse for as long as I could remember. Her father was one of the old-timers, a Rose who had likely already died or moved on to a different chapter. I might have even called her a friend until she dicked around with Jer's emotions for all those years. But I'd been willing to overlook that because she'd always been a part of the tribe. If she and her idiot husband hadn't gone all *Et tu, Brute*, she likely still would be.

Marissa should have reached out to Crow or Thor. She should have taken this to the club. But she came to me because she knew what it was to be a woman in an MC. She knew I'd handle it.

"How's Leo?" I asked, changing the subject.

"Pissed off and silent." Thor ran a thumb over his eyebrow.

After Nikki and the Caputis came after us, the Roses had wanted blood. In September, they had gone after the remaining Caputi heir, Leo, but he was only the kingpin because his uncle and elder brother had died. He'd never been cut out for the crown and preferred to snort his inheritance away instead of control it. By the time we'd gotten to him, he was so tweaked out that it was surprising he could hold his head up. The Roses had been sent there to kill him, to repay blood with blood, but Saint had a crisis of conscience and brought him back to the clubhouse, where Leo had been drying out ever since.

I'd been a big part of bringing him back to life, especially once he stopped eating. Now, he'd resigned himself to our food but hadn't uttered a word in over eight weeks. They were running out of ideas, and Leo was quickly losing his potential value.

"We shoulda killed him when we had the chance," I said.

Thor shrugged. "Jury's still out. He might talk."

"Would you?" I laughed out a sad noise.

He raised an eyebrow, running his tongue across his lips. "We don't have the right motivation."

"What are you suggesting?"

Thor shook his head, giving me a look that reminded me it was club business, and I should mind my own. Instead of answering, he held his fists up and nodded. "Again."

He went harder on me that time, quickly getting me in a choke-hold before twisting my legs out from under me so he could tumble me onto the undergrowth.

"You're thinking too much," he said. "You're up in your head."

"Yeah, no fucking shit." I climbed to my feet, but Thor was already there, tripping me up so I fell face first on the ground.

"Stop fucking around," he said, crouching so he was closer to eye level. "How are you going to go up against Nikki and the entire Caputi family if you can't even take me down?"

A raging fire built in my gut, part fury, part humiliation. He was right. I *was* distracted, and it had everything to do with this stupid, annoying thing between us. I hated that Thor could read me so well. I hated that I'd been forced to live with him for the last fifteen years. I hated that my brother had found his soulmate and moved out, leaving me to deal with Thor by myself.

I had nowhere else to hide anymore.

Maybe I never did.

"Get up, Montgomery." Thor pushed to his feet, moving his toned calves toward his water bottle again. Fuck him for being so beautifully made. At six-four, he was practically a giant, and his long, dark-blond hair and gunmetal-gray eyes had contributed to his nickname.

Thor.

A fucking Viking God come to life, and I was the stupid human that had developed this ridiculous co-dependence on him. I couldn't live with him, but the thought of leaving him made me want to peel my skin off my body. Ru thought I was in love with him, but such a minuscule concept had never encompassed the depth of decadent vileness in our relationship.

I pushed to my feet and took a deep breath, focusing on the way the air circulated through my body. The trees rustled in the crisp autumn wind, whispering a soothing melody that brushed against my cheeks in a healing embrace. Curling burnt-amber leaves rustled along the ground, reminding me of the world's cyclic nature. Everything around me was dying, long since wrestled into submission by the stillness of November and now preparing for the ultimate death of winter.

With my mind more focused, I looked at Thor and held my hands up. "Again."

This time, I kept up with him. I dodged his first few blows, backing away when he advanced. I was only five-ten to his tall, muscular frame, so I had to use his momentum against him if I ever wanted to win. He was big, so he tired easily. I only had to block him for so long before he got slow, and despite having an impressive military background, Thor was ten years older than me, thirty-nine to my twenty-nine. He was still in amazing shape, but forty hit everyone like a ton of bricks.

Even so, he tripped me up with an ankle I didn't see coming, and when I couldn't maintain my balance, I tried to use his weight to throw my other leg up on his hip in an effort to bring him down. It didn't work. He caught me and slammed my back up against a tree.

I winced on impact, ignoring the sharp pain that shot down my spine. With my hands wrapped in his between our chests and our legs tangled together, we were at an impasse. I couldn't move without submitting to him, but he couldn't back away without me letting him go.

"Give," he snarled.

"No." I tried to pull away, but he tightened his grip.

"Give!" His breath hit me in the face, minty and warm and *him,* and I shivered at how close we were. His lips hovered centimeters from mine, his fiery molten irises burning into me, our hearts pounding in time against our combined embrace. His knee was shoved in between my legs, his hard thigh pressed firm against my leggings, rubbing my vulva in the best and worst way. We danced on precarious battleground, one minor slipup away from total disaster.

This wasn't the first time we'd sparred; Thor taught me everything I knew. He'd held me down in hundreds of sessions before, grabbed my hair and yelled in my face, but none of it had ever been as charged as this one moment. Pressed up against a tree, nothing but our pride and our clothes between us, the mood shifted. My blood boiled and my skin shrank, making everything so fucking hot and untenable. I'd never been so aware of every inch of him, and I licked my dry lips, hoping to cool down. Thor dropped his gaze to the movement, and my heart pounded harder.

He was going to kiss me, and I desperately wanted him to. It was wrong, but for one moment, I imagined a world where a love like ours would be okay, where our relationship wasn't so damned unhealthy, regardless of the title society had put on us. We were toxic and possessive of each other in ways that should have made me uncomfortable, and the whole cycle had become so strangely addictive that I couldn't get away. He claimed not to want me, but no one else was allowed to have me, and everybody knew it.

"You live with monsters," he'd once told me. *"Don't be surprised if you turn out to be one."*

Yes, I was his little monster, and he'd made me this way.

Thor gripped my chin with his massive hand to hold me in place while he stared down at my frenzied state. Analyzing me. Regarding me. I tried to pull up my defenses, to file away all my errant thoughts before he could see them. But he knew me so fucking well. I could never hide from his calculating eyes.

"Training's done for the day." He took a step back, bent over to grab his water bottle, and walked away. "See you at the clubhouse."

My knees shook as I struggled to hold myself upright, cursing him with a one-finger salute as he walked away. For fifteen years, I'd danced around my attraction to him like it didn't exist, and any time someone came close to finding out my depraved little secret, I lied and pretended it was nothing, reminding the world he'd married my aunt so we could never cross that line.

Even if she'd died so long ago that I could barely remember her voice, Thor and I lived a life where a romance like ours would ultimately end in soul-shattering heartache, no matter what. If I didn't die caught up in the middle of this stupid war between the Roses and the Caputis, then he'd perish out there in the trenches, a measly piece of cannon fodder, and for what? Who could even remember anymore? They killed our people, we killed their people, and on and on it went.

Arbitrary words like uncle and love and broken hearts would never describe the relationship between Thor and me. He was there when even my brother wasn't. He'd done things for me that we swore we'd never speak of again. I'd confessed to him every dark, delicate secret I'd ever had, and he'd listened without judgment, only to convince me I wasn't a piece of shit for doing what I had to in order to protect the people I loved.

Thor always had been and would remain everything to me. And that made me so frustrated, I couldn't stand it.

KEEP READING

ACKNOWLEDGMENTS

Dear Reader, thank you for checking out this little age gap. You truly make it all worthwhile, and your support has been astounding. Extra love to my ARC volunteers — you are awesome, my friends. Thank you for spreading that good word across the reader-dom.

Thank you to my husband / best friend for supporting me on this journey, and thank you to my family (both biological and found) for providing the book-positive atmosphere for me to do this type of work in the first place. Like many an elder millennial, I read Anne Rice's *Interview with a Vampire* wayyyy too young, and that has made all the difference.

A HUGE shout out to my beta readers: Shannon, Maggie, Leslie, and Jen. You literally get the shittiest version of my stories, and I regret that you have to read it again in order to see how you've helped. You have shaped my stories more than you know, and your feedback is so incredibly precious and inspiring. Extra special thanks to Shannon and Steve for allowing me to use their beach house as inspiration for Leo Caputi's fuck pad. I will neither confirm nor deny the types of activities that we used to get up to at that place... but there were definitely no shoot-outs. ;-)

To my editors, Misha and Kim, you are the best. Thank you, thank you, thank you. I bow to your humble and generous wisdom.

But, most of all, thank you to my dad. We weren't always perfect, but we did our best. I never doubted for a second that you loved and supported me. I hope I make you proud. Love you, Pops.

Cheers!

ALSO BY JENA DOYLE

MIDSUMMER

We Wild Things (Novella)

Midsummer

Samhain

Solstice

Beltane

STEEL ROSES MC

They Called Him Saint (Novella)

Crimson Chaos

Savage Saint

Oleander Oaths

Mischief Mayhem

Ruthless Reign

ROYAL BASTARDS MC: HELENA, MT

Blood and Whiskey

Caves and Claws (Novella)

Blood and Magic

Heats and Holidays (Novella)

Blood and Trouble

ROYAL HARLOTS MC: ASHEVILLE, NC

Filthy Little Witch